The WRONG MR. DARCY

Also by

Evelyn Lozada with Holly Lörincz

The Perfect Date

The WRONG MR. DARCY

Evelyn Lozada
with Holly Lörincz

ST. MARTIN'S GRIFFIN
NEW YORK

This is a work of fiction. All of the characters, organizations, and events portrayed in this novel are either products of the authors' imaginations or are used fictitiously.

First published in the United States by St. Martin's Griffin, an imprint of St. Martin's Publishing Group

For information, address St. Martin's Publishing Group, 120 Broadway, New York, NY 10271.

www.stmartins.com

Designed by Devan Norman

Library of Congress Cataloging-in-Publication Data

Names: Lozada, Evelyn, author. | Lörincz, Holly, author.
Title: The wrong Mr. Darcy / Evelyn Lozada with Holly Lörincz.
Description: First edition. | New York : St. Martin's Griffin, 2020. |
Identifiers: LCCN 2020006769 | ISBN 9781250622143 (trade paperback) | ISBN 9781250125026 (ebook)
Subjects: GSAFD: Love stories.
Classification: LCC PS3612.O954 W76 2020 | DDC 813/.6—dc23
LC record available at https://lccn.loc.gov/2020006769

Our books may be purchased in bulk for promotional, educational, or business use. Please contact your local bookseller or the Macmillan Corporate and Premium Sales Department at 1-800-221-7945, extension 5442, or by email at MacmillanSpecialMarkets@macmillan.com.

First Edition: 2020

10 9 8 7 6 5 4 3 2 1

To our sons Carl Leo Crawford and Auggie Mar Lörincz.
Two young athletes who are on the path
to becoming exceptional men.

The WRONG MR. DARCY

CHAPTER 1

There are few people whom I really love, and still fewer of whom I think well.

—*Pride and Prejudice*

Hara Isari turned off the engine and sat, not moving, her heart beating with the *tick-tick-tick* of the cooling engine. She'd been immersed in a Jane Austen audiobook for the past hour, hanging out with her favorite characters, but now it was time to ease back into her own reality.

The familiar line of old firs at the edge of the parking lot were monstrously huge and fiercely beautiful, their limbs pronounced against a light gray sky, swaying in the winds of fall. Try as they might, however, the trees could not entirely camouflage the buildings just beyond the greenery. Or the crumbling, twenty-five-foot-tall stone walls that held in her father.

Touching her forehead to the steering wheel, Hara's long, wavy hair lay heavily across her back and her glasses pressed into the bridge of her nose. The resulting hint of pain flickered a warning: *more pain to come.* Or was it a metaphor for the moment?

She sat up and shook off the drama queen moment. Hara liked to find reasons to be happy, not emo. Visiting Thomas Isari challenged the twenty-two-year-old's equanimity sometimes, but not today, not when she had such exciting news to share.

She climbed out of the driver's seat and straightened slowly, pushing her eyeglasses into place. Then, the young woman turned to face the Oregon State Penitentiary.

She'd been coming to the prison for ten years, first by bus when she was in middle school, then by car as soon as she could get her license. Her mother refused to come with her, to see the man who'd ruined the reputation of their family. "I'm a black woman married to a Japanese guy who's now a *felon*. Does he know what they say about me? About us? You can tell your father to kiss my ass."

Even Hara's Grandma Isari, now addled by Alzheimer's and living in a home, had not made the short trip to see her son. Grandpa Isari never had the chance; seated on a hard bench behind his son in the courtroom during the sentencing, he'd grasped at his chest and keeled forward, dead of a massive heartattack.

Harsh way to escape reality, but maybe it was for the best, Hara thought sadly, as she tromped across the vast field of parking lot cement. Her grandparents had met as children, behind razor-topped fences in a World War II Japanese internment camp, ten miles from the small Oregon hospital they'd been born in. The image of their adult child behind bars, sleeping on a thin mattress in a five-by-ten cell with no window, permanently traumatized them.

No one but Hara visited Thomas Isari. The man who'd wiped the gravel and blood off her dimpled knees when she fell off her bike, the man who'd taught her to swim with the current in the river behind their farmhouse. The man who'd lifted her to dunk the basketball into their garage hoop, again and again. The man who'd run the family apple orchard and taken care of his aging parents. And the man who was the reason the FBI flooded into their small town. The man who'd operated an extensive, illegal sports betting operation that, when he was caught, ended several professional athletes' careers. Ended their family.

Now he sat in a cell, leaving her mom to run the farm. *Thanks, Daddy.*

Solo traveling to and from the prison did provide time to listen to books, Hara reasoned . . . but, damn, did she hate going in alone. Between the hillbilly guard who tried to cop a feel during pat downs, and the visiting room full of sex-deprived prisoners and their wives and girlfriends who dripped sour helplessness, Hara grew up learning to keep her shoulders back, exude confidence without arrogance, and use witty banter to distract anyone trying to give her shit. She'd also learned to size people up very quickly, and keep her distance if she didn't like them. First impressions could save a lot of trouble.

If her father could take it day in and day out, she could take it for an hour every few weeks. She wasn't about to abandon him just because of a few jerk bags.

Her sneakers squeaked on the industrial tile as her long legs carried her through the metal detectors and down the never-ending hall, halogen lights buzzing overhead and the tang of urine and bleach stinging her nostrils. She stopped for the armed corrections officers at multiple checkpoints and then for the pat down just outside the visiting room.

"Thank God it's you today, Roland," she said with a friendly smile. The older guard just nodded and sent her through. He wasn't much of a talker but at least he wasn't grabby. Most of the guards rarely bothered with her anymore, having known her for years. She knew not to draw attention, to wear not-tight-not-baggy clothes, wireless bras, no makeup or gang colors, and keep her pockets empty. She did not give the guards a reason to complain, or worse, turn her away.

The first few months, her visits with one of the most hated men in sports history had been from behind Plexiglas. Then her father was moved to general population, C Block, and allowed to have visitations face-to-face, in a room filled with discarded school furniture. The early years had been particularly rough for him, but as time passed, the prisoners seemed to have settled down. It didn't hurt that the Asian-American man helped tutor inmates. And was tall and built like a UFC fighter.

As she dropped onto a hard, plastic chair, she recognized some of the faces around her.

"Hiya Rita," she called quietly to the woman at the table next to her. Rita, with her fried blonde hair and hard wrinkles, could have been twenty-five or forty, it was hard to tell. "How's your little boy?"

The hard-faced woman shook her head. "These fuckers won't let me bring him back in here. Jonas is going to be pissed."

Jonas, a large black man with a bad back, was Thomas Isari's cellmate. A few months ago, Rita had been caught bringing in pain pills tucked into their son's diaper. Hara's father had an empty cell for a while, with Jonas in solitary, but it looked like Thomas had his bunkie back.

"Hey, baby girl," her father said, grinning as he slid his muscular frame into the chair across from her. Grasping her hands on the metal table between them, he leaned in and kissed her cheek, quickly, not giving the guards time to squawk. They saved a brief hug for the goodbyes. It was their routine.

"Nice bangs. My little hipster."

"Hey!" She smiled. Thomas loved her and it poured off him, made her feel safe. Even in this place.

"I'm just kidding. I'm glad you kept your hair long, but I like you with the short bangs, I can see your face." Before he let go, he squeezed her fingers, his dark eyes fixed on her. "Still hiding those baby blues behind specs, though."

Hara, about to respond, noticed her father's face for the first time. Squinting at his forehead, she asked, "What's that?"

A bruise yellowed at his temple, fading back into his short salt-and-pepper hair. She'd seen worse, much worse, like the time his pinkie fingernail had been ripped off when he'd taken too long at the microwave. There was also the long scar running down the back of his neck, from when he'd been shivved while lifting weights. She shivered.

He tapped his head, his forehead wrinkling. "You mean this? Nothing." At her frown, he said, "Seriously, there was a little misunderstanding but it's resolved. I promise you, I'm fine."

Hara forced herself to relax, letting her shoulders down. She'd learned long ago not to ask too many questions.

"I haven't seen a paper in two weeks," he said, "and the Norte are in control of the TV room right now. It's nothing but soccer all day. Talk to me about basketball. How are the preseason games going? Who looks good?"

"Oh!" She'd almost forgotten, her news overshadowed by the thick fog of . . . well, of prison. "You are never going to believe this! One of the owners of the Fishers called. I won the contest!"

Her father beamed. "No way."

"I know, right? I've got the exclusive interview with Charles Butler!" She clapped her hands in delight, like a child, but then interrupted her father before he could speak. "I know, I know what you're going to say, it's crazy that they chose me, a newb reporter—"

"No, I was going to say no one deserves it more than you."

Hara let the praise warm her.

"Damn. So proud of you. This is fantastic news. Now, you're sure no one is pulling your leg?"

"I swear. My editor says the man who reached out, O'Donnell, is legit, one of the five partners who own the team. They're flying me to Boston! I'm going to have a face-to-face with one of the biggest names in basketball!"

"Butler . . . I don't know how I feel about you being around that guy. I wish the interview was with anyone else. He's such a dick to the press. Worse, you might be from Podunk, Oregon, but you are drop-dead gorgeous, like a freaking runway model. He's going to—"

"Daddy, please. I've had to deal with d-bags before. You think I didn't know exactly what I was getting into when I decided to be a sports reporter? I spend all my time with athletes. I know what they can be like. And, frankly, I've been around *these* guys." She flipped her hand around the room, at the prisoners in their matching blue chambray shirts. "I'm pretty sure Butler can't say anything that's going to shock me."

"Hey, kid!" a voice boomed from beside her, making her jump. "I hear you're going to Boston!" It was Jonas, her father's cellmate. The big man nodded coldly at his wife as he sat down at their table, then turned to Hara and her father. "Good for you."

Thomas's face twisted into an ugly snarl, surprising Hara. He barked at his cellmate, "Jonas, you—"

"Hey, hey, you're right, man." Jonas held up a hand in peace. "I shouldna been eavesdroppin'. Heard ya when I came in, just wanted to say congrats to your girl."

The anger in her father's eyes dissipated as quickly as it had risen. "All right, sure. Rita, nice to see you." He turned back to Hara, putting an end to the conversation.

Hara raised an eyebrow at him. Her father offered a half smile and a shrug. "Sorry. He knows I look forward to my time with you."

She forgot sometimes. He was one way with her, but he had to be a different person when he left this room. Less of a person. It broke her heart.

"My little girl, the big reporter. Your mother must be dying."

"Oh no. You can't tell her."

"Well, lucky for you, there's no danger of that."

"I know, sorry. You know how she is, though. She hears I'm meeting a famous athlete and she'll go crazy. She'll try to come with me, make me wear high heels and contacts and giggle behind a fan."

Her father smirked. "You could go full-out, get your grandma to turn you into a geisha."

"Ha. Grandma would stab you with a pitchfork if she heard you say that." She and her father shared a sad look, missing the spunky woman whose mind was gone.

"You take after your mother, you know, much more belle than geisha. Good thing you've got her long eyelashes to flutter," he said, plucking at his own nonexistent lashes.

Hara laughed. "My daddy, the hairless wonder." She actually looked like both of them, and yet neither of them. Her height was obviously from Thomas, since her mother was tiny. A petite African-American woman and a tall Japanese dude.

Between them, Hara had ended up with thick, wavy black hair that fell between her shoulder blades and a caramel skin-tone that confused a lot of people, especially in contrast to her translucent blue, almond-shaped eyes. People were constantly asking her where she was from, or, more rudely, "What are you?"

"I'm from a small town on the edge of Portland," she would say. She didn't bother trying to answer the other question.

"Daddy, I'm not kidding. Mom's worse than ever. She hounds me to 'dress like a girl,' constantly leaving fashion magazines on my bed. I'm pretty sure she set up a Tinder account in my name." Hara pinched her old sweater. "I dress fine. I'm comfortable. I know how to look nice if I need to. What she really wants is for me to attract a rich dude with my 'feminine wiles.' Someone dying to get married. Then my life will be complete. She's a strong woman, running the farm on her own, yet I'm too muddled to take care of myself?"

"Willa just wants what's best for you. To have a bigger life than she's had, out of that town."

"Okay, first of all, I don't need a man to do that for me. I don't need *anyone* to do *anything* for me. Secondly"—she pushed up her glasses defiantly—"I know she loves me, I just wish she could see that I'm happy with what I'm doing. She'll see, I'm going to get a job on a big paper, covering sports. Look at Michelle Beadle. Great sportswriter. And Hannah Storm. And Jemele Hill. I can be—I will be—a damn fine reporter."

"You sound like you're trying to make yourself believe that. You *are* talented, Hara. But your mother is right about one thing. If you don't get your nose out of a book or a computer, you'll never meet anybody. Someday you are going to realize you *do* need somebody. I don't give a good goddamn who he is, as long as he's good to you. Or *she's* good to you."

"Uh, I'm happy to see prison has made you so progressive. But just because I like sports doesn't make me gay." She grinned at him. "I like sports because of you. It's all we talk about."

"Well, now, complain if you want, but it seems like your time with me has helped you get a writing gig. Let's see a little more gratitude, missy." He touched her cheek but withdrew his hand when the closest guard cleared his throat.

There was a moment of silence. It hurt. She was close to her mother in many ways, but her hugs always ended with a torrent of worries about Hara's future. Her father's affection was unconditional, yet was fleeting and controlled. But who was she to complain? It was far worse for him, stuck in a place where any human touch was rare and usually inspired by violence.

"You haven't given me the report yet," he said after a moment of silence. "Who's the starting roster for the Fishers? How they looking? What's going on with the other teams?"

This was Hara's job, covering the sporting world for her father, especially basketball. She used to love to play herself, then riding the bus to the prison to tell Thomas about her games, play by play, while he listened intently. As time passed, she found she was less interested in playing than in discussing strategy, plays, and analyzing coaching techniques with her father. She could say she did it for him, but it wasn't really true. She'd truly come to enjoy dissecting games and players.

"Boston did switch out a few guys this year, but the basic roster is the same. Of course, everyone wants to be on the team with Charles Butler. He has never been hotter. What's crazy is the Fishers brought back that rookie from last year, the one who sat on the bench."

"Are you talking about Derek Darcy? Is he healed?"

"His footage from training is good, but it sure seems like a crapshoot to hold on to someone who's been a dud. He is very fine to look at, I'll give him that, and he must be smart if he played for Pepperdine. I'm just not sure he's got what it takes to stick it out at the NBA level."

"You're pretty hard on him."

"He blew his first impression, whether the injury was his fault or not. Now he's going to have to earn back my respect."

"Butler is the one who should have to earn your respect. He gets away with too much just because he can throw a leather ball through an iron hoop. I don't like how he treats ladies. Or reporters."

"I don't know, Dad—they're all players. But, like I said, I'll be careful around him."

"Be careful around all of them. You go out there and you kick their asses if they need it. You show 'em, you ain't no sideline Barbie."

CHAPTER 2

For what do we live, but to make sport for our neighbors, and laugh at them in our turn?

—*Pride and Prejudice*

Hara strode to the back of the newsroom a few hours later, weaving through a cramped jumble of old desks. No one had bothered to turn on the overhead lights; the darkening gray clouds outside created more shadows than light. She wrapped a cardigan tightly around herself to fight off the early October chill.

Carter Hudson, owner of the *Tribune* and the only other full-time staff member, sat at a long table sifting through photographs for the next edition of the small-town paper.

"Hey!" she called out. When he looked up, she pointed to a framed photograph on the wall, an artful close-up of a wind-twisted pine tree. "This is new. I like it." Juxtaposed against the beat-up furniture and scratched flooring, the walls were freshly painted in satiny cream and hung neatly with dozens of blown-up photos in heavy gilt frames. Carter didn't like writing; he'd bought the newspaper so he'd have a platform from which to publish his photography, and he used the newsroom as a gallery. If it weren't for Hara, there'd be very little actual news printed.

"Good, you're back!" he called out. The forty-something man stuck a pair of pink leopard-print reading glasses on top of his mostly bald head and folded his arms, crinkling a silk shirt. "Mr. O'Donnell's assistant called. She'd like you to call her back. Don't mess this up, Hara."

Before she could answer, a familiar voice pierced the air behind them.

"Harrrr-aaaa!"

She winced, not turning around. "You told her, didn't you?"

"I'm sorry." Carter dipped his head. "I thought she knew—"

"That's right! *He* told me. Not you!" Willa Isari marched up to her daughter. "Hara! This is so exciting! How could you keep it from me!"

"Mother, calm down. I just found out today."

Willa looked like she just might vibrate apart, bouncing on her heels and grinning. The small woman flipped her long, dark curls out of her attractive face—vibrant, despite her years of picking apples and riding tractors in the wind and sun—and put a hand dramatically to her chest. "Hara. Please," she said quietly, "just tell me it's true. You've been invited to a cocktail party with the richest people in Boston?"

"What? No—"

"Actually," Carter interrupted them, "yes. The assistant said they'll fly you in this Friday. They're going to set you up in a guest suite at the O'Donnells' house. There will be a cocktail party to celebrate the start of the season. At some point in the evening, you will have twenty minutes with Butler, to ask him questions. Which, by the way, need to be preapproved." The editor in chief's lips twitched down. "They are footing the bill, but I'm not sure how I feel about limiting what we ask. I just hope Charles actually answers the questions."

I guess I will *have to wear high heels and makeup,* Hara thought. *Mom's dream come true.* Her thoughts turned into a swirling blob; an already highly stressful interview had just morphed into an invitation to the palace ball. *Wtf?* Now she not only had to worry about making a man who was famous for shunning the press actually speak to her, she had to dress up to do it.

"Well, I know how *I* feel about this!" said her mother. "We have so little time! We need to make an appointment immediately to get your eyebrows under control. You definitely need a bra fitting. And clothes! I have no idea how we'll afford it, but you are going to that party dressed to the goddamn nines. Those rich, eligible bachelors are going to swoon when you walk down those stairs. I will make sure of it."

"What stairs? Are you crazy? This is an interview—"

Her boss cleared his throat. "I can lend you a dress, Hara, from my mother's closets. And there are probably shoes that fit." Carter's very wealthy, socialite mother had passed away the year before but the son kept her closets intact, to be close to her, or so he claimed. "You will want to blend in. But it's more important to spend your time preparing for this story."

"More important—!" Hara's mother clenched her fists.

Hara put a hand on her mother's forearm. While irritated, she had to fight back a laugh at the anguish in the older woman's eyes. All over clothes and meeting men. "Simmer down, Mom. You're being ridiculous."

"I'll leave you two to it," Carter tossed over his shoulder as he rose and trotted back to his office.

Patting her mother's arm, gently, Hara said, "We'll talk about it later. Let's not do this where I work."

Willa peered around the room with an arched eyebrow. "Mm hm."

"This *is* my job." Hara pushed her black-framed glasses up her nose, the better to stare at her mother. "You know, how I make money. To help pay the bills."

Willa thrust an envelope into Hara's hand. "Here. Speaking of bills, here's your mail." She turned to go but then swung back around. "I do agree with one thing Carter said: This is a chance not to be wasted. I'll see you at home."

Hara dropped the student loan bill on her desk. The young reporter's head began to throb. Hearing the door slam behind her mother, she slumped into a chair.

I need to take up day drinking.

She wished her mother could get behind her on this. Hara's childhood had ended when her father went away, leaving her with a tightly wound Willa and only a few friends willing to stick by her. For years, walking through the aisles of the local grocery store had been a minefield of gossip and stares. She'd learned how to tune out people who were negative—though that sometimes felt like everyone around her.

She'd thought if she could prove she was smart and likable, the town gossipmongers would realize she was worthy and that her parents were still the same people they'd always been, farmers who'd grown up in this town and met at the local high school. At first, the young couple had struggled with bigoted bullshit aimed at their relationship, but both were so popular, they'd been named homecoming king and queen their senior year.

Hara struggled with plenty of her own bullshit at that school, and still graduated at the top of her class. She did have friends, but had spent zero time partying. Her free time consisted of picking apples, studying for AP literature, and re-

reading her favorite Jane Austen books. No homecoming title for her.

As a senior, she took on an internship at the local paper and started churning out her version of the *Bleacher Report*. Hara Isari liked sports and writing about sports. Carter encouraged her, printing her work and helping her get scholarships, but, according to a few of the town's loudmouthed hillbillies, it was just one more thing wrong with her, a girl who thought she was an authority on football.

It was too bad. There was a lot to love about her little town, including the tree-lined streets circling the quaint city park, and the artists and loggers who coexisted with tech workers and telecommuters. Most of the citizens were decent, hardworking people who kept to themselves.

She'd left for college and hadn't looked back. At least, until she'd graduated and realized she needed a full-time gig if she wanted to eat.

So here I am. Back in the thick of it.

The biggest difference between then and now was that now she had to cover the town beat in order to get paid. Stories on bunco games, drunken tractor driving, and the new flagpole in front of the Elks Lodge. Mind-numbingly boring, but it allowed her to spend her evenings writing and submitting freelance sports articles. So far, only a few had been picked up and nothing had gone viral.

To be honest, the biggest and most important difference between now and then was that now she realized she was partly to blame for her teen angst, that she'd pushed away the people who might have been there for her. Like her mother, and even Carter. Given a little time and space, she'd come to see that she'd hardened her heart. As an adult, she knew she needed friends, and was willing to look for the good in most people—though she immediately backed away if she sensed something off. Hara had perfected the art of living by first impressions.

Outside, clouds scudded across the sky like rocks skipping in slow motion across a darkened pond. Hara shivered. The wind was really picking up. She hoped it wasn't going to storm. They hadn't finished bringing in the apples yet.

Hara was staying out at the orchard for free, helping if her mom was short-handed, even if that meant giving her more opportunities to describe, in detail, how Hara could capture a man. She wasn't sure how much longer she was going to be able to take it.

It had been a very long and depressing year, in which she'd faced multiple rejections from bigger papers, the usual response being "we aren't hiring." The underlying, real message was "we aren't hiring young girls." Sportswriting was a tight field, anyway, but throw in her age and her sex and Hara feared she was going to have to settle for beat reporting until she could prove herself. It was one thing to cover the local stories and events for Carter in the interim, but she did not want this as a career. She wanted the excitement of action on the court or in the field.

She wanted what she couldn't get at a small-town newspaper and definitely not out at the orchard, drowning in apples and unwanted advice.

It wasn't as if she didn't want a boyfriend. But she didn't want someone because they were rich, nor did she want a man drawn to her only because she was thin and had shiny hair. She craved a man who would be drawn to her because she was talented and smart.

Hara wanted to be taken seriously—as a woman *and* as a reporter. Part of why she stuck with her big eyeglasses and wore bulky cardigans was to de-emphasize her sexuality. Admittedly, that got old, but better than people thinking she was stupid or shallow simply because her face was nice and her boobs were perky. She hated that. More than anything.

Well, okay, more than anything, she hated that she cared what other people thought. But she did.

Somehow the Charles Butler story had dropped into her lap. She had to jump at the opportunity. If she held back, she lost a chance to prove herself to the world. And to her mother. Hara closed her eyes and smiled, resolute not to let anyone spoil the mood.

Truth be told, she was also excited about the chance to go through Carter's closets. Maybe this was one of those times she could be a smart career-oriented woman *and* a girl who liked to dress up, and it would be okay.

Hara had a free trip to Boston. Why waste it?

She clicked on the computer and went into her Google Docs. There it was. The most current version of her résumé. She hit *print*, and then looked up the street address for Boston's biggest newspaper, *City Gazette*.

Her boss was back. Carter glanced at the résumé but pretended not to see it, instead handing her a slip of paper. "Here's the assistant's number," he said, drawing up a chair. "You know, I'm not sure why they're throwing this VIP treatment at an unknown reporter, including a press pass and a stay at the owner's residence. I want you to be careful, Hara. O'Donnell and the other owners are forcing Butler into this PR stunt and tossing a young reporter to the lion. You won the writing contest, but I'm not sure the prize is worth it. I feel like they are buying a story." Frown lines marched from his eyebrows back to the middle of his smooth, bald head. "I'm probably doing the wrong thing, letting you go."

"No way! I can do this! I promise, I'll be fair and unbiased, even if I have to use their questions."

"They're not really giving you a chance to develop much more than a puff piece. Is it worth it?" The older man tapped his chin, thinking. "I guess we can view this as a stepping-stone. Building connections. I just worry you'll get the reputation as a lightweight writer. Yet, I'd hate to take an opportunity from you."

"Then don't. I'm a big girl. I can do this."

"Should I get you a hotel room? I'll pay for it myself, if that'll make you more comfortable. This is just too weird, them offering to host you."

"Let me talk to the assistant, okay? See how long I'll be there and what it's like at the house?" Hara grinned. "I mean, would you turn down staying the night in a mansion? Come on, that alone makes the trip worth it."

CHAPTER 3

My good opinion once lost, is lost forever.

—*Pride and Prejudice*

The Boeing 737 finally landed.

It took a while for Hara to get her bearings. Business-class legroom—thanks to Carter—and a comfortable, oversize sweater with yoga pants had not been enough to overcome roller-coaster turbulence and a seatmate who whispered over a rosary for almost six hours.

The ground still swayed as she dragged her carry-on suitcase out of the Boston airport.

Thankfully, the Lincoln Town Car Mr. O'Donnell had promised waited for her at the curb, complete with a chauffeur holding up a small white sign reading *Isari*. Instantly, her equilibrium was back, righted by a flash of tingling glee. She felt famous. Discombobulated and in disarray, but famous. The driver opened the back door and helped her into the car.

Madeline Bingley waited for her in the vast back seat, separated from the front by a black tinted partition. The doll-sized, doll-faced woman was the executive assistant to the team's part owner, Mr. O'Donnell, and she was perfect and beautiful and terrifying.

"Hara, so nice to meet you." Madeline briefly offered a dainty hand, then smoothed back her short, white-blonde hair. She wore a striped business suit, cropped and tailored to fit her slender frame, paired with satiny pumps and an on-point popped collar. The fancy leather portfolio on the seat beside her probably cost more than Hara's monthly paycheck from the paper.

After the greeting, the executive assistant spent the ride turned away from Hara, speaking in code during a continuous stream of phone calls. Hara had to consciously unclench her jaw a number of times. Not because she was ignored, but because Madeline had the odd habit of fluctuating between a professional tone one minute to a baby voice the next.

"Teddy, we are going to need that account opened by this afternoon. Okay? Kisses!" the assistant cooed into the phone with a high-pitched giggle—yet her face remained stony. The woman dealt with sports stars and millionaires, apparently getting her way by adapting different personas.

They had been slogging through Boston traffic for what seemed forever, Hara pretending to answer emails, when Madeline suddenly pulled the cell from her ear, looked at an incoming message, and jabbed at a button on the car ceiling.

"Driver? I need to make a stop at the administration offices before we go to O'Donnell's residence. Do you know where that is?"

"Yes, ma'am," came the crackly response over the intercom.

Soon enough, they were pulling up in front of a row of high-rise office buildings. Madeline gracefully extracted herself from the back seat with a promise to return in a few minutes. Before the assistant could cross the wide sidewalk, however, Hara realized she was letting an opportunity slip by and rolled down the window. She called out, "Madeline? Do you think I could come in with you? Start getting the flavor of the organization for my story?"

The assistant blew air out of her dainty nose, running her eyes over Hara pointedly. "Hmm. Maybe another time." She went into the building without another word.

Deflated, Hara looked down at her street clothes, touched her messy bun. The woman might have a point but not manners.

Cacophonous city street sounds and Boston's clammy fall air flooded the car's interior. She tried to roll up the window but found it locked. When she pushed the intercom button, the driver didn't respond.

Before she could get up the gumption to lean forward and tap on the partition, a man's voice came from somewhere behind the Lincoln, surprising her not only because he sounded so close but because his voice was so deep. His baritone rolled across her like a smooth drum, resounding through her body, soothing while tantalizing.

"I told you, I won't be at the meeting. I need to fill out some paperwork," he said calmly. Then his voice went up in pitch, agitated. "Seriously? Why do we have to keep having this conversation?"

He must have been on the phone, considering the silent pauses. Hara wanted to get a look at the guy with the gorgeous radio voice but he was out of her immediate line of sight and she didn't want anyone to think she was eavesdropping, at least not on purpose. She jabbed at the window control, trying again to roll it up, but still a no go. She let her head drop back onto the seat and closed her eyes, faking sleep.

"Stop saying that. I'm not just playing at games. I'm good at what I do." Hara jumped when the invisible man barked out a harsh laugh, one which revealed quite a bit of hurt. "Oh, okay, Dad. Only you would be embarrassed to have a professional athlete as a son."

The man with the amazing voice and terrible father had to be a Fisher. He was standing in front of the Fishers' administrative offices; he had to be one of their basketball players. How did someone get to be a professional athlete and still have a father who put him down? *Never thought I'd feel sorry for a guy paid to play a game.* At least her dad believed in her, even if he couldn't be around. Slowly edging across the seat, she tried to poke her head out the window just far enough to see who was talking without being seen.

Leaning against the hood of the car parked behind her was Derek Darcy. The rookie she'd been discussing with her father.

In real life, this close, the full impact of his melodious voice and square jaw and height and his broad shoulders and his taut chest muscles was not lost on her. Not in the slightest.

"I take it you won't be at the game tomorrow—" He glanced over his shoulder and stopped.

Their eyes locked. Hara, caught spying on him, felt a blush sizzle up her neck to the top of her head. But his eyes . . . she had never seen anything like them. A stunning molten copper color, fringed with heavy black eyelashes, contrasting perfectly with skin that reminded her of a polished stone, dark, smooth, and glistening. His laser-focused gaze was reminiscent of that of a lion, noble and intense, possibly ready to attack.

Before she could duck her head back inside, he quirked an eyebrow and said evenly, "Can I help you?"

She didn't answer at first, hoping he was talking to the person on the phone, that he wasn't staring right at her. But, no. He hung up, lowered the phone, and kept eye contact, his coppery eyes revealing nothing.

"S-s-sorry," Hara stuttered. Quickly, she leaned back . . . and cracked the side of her head on the window frame. "Fuumphhh," she said in a moan, clamping down on a curse. Only she could be so brilliantly clumsy in front of a basketball star. Pressing her body into the seat, she put a hand to her head, mortification and pain combining to create a fantastic fireworks show behind her eyes.

"You might consider minding your own business," Derek Darcy's voice rumbled from out of her view. "That was probably karma." It was hard to tell if he was irritated or amused.

"Yep. You're right, thanks," she called out, trying to sound cheery, groaning internally. *Nothing to see here, move along now.* Hara scooted to the far side, as if that could rewind time.

She took off her glasses and covered her face with her hands, wanting to disappear, but then couldn't help but peek. She saw the player stride gracefully, like an athlete, toward the building, his gluteus muscles flexing under the tight slacks, revealing a perfectly shaped ass.

He stopped a few steps from the building, respectfully allowing an elderly, slow-moving gentleman in a suit to cross in front of him. Derek squinted back over his shoulder and once again caught her staring, this time through her fingers like a child cheating at hide-and-seek. The blood left her brain as she jerked her hands down.

He shook his head at her and sidestepped around the old man, making it to the doors in two long strides. The young, handsome ballplayer disappeared inside without another glance.

Hara had half hoped he'd turn back to her again, though she didn't know why. She'd made an ass of herself, sure, but he'd offered her no grace, instead making her feel even stupider. He'd been polite to an old rich guy, but he'd definitely been a jerk to her.

She lifted her chin and sat up straight, having established a proper response to Derek Darcy. Then she checked her throbbing temple for blood.

–*–

The massive brick residence on Beacon Street probably wouldn't properly be considered a mansion, since it was closely flanked by smaller but luxurious urban homes on the banks of the Charles River. But the gated complex had a large landscaped courtyard that led to the garages, and a private garden in the back, complete with docks and a small boathouse. Mr. O'Donnell's house boasted two elevators, five fireplaces, numerous bedroom suites, a library, a gym, and a living room with grand proportions.

This she knew because Madeline Bingley had been talking about the residence ever since leaving the administration building, making Hara think fondly back to when Madeline had been on her phone, ignoring her.

"The architecture and interior design have been featured in numerous magazines, including *Living*, *Dwell*, and *Architecture*. The O'Donnells have a small staff caring for the family and the home, including an on-site superintendent, so don't hesitate to ask if you need something."

The driver took her luggage from the car and began to wheel it inside.

"Oh, I can do that," said Hara.

"It's his job, it's fine," said Madeline, waving him on, and then running a hand over her white-blonde pixie cut.

"Let me get you back to your rooms." They pushed through the front door, a solid slab of satiny carved wood bigger than most of the walls in the Isari farmhouse. "You have a few hours before the guests start to arrive." Madeline raked her eyes over Hara's rumpled airplane clothes for the second time that day and lifted an eyebrow. "Do you have any questions about attire? Can we provide you with anything?"

Oh, you and I are not going to be friends, bougie. But Hara was amused by the condescension, Madeline reminding her of a classic Mean Girl. "No, I'm set. I have a dress. And my notebook with the approved questions. How long into the party will I be meeting Mr. Butler? Will we have a place to sit down for a few minutes?"

"Yes. I will come get you when Mr. Butler is ready, after he's had a chance to make his rounds. Shouldn't be too long."

"Will I have a chance to talk to any other players?"

Madeline's eyes narrowed. "I don't think so, not officially. This is supposed to be a piece about our lead player, is it not? Mr. O'Donnell was quite clear."

"Okay . . ."

"You don't have a mic with you, do you? No recordings. You and your editor have already agreed to that. I don't need to take your phone away, do I?"

"I'm not planning on breaking our deal. I hope Mr. O'Donnell knows how grateful I am he picked me for such an honor." Hara really wanted to answer with a wisecrack but quickly realized this woman was only going to be pleasant if Hara was submissive and pliable; she rolled out her meek, oh-you-are-so-amazing act, just temporarily.

"Yes, well, I know the owners thought your contest entry was impressive or you wouldn't be here. They need the basketball commission to see that the Fishers' star player will be compliant with the rules, that he *will* talk to the press this year. Starting with this exclusive. It's important you get it right."

Following the assistant down a long hallway on the second floor, Hara glared at her back. But then the reporter noticed the line of paintings on the wall; there were beautiful landscapes and abstracts mixed in with gloomy portraits of old people straight out of a horror movie. She was 95 percent certain that one of the paintings with an old Victorian woman clutching a parasol had moving eyes. Probably one of Madeline's minions behind the wall, watching Hara's every move.

Hara let her face grow impassive, but then almost lost it again when she realized that one massive painting was of a pagan orgy. She slowed her steps as she approached, trying not to be obvious.

The painting showed a field lit by moonlight, ringed by massive oaks and alders and fir trees, done in the finest detail. But Hara doubted the majority of viewers even noticed the needles on the fir boughs—there were dozens of cherub-figured men and women, naked and pale, writhing under and over each other, next to a massive bonfire, in the field of sown wheat stalks and in the tree line. She peered closer. Some were actually up in the trees. The bodies, coupled or in groups, were as painstakingly detailed as the leaves on the trees, and the imaginative positions . . . Hara gulped, suddenly flushed. One complicated entanglement showed a woman down on all fours, being used as a table by a very sweaty couple. But the table-esque girl didn't seem to mind, an O of delight on her lips.

"Uh hmm." Madeline cleared her throat.

Hara hadn't realized she'd stopped completely, leaning in, trying to decipher the many tangled limbs and crazy angles.

She stood straight, pushed her glasses up, and pretended to be blasé. "Well, I've seen better."

"Oh, I'm sure." Madeline smirked and moved on.

Who hung something like that in a guest hall? Maybe Carter had been right, maybe she should have stayed at a hotel. Hara would for sure be locking her bedroom door that night.

At the end of the hall, which had begun to feel like an interminable death march to the young reporter, Madeline finally stopped outside a door. "Here you are. Like I said on the phone, everyone will respect your privacy. But let one of the employees know if you need something."

Hara was left to her own devices in a light-filled room spacious enough to feel sparse, even with a plumbed bar, two couches, a massive desk, and a fireplace. The separate bedroom was almost as large. The bathroom reminded her of an expensive spa setting. *I can get used to this*, she thought, unpacking her toiletry bag. She also took the time to check out her head where she had cracked it against the car. It was still tender but there was no cut, thankfully. The only residue was her embarrassment at having a handsome, famous man witness her idiocy.

It didn't take her long to finish unpacking her small suitcase. The little black dress with subtly embedded sequins Carter had picked out for her sparkled in the light of the infinite closet.

Her boss did not live, or dress, like the average, barely-scraping-by journalist, thanks to family money. And, it was clear, he'd inherited not just his mother's riches but also her habit of being a label whore. When he'd first held up the expensive sequined dress, Hara insisted she wanted to exude professionalism, so Carter had layered the clingy cocktail gown with a silk blazer. Then, he told her he wanted to make sure she could hold her own with the moneyed crowd—and handed her a pair of embellished Christian Louboutin red sole pumps that fit like Cinderella's slippers.

As they'd peered into Carter's full-length mirror, the dress and shoes glittered against Hara's skin and accentuated her slight curves and toned limbs. They agreed, the combo was a hit.

"You sure you need these back? Louboutins are a must for the next office picnic."

Carter had put an arm around Hara's shoulder and squeezed. "Honey, honey . . . why in the world do you keep that bosom under wraps?" He adjusted a strap. "Your mom will be thrilled. You'll be beating them away with a stick."

"I have no interest in hooking up. Too much drama for little payoff. And I definitely am not looking for a boyfriend; I don't have time to train some idiot to be a good partner." The truth was, she was lonely. But she refused to be desperate.

"Oh, I get it, believe me. Men can be such assholes." Carter patted her shoulder. "But wait and see. You just haven't met the right man yet. Though, you never will if you write everybody off before you even talk to them."

Now, standing in a closet in O'Donnell's luxurious Boston home, about to conduct an interview that could change the course of her life, she let the soft material of the sexy dress run through her fingers.

What in the hell am I doing?

–*–

Derek Darcy blew out his breath hard enough to create a small circle of fog on the windshield in front of him and then stabbed at the screen on his dashboard until the two radio disc jockeys shut up.

What in the hell am I doing?

Why was he letting these guys and their amateur hour get to him? He couldn't do much about his father, unless he wanted to walk away from his family completely, but he didn't have to give credence to strangers. Let them riff—the media would be singing a different tune at the game tomorrow night.

Unconsciously, Derek reached down and rubbed his knee. He'd torn his meniscus at the start of the season last year; it was now long healed, but the surgical scar had not gone away. There was a line of tissue he could feel through his tuxedo pants, a constant reminder of the bullshit he'd had to put up with last year, as the rookie who rode the bench. And, apparently, still had to put up with. Imbeciles with a microphone or a pen loved to trash-talk Derek, but not for long. He was going to change all that, come hell or high water.

He jumped out from behind the wheel and slammed the door. Charles was supposed to have met him on the curb ten minutes ago. When his teammate had texted and asked Derek to pick him up at his mom's house, Derek was at first annoyed. But, surprisingly, Charles's mother still lived back in the old neighborhood and the thought of returning made him oddly sentimental.

Not that it had been his neighborhood, not really. No, he didn't have a community growing up. Instead, he'd had a waitstaff and absent parents, and resided in a historical manor that was ridiculously huge for three people and a couple of maids.

Derek met Charles Butler when they were in second grade, attending the same basketball camp. Charles had kept the bullies away and showed Derek how to play with confidence. And joy—something his father could never understand. They grew up together, shooting hoops and eating dinner at Charles's mom's house. Right here. This was where he'd found love and acceptance, in an old, rickety house on a long street of old, rickety houses and cracked sidewalks. It had been a while since he'd been here; he hadn't realized how much he missed it.

The curved sidewalk, lined with fall flowers and foliage, led to a newly refurbished Colonial-style veranda. *Not old and rickety-lookin' now,* Derek thought, noticing the new windows and siding. He rang the bell and heard Charles shout out, "Come in!"

Walking down the short hallway into the living room, he was amazed at the changes: Walls had been knocked out, a new fireplace and tigerwood floors had been put in.

"Wow! What happened in here? Your mom must have found herself a remodeling fairy godmother." He spoke to Charles, who sat on an extra-wide ottoman, tying his shiny black dress shoes. "Why didn't you just buy your ma a new house?"

Derek hoped that didn't sound rude. He didn't mean it that way. A lot of the players used their first-year contract to help set their families up. Especially the ones who came from low-income homes, like Charles, whose single mom had worked in the cafeteria of an elementary school.

"Oh, don't you go diggin' at him, I wanted to stay here," said Ms. Butler, coming into the room. "I fixed this place up a few years ago when he went to college, and it's just how I like it."

"Ma," Charles grumbled.

There was an edge to his voice that made Derek look around. Maybe he *had* insulted him.

"It's just Derek!" She paused, and then clicked her teeth, fluffing pillows on the couch, avoiding Charles. After a second, she said, "I don't have any intention of leavin' my neighbors behind. I ain't uppity. I got everything I need right here."

Charles sighed heavily and then squinted at Derek, not saying anything.

It hit Derek then, what his friend was worried about. Ms. Butler on her part-time salary had somehow managed to overhaul the house while Charles was in college . . . before Charles had an NBA contract . . .

Derek frowned, put a halt to that train of thought before it could go any further. She'd lucked into an inheritance or something. That was it.

She came to Derek then and gave him a squeeze. "Look at you! You a college man, *and* a big baller. Keep this guy close, Charles, he good for you."

"Yeah, okay." Charles stood up, towering above them. "Cuz we just sufferin' when he ain't around." He grinned and clapped Derek on the shoulder. "Sorry I'm late. Ma won't stop talking."

"I can hear you, Charlie." His mother's voice floated over from the corner, where she straightened magazines on a side table.

"Why am I givin' you a ride, anyway?" asked Derek. "What happened to your boys?"

Charles tugged his pant cuffs over his shoes and stood up. "Ain't you my boy?" He smiled. "They're not invited to this party. O'Donnell runs a tight ship."

"Besides, I wanted to see you!" Ms. Butler pinched Derek's cheek, making him blush. Then she brought a phone out of the pocket of her big cardigan. "You stand right there, let me take a picture. So handsome!"

"Christ, it's not like we're going to prom."

"Do not take the Lord's name in vain, young man! Now smile, dammit." She took a few pictures while Derek and Charles fidgeted with their ties and suit jackets, like nervous teenagers rather than wealthy athletes.

"We gotta go, woman." Charles bent down and gave her a peck on the head. "Thanks for dinner." He gestured to Derek then loped out the door.

Derek gave her a hug goodbye, clasping the older woman for a beat longer than necessary. There were very few people in this world that he loved, much less liked. "Nice to see you, Ms. Butler."

"You come back, you hear? I'll make your favorites for dinner."

His own mother and father preferred to eat at restaurants, the fancier, the better. They were regulars at their snooty club, had their own balcony at the opera house. They were too worried about money and appearance to spend many nights at home with their son. He realized the hypocrisy of these judgments, however, climbing into his GLS 550 Mercedes SUV wearing a Ralph Lauren tuxedo, but he also knew his materialism didn't rule him. That he could be grateful for the kindness shown him, even if it was from someone else's parent instead of his own.

"How's my tie look?" Charles asked from the passenger seat, as Derek backed out of the driveway. The big man's fingers fumbled with the material.

Derek laughed. "You're a hot mess. I'll retie it for you when we get to O'Donnell's."

"Listen . . ." Charles sat up straight, his head scraping the roof of the cab. "You're not going to say anything about Ma's house, are you? I forgot you haven't been out here since high school."

"Why would I? To who?"

"Never mind."

"Are you talking about the remodel? I was just kidding about buying her a new house. It sounds like she's happy . . ." He did not want to have this conversation. College scandals and payouts to student athletes were rampant these days, and the crackdowns were harsh. There was no way Ms. Butler would do something so wrong. Derek was determined to leave it at that.

"Yeah, you're right," Charles said, then cleared his throat. He clearly felt the same way about the conversation, abruptly asking, "Man, are you ready for tomorrow? How you feeling?"

"I'm more worried about surviving this party tonight than I am tomorrow's game. I hate having to talk to people. Especially ones I don't know. Okay, and most of the ones I know."

"Why you bein' a grouch? You twenty-three. Live a little. Boston loves us."

"Boston loves *you*."

"People might love you a little more if you actually said more than five words at the press junkets. And didn't have such a sour look on your face all the time."

"Oh-ho! If *I* talked to the press! You full of shit. The club had to make you do this interview tonight. The association has been bitching at you for a year." Derek glanced at him. "It always surprises me, you dodging the press. You're not some wilting flower. You actually like talking to people." He shifted down and changed lanes. "And now, you doin' this three-sixty with this big interview."

"Yeah." Rolling down his window, Charles let a light rain spatter on the inside of the car and on his face, staring out at the passing scenery.

They sat quietly for a few moments, each trapped in their thoughts.

"I—" Charles started to say something, but then stopped, his eyes dark when he faced Derek. "Man, I—" He cut himself off again with a deep sigh.

"What's up?" Derek had not expected the change in mood.

Slowly, as if choosing his words carefully, his teammate said, "O'Donnell hasn't wanted me talking to the press. But now the association is making a big stink about me not meeting contract expectations, so he's got this exclusive set up, to appease the powers that be."

"I don't get it. Why doesn't he want you to talk to the press?"

Charles wouldn't meet his eyes.

Derek gripped the wheel. "All right, man, what's goin' on?" First the house, now this shady business.

"It's nothing." Charles shrugged and then tried to lighten the mood. "It's okay, everything will be fine. No big deal. I just hate O'Donnell controlling my reputation with the public."

"There's obviously something."

"No, no," Charles said hastily. "O'Donnell just thinks I'm gonna say something offensive, I guess."

"Yeah, cuz nobody else is throwin' f-bombs or snark at reporters. That's just stupid." But Derek decided to let it go, since they were almost to the party. Instead, for the moment, he focused on the team's owner. "That dude is weird. I've never liked him." O'Donnell might have been the one to hire Derek, but Derek knew it was most likely due to Charles's insistence that he'd been picked up by the Fishers.

Charles seemed more than willing to change the subject. "You don't like anybody."

"That's not true. I like your mom. And I had this one nanny with a really big chest. I liked her a lot."

"Never would have expected that from you, choirboy."

Derek threw him the finger.

They pulled up to the front gate and were buzzed in. Parking, Derek turned to his friend. "You ready to be in the spotlight?"

Charles turned pensive again. "Sure."

A valet opened the door, ending their conversation. Derek followed the big man into the O'Donnell residence. There was something going on with his friend. He shoved his hands in his pockets and sighed. Nothing could affect the game tomorrow; Derek needed a win. He needed to prove himself off the bench. And he couldn't do it without Charles.

Am I really that self-centered?

"Hey!" he called after Charles. "Let me fix your tie!"

CHAPTER 4

They have none of them much to recommend them . . .

—*Pride and Prejudice*

Hara leaned against a pillar at the edge of the large, all-white living area. Five times the size of a normal room, the hard, glistening space was filled with marble and ornate gold trim and beautiful people in beautiful clothes. White-gloved waiters with golden trays of drinks and hors d'oeuvres wove silently through the guests and clusters of creamy velvet settees.

She felt like she was in a scene from her favorite book, the proud young woman at the ball surrounded by an opulently dressed crowd looking down their noses at those who were not in their private clubs. Thank God for her camouflage, the expensive LBD and Louboutins. Carter would have loved the decadence but it put Hara on edge. She'd wandered in a few minutes ago, hoping to come off as elegant, arranged against the stone column. A deep cold seeped into her shoulder blades as she dithered between giddy and terrified.

She shivered. *Oh, great.* Glancing down, she saw the light

blazer over her thin dress did nothing to hide the resulting hard nipples. She knew she should have slapped on Band-Aids when she was getting dressed.

The party in full swing around her, she pondered her next move. Her inclination was to force herself into a bold strut up to the nearest group of diamond-bedazzled octogenarians and insert herself "confidently" into a conversation, whether it be about the price of beef or redecorating a Manhattan high-rise. She could make shit up and tee-hee with the best of them—prison visitation rooms had taught her all about reading your audience. The most important thing was to assert dominance quickly without coming off as cocky. She needed to look like she belonged. *Fake it until you make it. Stop hiding!*

Before she was forced to make a move, however, a portly old man broke away from a clique of men fresh off the Monopoly board and approached her. "Ms. Isari?"

"Yes?" she stuttered.

"Hello, I am Connor O'Donnell." He twiddled his fingers at a spindly woman who had materialized at his side. "And this is my wife, Molly."

"Oh, hello!" Hara leapt to attention the best she could on high heels and the stone floor, and thrust out her hand. It took a beat for Mr. O'Donnell to shake. Finally, he grasped her fingers, crunched down like he was trying to squeeze the last drop from a tube of toothpaste, and pumped once. Mrs. O'Donnell's handshake, however, was so tepid Hara wasn't sure they'd actually touched.

"Is everything to your liking in your rooms? Is there anything I can do for you?" Mrs. O'Donnell asked, her voice as light and airy as her handshake.

"Honestly, I can't imagine what else I would need. Everybody has been very kind. Your home is beautiful, thank you so much for hosting me." Polite on the outside, her insides were agog over these two blue-blood conservatives pushing seventy who just happened to hang an orgy painting in the guest hall. Totally normal.

"That was completely my husband's doing, dear." The older woman lowered her eyelids and offered him an unreadable look before gliding away, saying, "You must excuse me, I will need to attend to those arriving."

Hara nervously turned her attention back to O'Donnell. She couldn't believe she was talking to an NBA team owner, weirdo or not. It was crazy. She smiled broadly at the man, hoping the wattage would blind him to any small town that might be peeking out from behind her edges. "Believe me, I know how lucky I am to have this opportunity, sir."

"That's true. We've struggled to get Charles to talk to journalists. The people at ESPN have been trying to get a full interview for months. He's finally agreed to an exclusive, though, and we thought a contest was the best way to put a positive spin on it. Sportswriters from every outlet entered articles. However, after reading your article analyzing the leadership potential in last year's All-Stars, I knew you were the one. Insightful and very thorough." He winked at her. "And the fact that you're an attractive, up-and-coming young woman is good PR."

Hara bit her lip. Had she been profiled? Was she picked because she was female? Her smile this time was forced. "Well, I'm the woman for the job." Hara would write the hell out of the interview, whether or not he liked her ass.

"Glad to hear it. We'll be meeting him in just a short while. Ms. Bingley filled you in?"

"Madeline? Yes."

"Good. Good. Well, I must mingle. There are plenty of

girlfriends and wives of the players here, you should have no trouble finding someone to talk to. Until later."

The old man hailed a small group farther off and wandered away.

Hara leaned back against the wide pillar.

Was she here because of what she looked like, rather than her talent as a writer? She grappled with that inner demon briefly but then decided to push it out and shut the door. The only thing she could do now was to go forward and prove that she deserved to be here—she'd been doing it for years. She *was* a sportswriter. A good one. And O'Donnell wouldn't have brought in someone unless they could do a decent job, she assured herself.

Hara forcibly shifted her concentration to the interview, going over details in her head. But it wasn't just insecurities distracting her: Her contacts were contracting against her rapidly drying eyeballs. She desperately wanted to rub them, furious with herself for giving into vanity and wearing contact lenses instead of her glasses. They always bothered her, and this was no exception. Blinking as rapidly as a ticking clock didn't help.

She was also trying to distract herself from the roomful of partygoers ignoring her. She didn't usually allow herself the luxury of feeling shy, but the intimidating crowd had no idea she existed. Streams of people flowed around her, including women too flawless to be real, with artful makeup and perfectly proportioned bodies wrapped in haute couture and gold and diamonds.

I'm just as good as everyone here, Hara told herself sternly, squaring her shoulders. She ran a palm across her flat stomach; the dress and jacket clung in the right ways, even if doing nothing to hide her hard nipples. With her hair pulled up loosely, she'd followed the directions from a *Vogue* video and added a dab of rose-colored blush to her angular cheeks, mascara to her already dark and long lashes, and a sheen of pink-tinged lip gloss to lightly lined lips. She felt sexy. Also professional, she reminded herself, fingering a rolled-back cuff on the silky suit jacket. But she'd let the jacket hang open, and it slid over her hips, not hiding her curves.

Hara found it amusing that O'Donnell suggested she would only find something to talk about with the young women in the room. Her job was to talk to everyone, and this was a varied crowd. The professional athletes tended to stand out, being at least a head taller than the other men. She recognized a few of the Fisher team owners, and a handful of movie and music people.

When she spotted Kendrick Lamar with Mark Wahlberg, she thought she might pee herself, just for an instant, but then got her fangirling under control. It was time for business.

–*–

Derek appraised the twin butlers in gold livery and white gloves at the entrance to the grand room, sentinels guiding and guarding at the same time.

His mother would have scoffed and claimed this was new money, whispering loudly about the gaucheness. But Derek could respect that people wanted grandeur in their life. They wanted a sense of import. Of magnificence. What was wrong with that?

Charles had stopped twenty feet from the entrance to the room, to let Derek retie his tie.

"Wreck, can I tell you something?" Charles asked, his head

craned up. "We good, right? You and me been buds since forever, since we was grommets, skateboarding to the courts."

Derek dropped his hands, done with the tie. "Yeah?"

"If something did come out about me, something that might make me look bad, you'd have my back, right?"

"Oh Jesus." Derek's heart lurched. He peered around, made sure no one was close. "Fuckin' A, man. 'Course I got you."

"I'll tell you about it later, but I didn't kill nobody, you can get that look off your face."

"Hold up." Derek pitched his voice low. "Is this about your mom? Her coming into money before you went off to play pro ball?"

"Goddamn it, I knew you caught that. Ma. The biggest mouth."

"You the one bringin' it up."

Charles walked farther away from the party entrance and the people, Derek following.

"She didn't know what she was doin' was wrong. Before I announced where I was going to college, the school came to Ma and told her they'd give her money if I went there. They called it a bonus, told her everyone did it. She knew that's where I wanted to go anyway, so she didn't spend too much time thinking about it, just accepted the money. You know her. So damn naive. I didn't know anything about it until I came back home on my first break and she was changin' shit up. She thought she'd surprise me." He groaned. "She did."

"Why you telling me this? Especially right now?"

"What if the press finds out? What if this reporter did some digging before she came here? What if I'm about to get jumped?" Charles eyes were wide, his nostrils flared.

"Goddamn it." Derek clenched his fists, not sure what to think. "How could you let this happen? It's not just your mother. Your school could be stripped of every title you won for them, and you'll get fired."

"I don't need the lecture right now. I need your support."

"You know what you need to do? You need to go in there and out yourself right now, get ahead of this thing, put your spin on the story. I know your mother, I believe you, there was no way she realized she was doing something wrong."

His friend was unable to meet his gaze.

Derek inhaled sharply, having thought of something else. "O'Donnell knows about it. It's why he doesn't want you to talk to reporters."

"Yes and yes."

"What a slimy fucker. Did he know before he brought you onto the team?"

Charles shoved his hands in his pockets. "We gotta go in. I'll explain more later. But will you come into the interview with me? Watch the reporter, see if you think she maybe knows something?"

"I . . . I guess." Derek's thoughts were in chaos. He struggled between his love for a friend and a sickening sense that his ethics were about to be challenged. "Charles, seriously, think of a way you can self-report, use this opportunity to get on top of it."

"Let me think about it." He stood up straight and clapped Derek on the shoulder. "Don't worry about it too much. I'll take care of it. I ain't lettin' this ruin our season."

Charles loped away from him, headed for the party. Derek could only stare after him.

The season. *This could ruin everything.* Why did shit always have to be so complicated?

Derek needed time to process. Normally, his was a black-and-white world. There was a right and a wrong, and that was it. But here, in this instance, he was mired in the rare gray in-between. Ms. Butler . . . he adored the woman. Charles was his friend. They'd lived in poverty, with a financial insecurity that Derek had never had to deal with. She'd accepted what the school had told her. She hadn't broken the law. But, ignorant or not, she *had* broken the rules and her son knew about it.

If Charles was dropped from the team, Derek would suffer, too. There'd be no one there to advocate for him, and the team would falter without their best player. He wouldn't get his chance to prove himself without Charles's help.

Derek frowned, shoved that dark thought back into the farthest corner.

He followed after Charles, who seemed to have thrown off his cloak of anxiety as he stepped into the crowded room with panache and waited a second for people to notice him. Derek's own steps were measured, guarded—he might have had more experience with the moneyed and the influential than Charles, but his famous teammate glided through the masses, confident and charming, no matter what was going on in his head. Derek wasn't jealous. They were a team. They always had been.

In the great room, he felt the energy building. Partygoers near the doors turned and beamed at Charles and Derek. The rookie twisted his lips into what he hoped was the semblance of a smile, trying to project pleasantness while avoiding eye contact with people he didn't know or care about.

Surrounded by happy, expectant faces, Derek felt out of sorts. For him, even when he was in the best of moods, parties were torture. He always felt unbalanced in a crowd, and more alone, and lonelier, than he did by himself at home. He did not know what to do with his face or how to hold his hands or where he should stand; yet, on the court, or even at a business meeting, he knew how to command, how to move without a thought. Groups of chattering people, though . . . he didn't understand small talk. Why would he want to discuss the weather? That was five minutes of his life wasted, unused time he would never get back.

Deep down, however, the real reason was because he froze when others expected something of him, especially human contact, and he was sure that eventually he was going to let them down. They'd find out he was boring, or too serious, and they'd cut him off.

He shook off the flash of self-awareness. Now was not the time for that.

A couple of suits raised a glass in salute to him, but the majority of the attention was on Charles, Boston's most popular player. Derek strove to keep his face blank while people fawned over his teammate and lifelong friend. He did not have a desire to become chummy or hang out with any of this crowd, but he did hope one day soon they'd also acknowledge him as a solid player, a local boy making good, just like Charles.

I know I gotta earn the star recognition. Derek purposefully slowed his roll, let Charles have more space. Let him enjoy his limelight.

He scanned the crowd, not really seeing anyone. But then a light twinkled in his periphery, catching his attention.

A young woman's sequined black gown reflected the warm glow from the chandeliers. He stared, mesmerized. She was incredibly sexy, a tall waif with the long body and stance of a ballerina, pink cheeks lighting up her smooth, tawny face, and shockingly blue eyes peering out from under a thick mane of black hair.

Wait a second. Is that . . .

It was. The young woman from the car earlier, the one who'd whacked her head on the window frame. He'd felt bad for her, but he'd also been pretty irritated to think she'd been eavesdropping. He was tired of never having a minute to himself. Yet her intelligent blue eyes, even behind glasses, had captured him. Now she was sans glasses and the translucent cobalt of her eyes struck a chord deep inside him, making him think of Caribbean waters. The sparkling dress showed off her lightly bronzed skin and a fluted collarbone.

He could picture himself kissing her there, in that hollow.

His skin prickled as she shifted slightly and their eyes connected. He saw the fire under the water.

Derek's chest tightened, his body flooded with thirst. He wanted to drink her in.

His automatic response was swift and surprising. He kicked himself internally, trying to snap out of it. He told himself she was probably bulimic. Or bitchy. He didn't have time for any drama. What if she was a stalker? He'd run into her twice in the last six hours.

Oddly, she blinked at him. And then blinked again, rapidly.

He forced himself to nod and keep moving. Talk about the worst time and place to meet a girl. Plus, the only reason a young woman would be at this party, alone, was to find a rich man.

Not happening, blinky.

–*–

The crowd around Hara had shifted their focus to two men entering the room.

The six-foot-seven Charles Butler, scrawnier than Hara had imagined but just as handsome, charmed the people around her with his smile and fist bumps—a completely different personality than the quiet, frustrating version he often presented to the press before or after games, answering questions with one or two words, if at all. Now the player strolled casually through the crowd, calling out to people by name.

But it was the man next to Charles who had grabbed her attention. She couldn't believe it.

Only a few inches shorter than his popular teammate, Derek Darcy was just as tall and as built as he had been earlier that day, and he looked damn fine. Once again, she thought of a lion as he moved, silent and lithe. His broad shoulders and biceps bulged through his suit jacket, not to be missed, nor was the strong square jaw. Hara felt herself drawn to him, wanting to touch him, to share space with this perfect specimen of a man.

Derek's glance was roving over the crowd, but then slid back to her. His eyes widened. The breath in her throat caught as again, the bold color of his eyes stunned her, the long black lashes framing brilliant, burnished-maple irises. Pinned in place, she had yet to breathe. Did Derek Darcy remember her? He stared and she couldn't look away, unsure of what to do.

Hara blinked, and then blinked again rapidly, her eyes painfully dry; that broke the spell.

He nodded, almost sternly, and then moved on. It took a second to catch her breath and let her heart settle back down.

A young woman about Hara's age stepped close. "Did he smile at you?" she asked dreamily, following the players with her eyes as the two men melted into the crowd.

"Who?"

"Derek! Oh my gawd, that man is fire," the girl said, fanning her face dramatically. She might have arrived straight from a photo shoot, wearing a neck scarf and a strapless, plunging jumpsuit that defied physics, with her nutmeg hair perfectly shaped in an au naturel puff. She was so well put together that Hara felt like a brace-faced, pimply kid standing next to a superstar.

"He didn't smile." Hara paused. "He did nod, though."

The girl pouted her perfect lips, shaded red, and said, "I like him. Even though he never talks to me. Or anybody." She reached out a hand to Hara. "I'm Naomi. Who are you?"

"I'm Hara. I'm a reporter out of Portland."

"Ah, lobsters and such. Do you love it there?"

"No, I'm sorry, I'm from Portland, Oregon. We're more about the salmon." Hara laughed. "So, you know Derek Darcy?"

"Kinda." Naomi fingered her scarf and continued to stare after the players. "I've been hanging with this crowd since I dated a player last season, but he was cut. Which was a bummer, but not really. I mean, so many fish in this sea." She smacked her red lips, humming at a cluster of men she spotted across the room, including Butler. Quietly, she said, "And Charles is the biggest fish."

Hara tilted her head. "You know Charles, then? Are you guys dating?"

Naomi's Afro bobbed as she whipped her head around. "Shhh. Tina will kill me, kill both of us, if she thinks we after her man."

She suddenly looked much younger than Hara, once Hara could see past her glamour.

God, hopefully Naomi is at least eighteen if she is roaming free in this crowd.

"Hey," Hara asked, trying to change the subject, "weird question, but do you have Visine in your clutch? My contacts are killing me."

Instead of answering, Naomi shifted her focus to a point behind Hara.

Madeline Bingley stood at her elbow. "Hara? Are you ready?" The sleek blonde woman eyed Naomi but didn't say a word to the girl. The assistant was fierce, and slightly frightening, with smoky noir eyes and an outfit Hara recognized from the cover of *Elle*, a Getty lambskin fit-flare dress and matching stiletto booties. "Charles wants to do this sooner than later."

Hara followed in her wake, with Naomi gaping at her. She gave a little wave, as if she were in control of the situation.

CHAPTER 5

You may ask questions which I shall not choose to answer.

—*Pride and Prejudice*

Approaching a set of double doors at the edge of the living room, Madeline abruptly swung around to face Hara. "Remember the rules. No recordings. Stick to the approved questions." She sniffed, her pointy nose in the air. "And for God's sake, get your quotes right."

As they'd crossed the room, Madeline had been accosted repeatedly by the well-to-do offering hearty hellos and asking her how she was doing; O'Donnell's assistant acknowledged most with little more than a tilt of the chin. Men in expensive suits created a deferential path for them.

Hara's first impression of the woman had in no way changed, but the reporter realized something: Madeline was definitely more than a glorified secretary. People were treating her as if she had power. Hara put on her respectful face. *And you will stay respectful, do you hear me, Hara? Do not screw this up.*

Madeline tapped her foot, waiting for her to respond.

The reporter shoved her ego into a box. "Yes. Of course. I understand."

"We have you set up here, in the library."

Hara nodded, but her doubts about the process crept in. She'd handed over her notepad and pen earlier, ostensibly so Madeline could put it in the library for her, but she'd seen the assistant flipping through the pages as she walked away. Probably checked the pen for a bug, too. Why was it so important Hara not go off-script? What were they worried Butler was going to say? He might get a little sexist, probably even misogynistic, but how was that shocking for a cocky athlete? She shook away the train of thought. They just wanted to control the narrative, like all ball clubs. Hara knew that when she agreed to this. It was fine. She either did it their way, or there was no way.

As the assistant moved toward the library, Hara buttoned her jacket with trembling fingers, covering her cleavage. She refused to use her sexuality to keep Charles Butler's attention. It was a tool in her toolbox, for sure, but not in an important moment like this.

A defining moment.

I'm in control. Pretend you're a competent adult, Hara. Use his name, keep steady eye contact, do not hunch. Project charisma and confidence. You got this, girl.

Madeline pushed open the heavy panel doors, which slid smoothly into the wood-paneled walls, and then threw open her arms like a game show host. "Charles! You look fantastic! Are you ready for tomorrow?"

The star player for the Fishers was sitting on a leather sofa in front of a low-burning fire, drinking a bottle of Perrier, but unfolded his lanky body into a standing position when they entered. He towered over the executive assistant. With a tug on his lapel, he said, "Do you mean I look fantastic in Armani? Because that's true." He grinned. "Or we talkin' on the court? Because that is also true. Chicago's goin' down tomorrow."

"Yes, *so* true," Madeline said, nodding. "Thank you for being here. Let me introduce you to the reporter, Hara Isari."

O'Donnell didn't give Hara a chance to speak. From across the room where he stood in front of an enormous bay window, the team owner butted in, "Hara's a whippersnapper, Butler, be careful of this one!"

The old man's tone had been lighthearted—but his lip stuck to yellowed teeth as he smiled, and the skin around his eyes tightened. The odd response confused Hara. Was he unhappy with his choice of reporters now?

Behind O'Donnell, the window framed a rosé-colored sunset, the rays sliding over the misted riverbanks just past the family's gardens. The quality of the light touched something in Hara, helped her take a breath, find a center in the swirling chaos of thoughts and emotions trying to overtake her.

There was another man standing by the window, staring out. He turned and she was again face-to-face with Derek Darcy. She almost laughed aloud at his double take; he hadn't known she was the reporter, of course, until just now.

She offered the handsome rookie a smile but his surprise had quickly been erased, replaced by smooth indifference. *Wow, Mr. Personality,* she thought with disappointment. Yet, as before, she couldn't look away, entranced by his strange, brooding eyes. Another flash of nature's beauty to appreciate.

His gaze was emotionless but intent, and did not shift past her or through her. It was as if this gorgeous stranger, a young man cresting on fame, was trying to peer inside of Hara. She felt seen.

But what did he see?

Luckily, Madeline broke the awkward stare, sliding in front of Hara. "Hara Isari, this is Mr. Darcy."

Hara, leaning to see past Madeline, offered a small wave but he didn't respond, only inclined his head and continued to regard her with an intense gaze.

The assistant didn't waste any more time on Hara. "Derek, I didn't know you'd be in here." Madeline's voice dropped to a fangirl purr. "You were on fire at training camp. I loved watching you."

"Thank you. I didn't know you were there," Derek responded in a polite monotone.

The timbre of his voice did something to Hara, sending a slight quiver down her spine. Derek Darcy had the sexiest voice she'd ever heard. She wondered what he sounded like when he laughed. If he laughed.

Madeline said, low and throaty, "I try to make all the practices . . ."

Hara, happy for the distraction, touched a fingertip to the corner of her eye, trying to readjust the contact, sticky to the touch. Dry plastic felt like grit rubbing against her cornea. Blinking did absolutely no good.

The assistant stopped her babbling finally and shifted her attention back to Charles, the reason they were there. "Isn't that right, big guy? Talk about being on fire!"

"Yeah, okay, Madeline." The star player twisted his lips in amusement. "Maybe we should get this show on the road." Charles stepped toward Hara and held out his hand. "You're a lot better lookin' than Eddie, the guy who normally covers the team. Hara, right?"

She forgot about her dry eyes. "Yes. Hello, Mr. Butler, pleased to meet you." Hara was much taller than Madeline but still had to lift her chin to look up at the basketball player.

His massive hand enveloped hers, which she prayed he didn't notice was shaking. His handshake was firm. Not trying to crush her bones. Not touching her like a delicate flower. She smiled and said, "And no worries, I'm almost past the whippersnapper stage."

His snort startled her, making her jerk back slightly, and then they both laughed, his demeanor easy and comforting. "Good for you, girl. We don't need no whippersnappers round here." He gave one final shake and let go of her hand. "Call me Charles. I'm not even sure what the hell a whippersnapper is."

She decided she liked him. He seemed so . . . normal. She'd been expecting a resistant, petulant asshole. More like Darcy. Her knees felt a little less wobbly.

Good, good, keep him on your side. Ooze that charm, Isari. "According to my grandma, it means I'm acting bigger'n my britches. But I was never exactly sure what that meant, either."

"Let's get you two started, shall we?" said Madeline, grimacing at Hara.

The assistant directed them to a pair of wingback chairs in front of the fireplace, then swayed over to Derek. A small, ornately carved table sat between the chairs, bearing Hara's notepad and the sheet of paper containing the questions. She lowered herself slowly to the edge of the deep cushion, arranging her dress so as not to let it ride up on her thighs. Then she tucked her legs to the side and crossed them at the ankles, making sure there would be no panty flashing. No one needed to see her Spanx.

Charles, on the other hand, took off his suit jacket, let himself drop into his chair, and settled back with a big sigh, loosening his tie. "What paper you say you're with? You don't look familiar."

"I'm—"

"She's vetted, Butler. Don't worry about it," O'Donnell said over her. "She's good at what she does. You read her entry for the contest."

The player shrugged. "All right. Whatever. Just makin' polite conversation."

Obviously, there was to be no chitchat.

Hara took a breath and dove in. "Let's start big picture, Mr. Butler. Charles. You guys suffered such a heartbreak loss in the championship game last year. Any predictions for your team in the upcoming season?"

"That's goin' big picture, all right." His dark eyes were earnest as he put a hand on his heart, as if swearing-in at court, and said, "I predict we're going to be a force this year. Our new guys are young but they fit right in, filling the holes. The depth of this group is somethin' . . . it's the most talent I've been with at any level. My boys worked hard these past months. The veterans, every one of them, are stronger and more amped than ever before. I know I am. Look at these guns!"

She glanced up from her notebook, in which she'd been frantically scribbling in shorthand. She didn't stop writing as his long fingers unbuttoned a cuff on his dress shirt, but that didn't mean she wasn't paying attention.

Yeah, okay, roll up that sleeve, she thought, biting her lip to keep a straight face. Men were ridiculous. What did she care if he wanted to flex his sexy bicep at her? She'd seen a hell of a lot more than that being flexed at the prison, and those guys were usually missing teeth or covered in flaming skull tattoos.

O'Donnell coughed. Loudly.

Derek, from where he stood at the window, made a scoffing noise. "Come on, man, totally unnecessary. Get on with it."

"You just jealous." Charles sucked his teeth at his teammate, but let his sleeve go and instead leaned forward, toward

Hara. Energy rolled off him. Good energy. "I'm proud of my team. You wait and see, Boston is going to go crazy when we beat L.A. in the finals."

"All right! You're a league MVP and considered the floor general for your team. How do you feel about that kind of leadership role when you're so young and relatively new to the team?"

"I work hard to deserve it. I'll make MVP again. But I do have a ton of talent who keep my ego in check. We've got personality skirmishes, sure, but we respect each other, and we bring each other up."

Hara wrote what he said and waited a moment for him to continue, but he didn't. She was surprised at how generous the young All-Star was being toward his team, and he wasn't nearly as egotistical as she'd expected.

"Any standout players this year? I mean, besides you, of course." She smiled. Sarcasm, even teasing sarcasm, was a risk, but she sensed he enjoyed banter and wanted to keep him tuned in.

Madeline shot her a look. Hara blinked. She'd asked an approved question. She blinked again, cursing her dry eyes.

"Uh huh, cute." Charles chuckled. "If I'm going to talk about someone who's almost as good as me, then I's got to bring up my brother Derek. Wave hello, Wreck."

Derek, not bothering to uncross his arms, rolled his eyes.

Charles continued, "Yeah, seriously, that grumpy bastard over there is the man. Thank God the rook is off the bench this year, he's the yin to my yang. With my shooting and Darcy's defense, we just can't be beat."

Hara pressed her lips together as she continued to jot down his words. She wanted to ask about Derek's recovery from his injury at the start of last season. He had to hate it that he had to endure another year of being called rookie.

But no follow-up questions were allowed. She had been so stupid to agree to that. Hara couldn't even ask Charles if he wanted to add anything.

Luckily, he went on without prompting.

–*–

The interview lasted ten more minutes.

"Well, that was my last question," said Hara. "Thank you so much for taking the time to sit with me, especially the night before the first game. I'll let you get back to it."

Charles sat forward, puckering his lips. "That's it? Wasn't as painful as I thought it'd be."

"I think she has everything she needs," said Madeline, stepping into their space. "Isn't that right, Hara?"

"I . . . I guess? I mean, yes, I'm good."

"Not that good," muttered a melodic voice from across the room.

She stiffened, the handwriting on the notes in her lap going fuzzy.

Did Derek Darcy just throw shade at her?

Charles stood up gracefully, despite his great height. "Congratulations on winning the contest, Miss Hara. Good luck out there."

"Right back atcha."

O'Donnell and Madeline fretted around their star, pulling him off to the side, a tree among the shrubs. There was a rush of whispers.

Hara gathered her belongings nonchalantly, trying to hear the hushed conversation while appearing not to have a care in the world. No use. They sounded like Charlie Brown's teacher. *Wahn wahn wahn.* Without looking around, she moved slowly toward the door. Disregarding Darcy's snide comment, she felt pleased with herself. *Nailed it,* she thought, suddenly flush with gladness that she had brought her résumé. City Gazette, *here I come.*

"Ms. Isari."

It was Madeline. "You did well."

Hara was surprised at the compliment. "Thanks."

"Before I forget, your press pass for tomorrow's game was delivered to your room. Don't lose it."

Hara had been so caught up in psyching herself up for the face-to-face interview, she hadn't even processed the extra thrill of getting to sit in an actual press row at an actual NBA game. The residue of Derek Darcy's insult washed away with the influx of new excitement.

Charles came up beside her, shrugging back into his suit jacket. "Don't mean to be rude, but apparently"—he glared at Madeline though softened when he shifted his glance to Hara—"I have to leave before I say something to ruin your opinion of me. Let me know if you need anything else." He threw a wave over his shoulder and headed for the door, where his teammate waited for him.

Derek's copper eyes matched up with Hara's once again, and once again, an electric zap made her shiver. Though ten feet apart, she felt like he was touching her, holding her in place, peering into her. She'd never experienced anything like it before. If only his demeanor matched his appearance.

He turned his gaze away. The players left the room.

The energy dissipated; Hara could swear the lights dimmed.

"Hey, Madeline, do you think I could sit in here for a bit? I want to finish writing out my notes before I forget something."

"Good idea." Madeline sniffed. A pause. "Just so you know,

the players will be leaving soon. They've got a curfew, according to their contract. I'd appreciate you giving Charles and the others space until then. They've got to focus on their game tomorrow."

Hara blinked silently in response. She'd been considering how to fit in more candid questions if she was to "accidentally" get into a conversation with one of the players out at the party. She needed to work on her poker face.

"Looks like we're all done here. Let me know if you need anything."

Everyone was always asking her if she needed anything, and then they ran away. Hara watched Madeline saunter through the open doors, catching up with O'Donnell; they appeared to be headed to the bar.

Hara settled back into her chair by the fire, pulled her notepad into her lap. Translating her shorthand went smoothly, most of the time. Despite having to stick to a script, she was pleased at the amount of material she had to work with. She would be able to write a decent story, thanks to Charles.

He'd treated her like a real reporter. She'd done it. She had defined herself. And someone else—someone important—had accepted that definition.

As she was pondering an indecipherable line of scribbles, two recognizable voices floated into the library. Derek and Charles. They were out of sight but close.

"I need a drink," said Charles.

A low rumble rolled out in response. "You can't be serious."

"Loosen up, Wreck. Go find yourself some female companionship."

"Here? In a room full of cougars and wannabe baby mamas?"

"Harsh. And not true. What about that reporter? She fine."

"Maybe if she didn't blink so much. Besides, come on,

you have to admit, she was weak. All her questions were soft, lucky for you." There was a pause, Derek's voice taking on a tone of concern. "But, still, Charles, I was hoping you'd change your mind about talking to the reporter, that you'd get ahead of this thing, before it becomes a thing—"

"Fuck, man, lay off."

Their voices faded.

She blinked rapidly, then, frustrated, dug the creased plastic out of her eyes and flicked the contacts toward the fireplace. The synapses in her brain buzzed with angst and excitement. The hum of satisfaction bled out. She'd had it in her hands for just a second. A solid reputation. She clenched a fist, as if trying to hold on to the last scraps of her dignity and her career.

Screw Derek Darcy . . . Wait . . . What thing?

What story was she missing?

CHAPTER 6

We all know him to be a proud, unpleasant sort of man; but this would be nothing if you really liked him.

—*Pride and Prejudice*

The wall clock in her suite claimed it was only 8:00 P.M.

She hadn't even lasted two hours. What a loser. She set the bottle of Prosecco she'd swiped from the party onto the bar, kicked off the Louboutins, and sighed in relief. She could have sworn she'd been at the party for hours, trying to make out who was who in the blurry crowd around her and then get past Madison's tribe of flunkies, young interns who proficiently cock-blocked her from every player and owner.

She slipped into her old, comfortable pajamas, gratefully put on her glasses, and stretched out on a couch with soft blankets, her notes, and her computer. She was typing away at the story, the now half-empty bottle of sparkling wine on the floor next to her, when her cell rang; she had to scramble out of the deep cushions in order to reach it.

"This is Telmate," said an automated voice on the other

end. *"An inmate at the Oregon State Penitentiary is calling. Your conversation may be recorded. Do you wish to accept the call from*—Thomas Isari. *If no, hang up. If yes, please press* one."

She pressed one. "Daddy?"

"Baby girl! So glad I got ahold of you."

"Isn't it five there? How'd you get permission to use the phone?"

"I swapped time slots with a buddy. Had to know how it's going. But I don't have much money left on my account, so talk fast."

"This has been the weirdest experience I've ever had."

"Is the interview over?"

"Yes. It went well. I've got plenty of material to write a good story, even doing it their way. But there's something going on, something they don't want me to find out about. I'm going to figure out what it is. That'll be my real story."

"Wait. What are we talking about? What story? You be careful. Leave it be—"

"It's Charles Butler. It sounds like he might have some scandal brewing."

A computer voice intoned, *"You have one minute remaining."*

She continued as if she hadn't been interrupted. "Which is too bad. I actually like Charles. He doesn't come off as a bad guy. He's not smarmy or painfully egotistical, not like some of the other guys. Not like Derek Darcy. Butler seemed to really believe in his team."

Her father let out a long swish of air. "You should probably stick to your deal."

"You don't have to worry, Daddy, I'm not breaking any contracts. I'll be fine. I didn't sign a nondisclosure or anything, they just insisted they preapprove the questions. I agreed to that, but they can't stop me from writing *another* article about Charles, not if I find something print-worthy. Besides, I'd make sure he got to tell his side of the story. He's been decent to me, I'd—"

"You have thirty seconds remaining."

"Sorry, little one, time's up," her father said. "I want you to know, I'm very proud of you."

"I know."

"You'll hate this, Hara, but could you message your mom? Ask her to put more money into my account?"

Hara cringed. What her father didn't realize was that it was Hara who put money into his account every month, so he could buy toothpaste and shampoo. "Sure, Daddy, I'll do that. And I'll try to send you an email tomorrow after the game, let you know how it goes. I love you."

"I love—"

The phone clicked and there was a buzz.

–*–

The next morning, Hara woke early, after a night of tossing and turning and grinding her teeth.

The only reason she knew she'd slept at all was because of a repeating, vivid dream.

She stood in a stone courtyard, just outside doors that opened up to a party inside. That's a castle, *she thought. She looked down and, oddly, she wore a gauzy Cinderella ball gown in brilliant shades of blue. Gold circlets wound around each forearm, digging into her skin. She started to remove one of the bracelets, but then a man in a tailed tuxedo was there beside her, holding her hand, his face shadowed. "These are stunning," he said, tracing his finger over a circlet, and she decided she'd never take them off. "And you're stunning," the mysterious man said, running his finger up her arm, then down the side of her breast.*

It was then she realized the shadows along the edge of the courtyard were moving. She knew, then, that the low rustling and moaning wasn't the wind, it was from the dark shapes, screwing at a furious pace around her, people from the painting in the hallway come alive.

Her breath came faster and faster as the man's hand went around her waist, to the small of her back. She slowly backed up against a wall, desperately wanting to keep his large, warm hand on her body. "May I kiss you?" he asked, and his face cleared and it was Derek Darcy.

"I'm not sure," she said, suddenly confused, but Derek laid his soft, full lips on hers, lightly. Instantly, her body responded; crushing against him, she opened her mouth to his. She felt him grow hard as she wrapped a leg around him, her skirt falling away, baring her flesh. His hand moved down to her leg, before gliding up to her bare hip, gliding, gliding. They both realized she wasn't wearing panties. And she was ready for him. He ran his thumb . . .

It was straight B-roll from old Cinemax porn.

O'Donnell's crazy painting had done a number on her, clearly. But why in holy hell did Derek show up in her dream? The man was a douche, not a dreamboat.

She rolled out of bed with a groan and dug out her running clothes. Hara needed to get outside and clear her head.

Fast-walking down the long hall, she avoided looking directly at the painting. Ducking out onto quiet, almost frosty streets just as the sun timidly began to poke its nose over the horizon, Hara ran for a long time, until her sweatshirt was saturated. Saturday-morning traffic along the Charles River was surprisingly slower than Portland's downtown traffic on the weekend. East Coasters ate dinner so damn late, they needed to sleep in.

Hara kicked up flutters of yellow, red, and green leaves with her worn running shoes. Turning away from the river, she slowed to a walk and crossed over Commonwealth Avenue. The city blocks were slowly filling with people. She occasionally overheard the catchy New England accent, with its broad *a*'s and short *o*'s. The whole "Pahk yuh car in Hahvuhd Yahd" thing. She adored the distinct sound. It was disappointing so few around her on the city sidewalks actually sounded "Boston."

As she passed down historic streets, the Colonial vibe emphasized that she was in one of the oldest cities in the United States. Puritans had turned old oak and hemlock forests into homesteads and markets and even the first public school, and, later, revolutionaries fought the British and suffered and bled on this ground so that American taxes would pay for American streets. The stories of hundreds of years of people and events hung in the air, clinging to the old brick structures. She inhaled deeply.

And coughed out the cold mist and smog.

A couple of backpack-wearing college kids startled her when they emerged from a building, throwing open the door unexpectedly. They almost ran her over, intent on their oversize pumpkin spiced lattes and conversation. "That one's ah slam pig. She wicked sheisty, too."

Finally! she thought, but they were gone too quickly for her to appreciate the native tongue for long.

Hara was in front of the famous Trident Booksellers and Café. She checked her watch. Plenty of time. The car picking her up for the game wouldn't arrive until late that afternoon, and tomorrow she hoped to tour the *City Gazette's* offices and—gulp—hand in her résumé, so now was the perfect time.

Inside, the smell of books and scones and bacon and coffee and more books permeated the air, and her glasses instantly fogged over. She sighed, took them off, and swiped at the condensation. She did not love running with her glasses on, but after last night, she was never wearing contacts again.

Her next bit of self-care was to sniff at herself surreptitiously; she was glad she was in a city where no one knew the bedraggled, stinky Hara. Her hair was huge with the humidity, barely contained in its ponytail. After ordering a breakfast sandwich and green tea, she settled into a chair tucked back in a corner by the window and picked up that morning's copy of the Boston daily paper.

She had to know. Her stress level rose, despite her long run, as she prayed she wouldn't find that another reporter had somehow scooped her.

A determined frown line formed between her brows. If there was something out there about Charles Butler, she was going to be the one to find it.

She had spent hours the night before wrestling with the ethics behind chasing down a story she knew the owners would not want her to investigate, the same people who'd paid for her to come out and give a once-in-a-lifetime interview. An even deeper, more painful struggle was with the demon who breathed life into her deeply rooted insecurities: Who was she to write an important story? She was a nobody. A crappy writer who worked for a small-town rag.

She'd stared at the ceiling and asked herself, over and over, *Who am I?*

However, each time she asked, she circled back to the fact that the universe had brought her, Hara Isari, to this place and this time and had pointed out, not so subtly, there was something more going on. Now it was up to her to take that opportunity and make something of it. To pull up her big-girl panties and take a leap of faith. *I can do this. Who am I? I'm Hara Isari. I don't back down from the scary things. I can do anything.*

But where did she start? She scanned the front page nervously, the thin paper gritty between her fingertips. If another reporter had already picked up the ball she'd dropped last night by not chasing down Charles or Derek . . . well, maybe she deserved that.

The front page announced the city's excitement at the Fishers' game one, as Chicago invaded the Bostonians' stomping grounds. But there was nothing scandalous about Charles Butler, only hype and hyperbole and Boston pride—Butler was one of their own, a local boy made good. They loved him.

Flipping back to the sports section, she found it was also free of negative stories about Charles, and anyone involved with the team. The wrinkle in Hara's forehead finally released. The articles in this section tended to be more factual and analytical than the front-page feature. Beat writers reported on the current roster of players, their stats, past performances, and current status. It was clear the town expected big things from Charles, as well as other players, but Derek Darcy was not one of them. The few times the second-year rookie came up, the writers hedged, saying, "We'll see."

An article at the bottom of one of the pages caught her eye: "Darcy Family Foundation Opens New Children's Wing at Mass Gen." There, below the headline, was a picture of Derek in a fitted tuxedo, alluring even with his brooding countenance. An older woman in a fur coat, who had to be Derek's mother, was at his side holding an oversize pair of scissors, ready to cut a ribbon. Hara had known Charles was from Boston, but she'd had no idea Derek was as well.

And not just any local. One of the elite. A rich kid on the court. No wonder he acted so sullen—he was used to everything being handed to him. Hara clucked. You had to earn your success at that level of play, no matter where you came from.

She jogged back to the residence, mentally preparing for the game that night, where she'd be working alongside peers. Older, male peers. She had some experience with the misogyny inherent with her job, but this was going to be on a whole new level. But Hara knew she had to earn her own success, and she was ready to put in the hard work. She ran faster, burning off nervous energy.

–*–

Derek threw up ball after ball.

"Dude. Enough. You're going to wear yourself out." Charles rebounded the ball, tucked it under his arm.

Hands on his hips, breathing hard, Derek said, "What you're trying to say, weak sauce, is *you* tired."

Charles shot the ball at Derek, a chest pass from five feet away.

"*Ow.* Dammit. That hurt, motherfucker."

"Who's the weak sauce, weak sauce?"

"All right, fine. Just trying to stay focused." Derek swung his eyes around the stadium; hundreds of early-arrival fans were filing into the tiers of seats.

His friend picked up a ball rolling past and bounced it to Derek, gently this time. "I know. First game since you went out last year. Big night. But you got this."

I do, Derek thought grimly, dribbling the basketball hard and tight by his foot. *I do have this.* Now he just needed to prove it to everyone else, but especially his father. "By the way, where'd you go last night? You disappeared. I looked for you to make sure you didn't need a ride home. And we have a conversation that we need to revisit."

"Don't you worry about me, boy-o. I always gotta ride." His teammate waggled his eyebrows. "And she was fine."

"Classy." Derek held the ball. If Charles didn't want to get into it right then, fine. But they were not done. "Please tell me you did not mess around with that reporter." He'd been shocked to find out that the girl from the car had been the reporter sent to interview Charles. The coincidence was almost too much. He hoped she hadn't been shadowing him, trying to get a story, but that was not out of the realm of possibility.

"I left her for you," said Charles. "I know you like the smart ones. But she a ten in the looks department, so your homely little self is gonna have to woo her with your money."

"She might have looks, but I'm not so sure about brains. I don't know why O'Donnell didn't bring in an actual journalist to do the interview. I am guessing the front line at ESPN"—he waved at the row of reporters standing in front of cameras at the side of the court—"would have jumped at the chance to hear you spill your guts."

"That girl did fine. She won some contest O'Donnell set up. He knows what he's doing."

"I don't trust her, or any reporter. And I definitely don't trust O'Donnell."

Charles frowned and tossed a ball to another passing player, then stepped closer to Derek. "Friend to friend, you're right not to trust him. Stay away from him, out of his sights."

Derek would have been startled, if it hadn't been for their talk earlier. "Why so mysterious, Scooby-Doo?"

"We'll talk later."

Then his friend's face lightened up. The coach had thrown a hand signal to Charles, who then yelled out to the others on the floor, "Come on, guys, let's run some plays."

–★–

The Town Car rolled through the darkening Boston streets, the traffic getting heavier as they approached the basketball stadium. The downtown was energetic, with twinkling lights and busy stores.

Hara caught sight of her reflection on the inside of the window. She pushed back her oversize black-framed glasses, smoothed down her bangs, and tucked loose strands into the tight bun. She then stroked nonexistent wrinkles from her pencil skirt and fitted button-down blouse, and straightened her favorite black blazer—it was actually a haori, a modern, kimono-inspired jacket, looser than regular blazers and with slightly deeper sleeves. And the lining was colorful, a flowery satin that made Hara happy when she caught a glimpse of it.

Carter always teased Hara about her take on the "sexy librarian" look, but Hara thought it was professional without being too uptight, and there was something fulfilling about acknowledging her Japanese heritage in this one small way.

The sparkly cocktail dress had been fun but, for now, it was back on its hanger and, sadly, her boss's Louboutins were back in their box. Instead, she'd pulled out a pair of kitten-heeled, red leather mules she loved. She saw no need to be totally boring. Plus, they matched the red leather satchel she carried around when she was on the job, a satchel that held paper and pens and a recorder and safety pins and a rape whistle and a tampon and lip gloss. The essentials.

She should have added Band-Aids. What if it was cold?

Her newest accessory hung from a lanyard around her neck. The lovely press pass. It was a good thing she'd remembered the pass, too, because she hadn't seen or heard from the O'Donnells or Madeline all day, except for a note delivered by a butler, telling her what time to meet a car in the brick courtyard. She'd assumed she'd be riding with others from the house but she was alone. Which was fine with her. The ride was short and quiet.

The security guard at the arena entrance ran her pass through some kind of authenticator, peered closely at her driver's license for what felt like forever, and then asked her questions about her address and birthdate. The final nod to let her through was solemn.

She stepped through the metal detector but then asked, "Where do I go?"

"No one told you?"

"No."

His eyes slanted suspiciously again. "To the right of the team's bench, beside the tunnel from the locker room. You'll see the TV cameras back behind the sidelines."

Hara felt a thin line of nervous sweat trickle down between her shoulder blades. She was too scared to look down, positive she had wet rings under her arms. Sure, she'd done a big-time interview last night, but this was a whole different beast, having to deal with her peers. Her older, much more male peers.

The place already teemed with fans and employees. On the gym floor, TV and radio reporters lined the front of press row, talking into cameras and mics. Her heart ratcheted up to an impossible rate. Over half the press seats were taken, laid claim by jackets and bags. Most of the reporters stood on the sidelines, hoping for two minutes from one of the players in warm-up suits shooting on the court.

Charles Butler led passing drills in the middle of the gym, but held up a second to flash a peace sign at her. She was just as surprised as the other reporters, who craned their necks to see who the star had acknowledged. Her lips curved up in a smile but he'd already turned back to his team.

"You know the big guy, huh?" A short, ginger-headed thirty-something with a woolly beard and big eyes stood next to her on the edge of the court. He held a recorder in one meaty hand, the other jammed into a pocket of his chinos. He had the face for print.

"I met him at Connor O'Donnell's last night."

He nodded at her press pass. "You're a reporter?"

"Uh, yes. Newspaper on the West Coast." It took her a second, but when she was able to get it out, she said it with confidence.

He tilted his head, a curious, hairy bird. "There was press at O'Donnell's party last night?"

"I was the only one. I think." She pushed her glasses up her nose. "I had an interview with Charles."

Am I bragging? I think I am.

A flare of emotion lit up his face, bulged out his eyes, but his voice was steady. "Huh. That's interesting." He reached out a hand. "I'm Eddie. I cover the team for the Boston paper. I've been trying to get face time with Butler for over a year."

She shook his hand, her stomach twisting. Gloating had led to insulting the first big-time reporter she had met. "It kinda came out of the blue. The organization got Charles to agree to do an interview, and then held a writing contest to assign a writer. I won." Her laugh was self-deprecating.

"Huh. Interesting," Eddie said again. "I entered that contest." He jerked a thumb over his shoulder. "Every one of these guys sent in articles, trying for that interview. You must be good."

Before the scintillating conversation could go further, there was a shout behind her.

"Watch out!"

As she turned, a ball heading for her face changed course at the last second, swatted away by a large hand. She felt the tips of the fingers brush her nose before she had a chance to step back.

Derek Darcy. Panting. He'd obviously sprinted to her rescue.

She adjusted her glasses, which had been knocked askew. "Thank you." She had no other words. The last time she'd seen him, he'd had his dream hand between her dream thighs.

His copper eyes gleamed with annoyance, his real hands on his hips. "You're the reporter, right? Hara?" At her slow nod, he said, "Well, if you can't pay attention, you shouldn't be doing this job. You can't afford too many more blows to the head."

Before she could stop herself, she said, "I'm sorry." But then she straightened her back and glared at him. "I appreciate your efforts, but you don't have to be rude."

He grunted and loped away, the muscles in his back working as he scooped up the ball and flung it to a teammate. Luckily, *he* was paying attention.

It was hard to break her stare. Her subconscious had decided this jerk was the best choice for a sex dream? She bit her lip as he practiced a jump shot, every muscle in his legs, thighs, and ass taut. Her brain wanted a kind, smart man but apparently her stupid lady parts were hoping for a long, sweaty visit from Mr. Muscles. As long as he didn't talk.

CHAPTER 7

> There is a stubbornness about me that never can bear to be frightened at the will of others. My courage always rises at every attempt to intimidate me.
>
> —*Pride and Prejudice*

She couldn't believe it. The game was over. The plays had been nonstop, with no time to breathe. Every time Hara glanced down to make a note, she missed something. She'd started writing without looking; the transcription was going to take a lot of guesswork.

The mood in the stands behind her was sour.

Boston had lost by two points. A heartbreak, so close right up until the bitter end. Then, in the last few seconds, Derek bungled a pass from Charles and that was it. The game was done. Too bad, too, because the rookie had played well up until then. For a defense guy, he'd scored quite a few points.

The reporters were bounding out of chairs, flowing into the tunnel behind the team, their curse words echoing off the walls.

The head coach led the press into a conference room. But by the time she could squeeze her way in, the cameras were rolling and print journalists were taking notes as the coach spoke in monosyllables from his spot in front of a wall covered in sponsor logos and imagery for the team. He called on the TV reporters first.

Beside her, Eddie shook his head and muttered, "This fuckin' guy. He always does that. Gives the talking heads priority." He grunted. "Listen to the questions they ask. They're clowns. They pay more attention to their hair than the game."

Listening to the dialogue up front, she couldn't disagree—at least, not with this particular bunch. The coach didn't seem to be saying much to them, anyway, almost every response consisting of, "I'll have to watch the game tape before I can answer that," or "We played with heart."

After a couple of minutes, the coach depleted his catalog of one-line, innocuous responses, so the group hustled into the hallway and over to the locker room. Just outside the door, there was a vastly oversize photo of a deceased coach, his eyes watching them as they jostled to be the first through the doors.

She'd known this moment was coming, when she was going to have to go into the locker room. A lot of female reporters before her had fought for her right to capture the post-game energy and hype along with the male reporters.

She was no quitter.

Hara followed. She'd never had the opportunity to interview anybody right after a game, especially not well-known players. There was no way she was going to shy away from the chance.

She'd read the stories. She knew what other women had gone through. And still went through, both in the locker room and in the abusive world of social media, from verbal harassment to physical attacks. Which explained why there weren't many skirts in a sea of gray suits and khakis.

The room was smaller than she expected, but a far cry from her high school locker room with its pitted cement floor and a grimy shower room facing rows of bent lockers. The Fishers had a well-maintained space, including a line of glass tables and leather office chairs in the center, and a thick, low carpet underfoot with a massive picture of the team's emblem embroidered into the center. One wall had a wide hallway leading back to the shower rooms and training room and medical bay. There were floor-to-ceiling lockers, and seats along three of the walls, each of which bore a plaque with a name and number, set apart by walnut partitions that offered no privacy whatsoever.

The damp air and bite of body odor was the same as at her high school, though. Worse, even.

The scrum of reporters hummed as the players returned from the shower rooms.

A young rookie, Gus Lawrence, was using a wet towel as a snapping weapon and came close to getting punched by at least one varsity player. Most of the guys weren't in the mood for horseplay, exuding sullen waves of disappointed energy.

When she realized just how much skin she was seeing, her eyebrows shot up in surprise. The ridiculously tiny towels looked like they had been stolen from a Motel 6; they were unable to close around the players' above-average-size bodies. Hara had thought she was prepared. But when a few guys strode past naked, their man parts free and bouncing off a leg with each step, her stomach twisted in anxiety. It was surreal. And very, very awkward.

Psht. Naked. Big deal. She forced her back straight, her face impassive. Hara had been flashed before, by far less attractive men. Her father's fellow inmates, and even the guards, had provided years of unwanted lessons on how to deal with sexual taunting. The reporters were breaking apart, surging as small groups around individual players, who were yelling at each other and, oddly, slathering their entire bodies with lotion before getting dressed.

"Hey, jersey chaser. Who let you in?"

It wasn't a player. The comment came from a sneering reporter to her left, his hairpiece a different shade of brown than his natural hair.

Hara pushed her glasses up on her head and batted her eyelashes at him. "My daddy said it was okay."

Charles Butler emerged, a towel loose around his waist, steam trailing after him. The room erupted. "Hey, Charles! Charles! What happened tonight? Charles!"

The crowd followed him to his locker, including the loudmouth who'd been next to her. From their excitement, it was clear they were hoping he'd actually say more than his usual two-word responses, now that he'd given in and done a full interview.

His post-game style didn't change. He was polite and friendly, but once again kept his answers to the bare minimum. Hara was happy to keep her eyes on her notepad, scribbling away while Charles dressed. She didn't want anyone to accuse her of being there just so she could ogle the meat sacks.

A few more ballplayers trailed out of the shower room. Then Derek emerged and once again his appearance made her catch her breath.

His lean, muscular body, dark skin slick from the shower, moved gracefully. Yet, he also walked with a slight stiffness, holding a towel around his waist with a tight fist. Was he sore? Or was he uncomfortable? Hara didn't know how any athlete could stand to have their privacy invaded like this, whether or not the reporters were male or female. Would it be so terrible if the press, male and female, had to wait in the conference room? Or the hall? Would the excitement of the moment be lost between toweling off and pulling on shoes? The controversy had raged forever. But if male reporters were going to be allowed access, then so was she. Women had busted open the glass locker room door and Hara was staying in there until they all had to leave.

The majority of reporters still clustered around Charles, trying to pry something headline-worthy free.

Derek was alone, now in compression briefs and socks. He slid on a pair of basketball shorts as she approached, glaring at her. She controlled her own stare, trying not to linger on his broad chest or how it narrowed down to a subtle six-pack. She could see why women might want to sneak in and get a peek at these men.

He spoke in a growl. "I mean, seriously, don't you feel weird watching me dress?"

"Don't worry about me," she said loftily, as if annoying an NBA player was an everyday event. "Let's talk about tonight. That was a pretty impressive showing, racking up the points like that."

"Maybe you hit your head harder than I thought. Didn't you notice? We lost." He tugged a polo shirt over his head, his biceps flexing naturally.

"A tough game, for sure." She didn't take his bait. "You were brought on because of your defense skills at Pepperdine. Looks like you're expanding your role on the court. How's the team feel about that?"

"I think it's important that I can be versatile, knocking down their balls *and* making the swishes—"

"The Wreck really put 'em through their paces tonight," Charles said loudly from his own locker. Now dressed, he came over to Derek and slapped him on the back. "I'm a little jealous. My bro here is tryin' to steal my crown. At least he's on my team."

Derek smiled slightly, more than she'd seen from him yet. "You know I got your back."

Charles turned and pointed at Hara. "You got a question for me, girlie?"

The room went quiet. "Who's she?" someone whispered.

I'm Hara Isari, bitches. She paused. There was a choice: Ask a question about the game, or ask Charles if he was hiding something.

"What made tonight's game so tough, you think?" It rolled out, confident and smooth, like she knew what she was doing. Like she wasn't a big, freaking coward.

As the other reporters shifted and filled the space around her, he responded, "You know, our problem was defense right from the start, but that was a matter of everyone not being on the same page. We're gonna get there."

Eddie, the bearded ginger, beat her to the next question. "Are you saying the loss was Darcy's fault?"

"Come on, man, you know I ain't sayin' that." The star went back to his space and grabbed his gym bag. "Well, I'm out." Charles offered Hara a two-fingered salute. Then, making his way to the locker room door, he slapped Gus on the ass with a ringing smack, surprising a yelp from the rookie, but he didn't say anything more to Derek.

As the star exited, Derek quietly tied his shoes, ignoring any further questions directed at him. The other reporters faded away, seeking interviewees more talkative than Derek. She stood her ground. "Do you think he meant it how it sounded, Derek?"

"Naw, my boy wouldn't do me like that." But he kept his face down.

Hara felt bad for him. The young player had worked hard out there on the floor, performing better than expected. He wasn't getting the attention he deserved. Then again, Derek wasn't making it easy for the press, emulating Charles's minimal-words policy but with a lot less friendliness.

–*–

Hara kicked away popcorn and avoided puddles of beer on the smooth cement floor as she made her way down the rapidly emptying main entranceway. She'd quickly written up a review of the game and amended a few sentences in her interview, and sent both off to Carter. Now she was free. That was that. Hara had covered the Charles Butler story and then made it into the locker room after a big game. *Yay for notches in my portfolio. Life changing! So exciting!*

Then darkness descended and that snide voice from the locked closet in the recesses of her brain started whispering. She could have asked Charles anything. Instead, she'd chosen not to rock the boat. She was an idiot. A freaking coward.

She'd shifted into the mindset of a manic-depressive. Her stomach surged with the emotional swings.

"Hara!" Naomi, the stunning girl from the party, stepped out of an elevator, waving.

The surge swung back up. She wasn't completely alone here. "Hi! I'm so happy to see you," Hara gushed, before she could stop herself. Swallowing, she brought it down a notch. "Whatcha up to?"

Naomi sang out, a smile on her young face, "I'm hittin' Tunnel. Come with me!"

"You're going to a tunnel?"

"Ha! A nightclub. Some of the players and the girls are

going, we're in a VIP section. D'Luxe is the DJ tonight, it'll totally be worth it."

They were walking past Eddie, who sat on the edge of a cement garbage bin, intent on his small laptop computer, clacking away madly on the keyboard. Maybe she should have spent more time on her own story.

Too late now. "Are you sure the players will be okay with me there?" Hara asked. She knew Naomi was only inviting her along because she thought Hara had some cachet with the team, having watched her being escorted to a private meeting with Madeline at the party. But what did she care if Naomi genuinely liked her or not? She could use Naomi's connections, just like the girl was using her.

Hara was being offered another shot at Charles.

"Come on. Don't be stupid," said Naomi. "You are an exotic beauty. Beautiful women are never turned away, not when Charles is around. But you can't wear your accountant clothes."

"I don't look like an accountant!"

"What do you have on under that button-up?"

"My bra."

"What's it look like?" Naomi asked. "Never mind. We'll make a stop on the way."

"I don't know . . ."

"You're goin', girl." She grabbed her hand. "It'll be fun."

The universe was giving her one more opportunity. Damn it, she needed to get over herself and take it.

Naomi did not live far from the stadium. Surprisingly, though she was in an amazing part of town, her apartment was tiny, a walk-up above a Chinese restaurant. Hara had assumed because she hung out with the hoity-toity crowd and dressed like a movie star that the young woman was wealthy.

The modest well-kept studio was done in light grays, with

small pops of black and red. Hara loved the chic decor. The "bedroom" was basically a nook big enough for a bed, though it did have a sliding door for privacy. In the main room, Naomi used black Ikea bookcases to cleverly create a closet that covered an entire wall, floor to ceiling, and fronted them with sliding barn doors. There was even a mini dressing room.

"Wow. This place is seriously cool."

"I know, right? My friend's dad owns the building. I love it." Naomi slid open a closet door. "What would you like? Maybe a little Asian flare? This would be so pretty with your skin tone and dark hair." She handed Hara a satin lilac dress with a mandarin collar and plum blossom embroidery.

Hara held it up to herself and then handed it back. "Very pretty. Not my style, even if it wasn't sized for a starving child. I'm not opposed to wearing Chinese styles, but I'm Japanese. Much different."

Naomi rehung the dress and continued rummaging through the hangers. "Are both your mom and dad Japanese?"

"Nah, my dad is Japanese American and my mom is African American. Guyanese, actually, but like four generations back. If I did one of those DNA tests, I think they'd find a little of literally everything."

"I hear ya. My family is the same way. Here. This should fit. We can adjust the laces in the back." She handed over a patent leather corset, complete with black lace that covered the cleavage area and ended as a high ruff around the neck.

"I don't know. Why—"

"If you're not dressed right, you ain't gettin' in the door."

"Okay. Well." Hara held the corset up to her long frame. "Victorian meets steam punk meets S and M. How do I even put it on?"

The process of getting it over her head took both girls,

and nearly scraping off Hara's nipples as they yanked it down. Once the piece was relaced, it was surprisingly comfortable and appealing. The boning held up her breasts and, while the corset was cut low, the lace was fairly thick enough to keep her from pole-dancer status. The smooth, shiny leather came to a point over her clingy, almost knee-length skirt, creating an hourglass. She couldn't stop looking at herself in the mirror.

"Where is this from? Is it Vera Wang?" she asked, as if she knew what a Vera Wang corset would look like.

"No! I made it." Naomi pointed to a sewing machine in the corner. "I bought a cheap corset off eBay, covered the boning with patent leather, and added the neck ruff. What do you think?"

"This is amazing. I'll get it back to you, I promise."

Naomi sighed. "Don't worry about it. My boobs are too big."

"You could sell this for a ton of money!"

"That's how I got started—someone needed a seamstress. Now, I have an online business. I'll show you sometime." Naomi handed her a bundle of red metal bracelets and dangling red earrings. "There. Matches your heels and your bag."

"That's a lot of red."

Naomi snorted, sitting on the edge of an overstuffed chair, reapplying red lipstick. "Whatever. Own it. Red is a power color. Be powerful." She leaned toward her and dabbed some of the red on Hara's lips. "You look phenomenal in red. It's the perfect color for your perfect skin. With your height and unique look, you could easily be a model."

"My mom would love it if I'd try modeling." Hara rubbed in the lipstick and then pushed up her glasses. "Ain't gonna happen. I'm too clumsy and I like to eat."

Naomi tilted her head to the side, squinting at Hara. "Do you have to wear those glasses?"

"Yes." The young reporter touched the frame. "Though I obviously need to get them tightened. They keep sliding down and it's driving me crazy."

"At least keep them off the tip of your nose. No offense. How about that bun?"

Hara shrugged, pulled the fasteners free, and shook out her hair until the shiny black locks waved down between her shoulder blades. She sighed in relief, rubbing her scalp.

"Ahhh. So much body." Naomi fluffed Hara's hair with her fingers, then twisted a few strands of her bangs. "Your hair is almost as big as mine."

"I wish. Instead, it's this half-assed mess, curly in some spots and flat in others."

Naomi, running her fingers through her own fluffed-out, kinky hair, said, "Girl, with that beautiful skin and those crazy blue eyes, you all Vanessa Williams. You know, wall-poster Vanessa, from back in the day. Maybe a blend of Vanessa and Zooey Deschanel, sporting those cute bangs and trendy glasses. Don't even pretend you don't know how striking you are."

"Psht. Right. Come on, let's go if we're going to do this." Hara slid on her jacket over the corset. "I think this looks all right."

"The point is to show off your figure, not hide it. Never mind, they have a coat check."

–*–

Tunnel turned out to be a narrow underground dance club with soft overhead blue and lavender lights pulsing on a seething wall of bodies. Sofa benches lined the walls, and VIP sections were roped off in the back. Hara had been allowed in because Naomi was on a first-name basis with the bouncer.

The hard, hip-hop beat reverberated in Hara's chest as she followed her new acquaintance into the crowded room.

She tugged on the top of the corset nervously. She kept thinking of the story about the country mouse in the big city. It took every last drop of her willpower not to shrink into the shadows. She refused to allow herself to give in to insecurities and fear, not now. *I'm going to party with the Fishers and I'm going to like it, dammit.*

A gathering of women Hara had seen at the O'Donnell event were lounging on or around some of the players, tucked back into a corner. There were also the friends of the players, the posses who ran errands and made sure the drinks flowed.

She spied Gus, the towel-snapping basketball player with blond, floppy hair and wide surfer shoulders. He sat on the edge of a chair, entertaining a circle of young women nodding and giggling at his every word. Of course he was popular with the girls. If only he had a brain.

"Oh, I adore Gus," Naomi gushed, pointing at him before wriggling through tight clumps of people to reach the bar. By the time Hara caught up to her, she was flagging down a bartender, who had an outrageously twirled mustache, and ordering them Camparis, heavy on the Prosecco. "You'll love it. An aperitif my Italian friend likes to drink. Very sophisticated."

"Unlike Gus," Hara teased. "I don't know why you'd adore *him*. Kind of seems like he got hit with the simple stick."

"You should give him a chance. He's nice, and smarter than you think."

"I don't know. My first impression is usually right. I'll go with my gut."

Naomi *tsked.* "Are you always so stubborn? What if you're wrong?"

"I'm not too worried about it, especially when it comes to surfer boy over there. He's all yours."

"I guess I'm not sophisticated, either," said Naomi, making a face after a small sip of her drink. She handed it to Hara. "Here, you can have mine. I've found who I'm looking for, right over there."

Hara followed her line of sight. She expected to see Gus. But no, Naomi was fixated on Charles Butler, sleek in a motorcycle jacket and tight jeans. He had women crushed up against him on a narrow couch. He ignored the females, however, instead leaning forward, waving his hands around and talking animatedly to the man across from him.

Hara was surprised when the man in the chair turned slightly and it was Derek, his elbows on his knees, a bottle of beer in one hand, paying close attention to his teammate. It was funny, he hadn't seemed like the nightclub type. Too many people he might have to talk to.

"See. Like Derek Darcy," Hara shouted to Naomi, pointing through the crowd and continuing their conversation. "From the second he opened his mouth, I had him pegged as a blowhard. I couldn't have been more right."

"You were only around him for five seconds. He might be a nice guy. Maybe he's shy."

"Derek is not timid," Hara said, and then downed her drink in three gulps.

"Okay, then." Without any further comment, Naomi nudged her discarded drink in Hara's direction.

Hara grinned. "I don't really like this, either," she said, and took a hefty sip before continuing her rant. It felt good to unleash. "He's a snooty meat bag with money and the ability to play ball and that's it. Though, I could probably forgive him for being an arrogant asshole if he hadn't insulted me. He told Charles I'm a terrible reporter." Hara set down the drink and pushed her glasses up her nose. "And he made fun of me blinking. It was mortifying. He thought I looked like an idiot."

"I'm not sure I believe that," Naomi said. "Who in the hell gonna knock what you got goin' on?" The confident young woman put the Campari back in Hara's hand. "Come on, I need to talk to Charles. Let's go show these men who they dealing with."

Naomi strode through the crowd, and in an impressive maneuver, wedged herself between Charles and the girl closest to him on the couch, who practically convulsed in rage. *Honey Badger don't care,* Hara thought to herself and laughed, as Naomi leaned in and commenced a whispered conversation with Charles that left his teammate hanging. She obviously was not worried about pissing off the Tina she'd mentioned at the party last night.

Sitting back in his seat, now ignored, Derek scowled with irritation. Hara felt a twinge of satisfaction.

The rookie stood up as she approached, which surprised Hara. Despite her dislike of his personality, his physicality continued to throw her, with his solid, lean build and chiseled chest highlighted by a tight, black T-shirt. And those impossible copper eyes, intent on her.

"Here. Please. Take my seat." His voice was deep but pleasant, a perfectly toned drum.

"What?" She caught herself. She could smell him now, a spicy earthiness that made her inhale involuntarily. "That's nice of you. Are you sure?" He'd probably spilled something on the seat. She would sit down and end up with a wet ass. But inspecting the cushion, and then his face, she could find no evidence of foul play. "Thank you."

He nodded. After she sat, he stayed next to her, occasionally shifting from foot to foot, not saying a word.

"Sooo." Hara couldn't bear the awkward silence. "Now that you've had some time to process, what do you think about the game?"

"I don't want to talk about it."

Hara sipped her drink stoically. This was shaping up to be the exact opposite of a good time. Every bit of her wanted to walk away while she still had some dignity left. But there was Charles, who was much nicer than Derek. Right there, across from her. All she had to do was tap him on the knee, interrupt Naomi, and see if she could get the star to talk to her alone for five minutes. *Go big or go home.*

She bent forward and said, loudly, "Hi, um, Charles? Would you mind if I talk to you for just a minute?"

He didn't answer. Granted, it was impossible to hear anything over the music, but Charles was immersed in Naomi, his fingers in her thick hair. He didn't even know Hara was there. She was going nowhere, fast. Charles was ignoring her. Derek was ignoring her—and he could use some good press in order to build his reputation. What was she doing wrong?

Derek stared at his beer bottle like it was talking to him. On the couch, Naomi had her lips pressed against Charles's ear, either offering words or a tongue. It was hard to tell. He wasn't hating it, letting his fingers trail down her side.

If Hara tried to engage him now, she'd just come off as a freak.

The rest of the basketball crew, the friends and hangers-on, laughed and gossiped, clumped in small groups around them. Hara struggled to not be envious of her new, younger acquaintance. Naomi, unashamedly going for what she wanted. The girl knew she had an audience and made the best of it, running her hand through her hair, or licking her red lips with a slow, languid motion—Charles was mesmerized.

When Hara grew up, she wanted to be able to flirt like her.

Charles was a baller but Naomi was, frankly, a bombshell. The power of a woman over a powerful man.

Hara sighed. *Maybe it's time I found myself a boyfriend. Or at least a date.* She'd settle for someone to talk to right now. The young reporter glanced at Derek standing next to her, his hands in his pockets, face averted. He wasn't interested in talking to a human.

She tried again, anyway. "This is a fun place. Is this where you guys normally hang out after games?"

"Not me. Not my scene. Everyone trying to get with someone else."

"I don't know, I guess it's not so bad when you find someone you get along with." Someone who was at least interested in good manners.

He shrugged. "Maybe. But desperation isn't attractive. And everyone here looks the same, acts the same. Even you, all dolled up. Beautiful and dressed for attention. You sure you not here looking for a star to warm your bed in a brand-new house?"

"You—" She stopped herself, but not for long. "Are you serious right now? I'm out here because I'm trying to launch my career; I need to look like a rag while I do it? I'm not allowed to be attractive *and* successful? Pretty women can't be smart and independent? Because I sure the hell don't need some man to complete me. But, like a normal woman, I don't mind having one around. As long as he's not a dick."

It was disappointing, really, another successful male exposing his feet—and brain—of clay.

She turned her back to him, fuming.

—*—

There is no reason for me to stand here and look stupid, Derek thought, glaring down at his beer bottle again, trying to avoid looking at Charles and his fling, or the sight of the humping couple in the corner, or the hot, quarrelsome woman next to him.

This was ridiculous. Charles was determined to fuck up. Who was Derek to stop him? And now he had to make sure this reporter didn't walk out with a story. Charles could not afford any unnecessary attention right now.

A light perfume floated up to him. He breathed in deeply, almost unconsciously. *Mmmm.* She wore something that reminded him of lathered soap and a sunny hayfield.

He shook his head.

Inhaling again, savoring her aroma, he let his breath out slowly. The girl was definitely a distraction, whether he liked it or not. Derek could feel the irritation rolling off her, which did make it easier to keep his distance. He knew it was his fault, that he'd insulted her, but it hadn't been his intention. He had just been honest.

But in retrospect, maybe too blunt. He shouldn't have said anything about her appearance. It was true, she was beautiful, with the most stunning eyes he'd ever seen . . . but she was probably on the prowl for a rich boyfriend just as much as a story to cover. Derek supposed she didn't care to be called out publicly, though. And his not wanting to talk about the game—well, that was because he would have to think carefully about what to say and how to say it before feeding details to a reporter, making sure his comments stayed glib and positive even if taken out of context. Frankly, exhaustion had killed off what little interpersonal skills he had. He didn't have it in him to parse words.

The adrenaline high from the intense game gone, and no winning glow to keep him going, he was bone-deep fatigued and filled with regret about decisions on the court that may or may not have cost the game.

Charles. He'd dropped a major bomb on Derek, leaving him all wrapped up in worrying about his friend and his mom, then he acted weird about Derek's performance, and here he was now, behaving like a horny teenager, no cares in the world. Charles and Naomi were laughing over some secret, oblivious to the reality around them.

Derek, on the other hand, couldn't let it go. It wasn't just that Charles was getting away with breaking the rules. When his mother took that money, she became part of a growing national controversy, a trend that could ruin colleges and kids' lives. If an athletic kid could be bought, then the rich schools were going to get the best players. The colleges that couldn't afford blackmail bids would lose the ability to draw athletes, and then their funding was going to go down the toilet. Which would affect all the students at that school.

The professional basketball season was lurching into full tilt. He didn't need this crap. Derek shut his eyes and had a brief flash of intense hatred for . . . not for Charles, but for the ethical quandary he'd put Derek in the middle of. What was he supposed to do with this information? What was the right thing to do?

Derek needed to stay focused, to get back the respect he'd lost last year, sitting on the bench like a loser, taking up valuable space and giving nothing to the team. He had the next few months to prove he deserved to be back, maybe even as a top scorer. He could do it. He just had to put his head down and work for it. Charles's problems weren't his concern.

So, no distractions. No more worrying about Charles.

Stop smelling her.

He moved back a step, but was caught once again by the reporter's eyes. There was no denying Hara was an attractive girl, gorgeous, even, with her unusual eyes, her long black hair, her cute glasses. Her bare, creamy-caramel shoulders and pert breasts in what had to be the sexiest top ever created, yet almost queenly with the ruff neck. He'd seen her with her hair up and down, glasses and no glasses, dressed for a cocktail party, dressed professionally, and now dressed for clubbing . . . the woman could work a grain sack. He'd love to see what she looked like in the mornings, naked on satin sheets.

Derek sighed. He had to get his house in order before he could let in a girl.

–★–

Well, I can sit here and look stupid, Hara thought, *or I can put myself out there, maybe gather some intel.* She slowly stood up, gratefully putting distance between herself and Derek, joining the crush of women. They were hardly less intimidating than the athletes.

"Hi there. Are you a reporter?" asked a pretty young woman with an Italian lilt to her vowels. "Did I see you talking to the team last night?"

"Just a couple of them. The owners brought me in to do a feature on Charles."

"Ah ha! Of course they did. They need to make sure the public is behind their rising star." The Italian girl stuck out her hand, a large ruby ring face out. "I'm Kitty."

Hara realized she was talking to the famous young heiress Kitty Morretti. Kitty kindly went out of her way to introduce her to the other women. None needed Hara to give them publicity, since many of them were recognizable models or TV personalities, but most were friendly. One woman was a famous trial lawyer, another owned a successful fashion line. All of the women were draped in gold and diamonds, to the point that Hara felt like she was in a jewelry commercial.

Kitty said to her, "These fine ladies are known as the Wives Association. No one messes with them, not if they want to keep their hair extensions. They're our Queen WAGs." At Hara's raised eyebrow, the woman added, "WAGs. The Wives and Girlfriends. The wives and fiancées rule the kingdom, then the girlfriends."

"And, of course, there's always a coupla hoes hanging out, trying to be a WAG." A woman with cute bleached curls pressed against her mocha skin laughed and added, "We like our men to be good with their balls. But we good with everything else, including managing the money, the families, and their extracurriculars. They have capable hands—"

"Very capable hands!"

"—but we are the ones who make sure they survive. And that those hands and balls don't get into trouble."

"Nobody can bounce me like my man. I'm gonna make sure that don't stop."

Names were thrown at Hara, but she simply smiled and nodded, her brain on overload. These were the long-time partners of the players. She sensed they were a tight crew.

"Speaking of hoes, you need to get ahold of your girl." One woman pointed a long, zebra-striped nail at Naomi, still cuddled up to the Fishers' star player. "You came in with her, right? Tina goin' to scratch her eyes out. And if she don't, I will."

Hara shifted back and forth, worried for her friend. And her own immediate safety. "Tina? I thought I read somewhere they broke up?"

Kitty shrugged. "They break up twice a week. That doesn't mean Tina is going to be lenient."

"You son of a bitch!" someone screeched from behind them.

"Uh oh. Too late."

Charles leisurely glanced over but didn't move. Naomi, on the other hand, rose from the couch slowly and stood with her feet apart, a firm stance. A basketball stance. Hara almost smiled.

"Baby . . ." Charles started to say, as if bored.

"Shut your face." Tina, a famous reality TV star a few years older than Naomi, was hourglass shaped with a dreadlock high bun and perfect wing-tipped eyes. She reminded Hara of her mom, when Hara was young and her mother would still get made up and go out with her father.

"You. You bitch." The woman poked Naomi in the chest, hard. "That is my fiancé. I'm gonna snatch that Afro bald. You do a sister like this?"

Naomi, big-eyed, looked to Charles. Hara heard her whisper, "I thought you said this was done?" He didn't answer.

Tina snorted. "Uh huh. That's what I thought." She tugged out her earrings—large, dangling plates of ivory—and handed them to the person closest to her. That person was Derek.

Derek raised an eyebrow. "Really, Tina? You're not on camera. Give it a rest."

In response, she handed him her stilettos. It was so over-the-top dramatic, Hara looked around to make sure there really wasn't a film crew taping them.

Derek stepped between Naomi and Tina, thrusting the shoes and earrings back at the raging fiancée. "This girl is here to see me. She was just talking to Charles."

"Now that Charles is intimately familiar with this little bitch's bra size, it's time for the conversation to end."

Derek grabbed Naomi's hand and drew the young woman to his side. She slid under his arm, tucked against him, using the rookie player as a shield.

Hara's heart hammered. Partly because she had no desire to be part of a battle scene. But oddly, it was also because of a surprising spike of jealousy. Derek had his arm around Naomi. They were a perfect fit, a beautiful couple.

One of the WAGs grabbed Tina and whispered something.

Tina swung her head toward Hara and slit her eyes. "Oh, you idiots invited a reporter in here and then didn't have the decency to squash this shit?" She flipped her fingers at Charles, still lounging on the couch, placid. "Fine." She turned to Derek. "I'm gonna pretend your heartwarming little story is true, Derek. For now." She grabbed back her shoes and earrings. "But I'm gonna ask you to get outta my face."

Derek shrugged, unfazed.

Naomi, with a hint of the shakes, said, "Let's get a drink."

Tina cursed at their retreating backs, and then dropped onto the couch next to Charles. Hara winced when the angry woman dug her pointed nails into the man's leg. He yelped in pain; she dug harder. The crowd busied their attention elsewhere.

The reporter joined Derek and Naomi at the bar.

Naomi had been enjoying her affiliation with the WAGs. And with the men. Now, the beautiful clothes designer leaned against Derek, despairing over her jeopardized access to Charles and to the behind-the-scenes life she loved. When the ballplayer remained politely quiet, Naomi shifted to describing the many ways in which Charles deserved better than an unhinged drama queen. Her naive rambling was hard to listen to, but Derek, surprisingly patient, said nothing.

With eyebrows furrowed and lips pursed, he drank his beer and occasionally patted the babbling girl on the back, probably getting ready to tap that himself. Hara cringed but then found that her eyes were constantly drawn to his flexing shoulder muscles despite herself.

Everyone around her was in conversation. It was like she was back in high school, sitting by herself in the library.

Catching her reflection in the mirror behind the bar, Hara frowned, seeing a young woman in glasses, alone in a crowd of people under throbbing colored lights. Her wavy black hair fell over the fancy lace ruff and her bare shoulders; high emotions added a flush to her cheeks and deepened the blue of her eyes, vivid even from behind her glasses.

Well, I did what my mom wanted. I'm dolled up, surrounded by rich men.

A thirty-something in a suit sat a few feet down the bar, his hair brushed back in a hipster pompadour. He caught her eye in the mirror and smiled. Hara, startled, quickly flashed her gaze down, breaking eye contact.

She took a deep breath. As deep as she could, anyway, wearing the old-fashioned binding corset. Then, ready to engage, she looked back up.

He'd turned away.

CHAPTER 8

. . . She cannot be too much guarded in her behavior towards the undeserving of the opposite sex.

—*Pride and Prejudice*

On either side of the massive bar mirror, there were backlit glass shelves reaching from the counter to the high ceiling, with a wooden ladder on a ceiling rail providing access. The soft, dreamy light shone through the liquor bottles.

Hara spotted one of her favorite whiskies and ordered a glass of Angel's Envy rye, neat. Waiting, she tried to decide if she was going to stick it out a little longer or head back to the O'Donnells'. Her flight didn't leave until the following night, so she could sleep in tomorrow. Or she could pretend she was good at adulting, go back and pack, and have time to tour a few historic sites in the morning.

Her opportunity to speak further with Charles was blown. Sure, she could write about what she'd seen tonight, that Charles Butler was as much a dog as everyone suspected, but that wasn't news, or even remotely unusual in the world of sports.

She had nothing to feel bad about. The young reporter was going home with a solid interview under her belt. Life was good. But, Hara *had* started the day adamant she was going to dig out some story that would end up going viral, setting her up for life. Could she still make that happen?

Taking a deep, calming yoga breath, she winced. The corset's ties dug into her back.

The bartender placed the glass of amber liquor in front of her. Calm now, she settled onto the stool, letting the heat of the whiskey slide down her throat, warming her to the tailbone.

Derek was suddenly next to her, ordering a beer. His muscular forearm was so close that she could feel his body heat, and his spicy smell had her pheromones in a twitter. It made Hara's arm hair raise and, swear to God, it felt like the hair was reaching for him. Her body continued to respond to him even when her logical side did not.

He held out his bottle. "Cheers."

She clinked, warily, but allowed herself to smile. *All right. Friendly is as friendly does.* "Where'd Naomi go?"

"I believe she went to the restroom."

"What you did for her was nice."

"I did it for the team." His eyes burned into her. "We don't need the bad press."

Hara maintained eye contact, refusing to squirm. "Listen, I'm not here to catch a man, nor am I in search of gossip. I don't write for a rag."

"Glad to hear it. Charles is a good guy, he just forgets to show it sometimes."

Pot, black, buddy. "You guys are close?"

"I've been friends with Charles since we were little kids. He's the reason they didn't cut me this season, after being a waste of space last year."

"Ah. How's your meniscus, by the way? You seem strong now." She flushed slightly, hearing herself.

"Uh, thanks. Yeah, I'm a hundred percent."

"How was the bench? That had to be pretty boring."

"You have no idea. My biggest thrill was getting away with sneaking Skittles onto the floor in a water bottle."

She laughed, warmed by this small, human detail. "So, I have to ask, why stick it out? If I can believe the interwebs, your family owns half the East Coast. You could have paid back your contract and gone on your merry way. Why play ball, anyway?"

"Oh God. Here we go."

Hara sighed, the warmth dissipating. "Fine. We can sit here silently, I guess."

"It's not like you're trying to engage me in conversation. No, you're diggin' at me so you can get a byline."

Hara shrugged. "Whatever."

Charles saved her.

"Hey, Derek!"

Twisting in her seat, Hara saw Charles coming toward them, parting the crowd, some of whom reached out to touch his arm or back. He ignored the hands, stepping closer. "Bro, you drove, right? Can you give me a ride home?"

"Sure." With no hesitation, Derek stood up. "Let's go."

"No. A half hour. My boys are hooking up, and Tina left me here, she's pissed. Now that she's gone, I wanna make sure poor Naomi is going to be okay."

"I don't think—"

But he was already making his way to "poor" Naomi, who was returning from the restroom. Charles stopped next to the girl, ignoring the small clutch of WAGs who had moved closer, holding Louis Vuitton and Hermès bags like possible beating tools. The women stared at Naomi, who was now rigid and nervous, flicking her eyes back and forth between them and Charles.

Hara shifted around to face the bar. She felt sorry for Naomi. Sort of. The girl could leave if she wanted to avoid escalating the drama. Slugging back a gulp of Angel's Envy, Hara thought, *I should go. This is so not my scene.*

Next to her, Derek exuded frustration, grumbling under his breath and drumming his long fingers on the bar top. Loudly.

She was about to text an Uber when the basketball player said, "I've got time to kill, I guess. Any possibility you've got anything interesting to say?"

"Wow. You really are a dick."

He narrowed his eyes at her but said, "You're right. I don't need to take this out on you." He took out his phone.

"Fine," Hara said. She swirled the liquor in her glass. "How about if I swear everything is off the record?"

He twisted to stare at her but then sat, and said lightly, "Pinkie swear?"

That surprised another laugh out of her. Hara crooked her finger and offered it to the professional athlete and multimillionaire hulking on the stool next to her. Even his smallest finger felt like an iron bar.

He held her finger for a beat and then let go. "How about I answer your question about why I play, and then I get to ask you a question."

"What, are we in third grade?"

"You got something better to do? Gonna go follow the Paul Revere Trail?"

She tipped her glass at him. "I was thinking about it." She paused. "So . . . then . . . okay. Why did you stick with the game?"

He nodded, took a sip of his beer and put it on the bar in front of him. "You see a player out there, and he's taking a charge, skidding across the floor, or running up and down the court until he's about to stroke out, and it's easy to think, 'Jeez, it's just a game, dude, take it easy,' but I don't see it that way. I'm not sayin' it's life or death . . . except, maybe I am. But not in the way you think. It's not about the winning or losing for me. It's about the fact that for two hours, I have a very specific job to do, with a very specific goal. I know exactly what is expected of me and, for the most part, I get it right. I'm good at basketball, a game that has rules, and a beginning and an end." He took a slug of beer. "I earned my spot on this team. My money or family didn't get me here. I did."

"You know, I overheard your phone conversation with your dad yesterday, before the game—"

"You mean when you hit your head, after listening in on a private conversation?" He said it in a friendly tone, though, and with a slight smile.

Hara pushed her glasses up her nose and tried to look dignified. "Um, well, okay, but to be fair, I did try to roll up the window. You're the one who chose to stand right next to the car. Anyway, I could tell your dad was being hard on you. And I just wanted to say I'm sorry. I swim in a much, much smaller pond, but I can empathize—my mom hates what I do. But you're so obviously good at basketball, I don't get why he'd have a problem with it."

"Yeah, well. My father is a wealthy, powerful black man who is embarrassed that I'm embracing the 'stereotypical African American's role, as entertainment for the masses,' as he says. An elitist accusing *me* of being a stereotype." His voice had started to rise, but he calmed himself. "You know what my family does? We buy up homes and city blocks and turn them into commercial property. My whole life, we've taken from others to make a profit. My father would make me go with him to clear 'sites'—we were clearing away run-down apartments or row houses, places people still lived. As a child, I watched other kids lug Hefty bags of their belongings down the street as their homes were razed." He took a short, hard drink of beer, his eyes closed. "My father doesn't play by the rules. No one ever sees what's coming. I don't play like that. Like I said, I earned my way here, not just with talent, but hard work and playing by the rules. I almost lost my spot on the team last year. Now, I need to prove to people, and to myself, I deserve to be here."

Hara tried hard not to gape. Was he for real? "Why are you telling me this?"

His face shuddered. "Sorry."

"No, no, I'm sorry, that came out harsh." Conciliatory, she laid her hand on his arm. He'd been honest and open with her, in a way that made her feel like she was seeing past a public facade, and she appreciated what he was giving her. She hadn't meant to shut him down. "I just . . . you haven't seemed like the type of guy who likes to share." She was struggling with the dichotomy between this thoughtful, deep man and the sullen, righteous jerk from earlier. She removed her hand but put her arm back on the bar, close to his. It was true what she'd said, and she'd forgotten he was human, too, struggling with family just as she was.

"I'm not good at small talk." Derek set down his beer and put his square chin in his hand, peering at her through half-lidded eyes. "To be honest, I'm not good at talking with people in general. I never seem to be able to say the right thing, so I usually don't try." He shook his head and sat up, like he was shaking away his thoughts. "Anyway . . . it was a big night, right? I made some mistakes, but I did all right, don't you think?"

He was seeking approval? From *her*? "Not that my opinion counts, but you did prove yourself. It's just that you'll have to keep doing it. And maybe win a game."

"Funny girl."

"It's not like you're going to get fired. You're contracted. You've got all season to make your mark."

"You'd think so, but I have no desire to ride the bench again. There's a lot of talent on my team, I've got to find a way to stand out."

"Is that why you went for so many buckets tonight?"

"That's right. I'm gonna be a double threat, dammit."

She nodded. "Smart."

He cocked his head and smiled, an honest smile. "You know, you're not bad. For a reporter."

"That's not what you said last night."

"Hmm?"

"I heard what you whispered behind me during the interview." *And outside the library.* "You said I wasn't very good. Just so you know, I wasn't allowed to ask any follow-up questions, per an agreement with O'Donnell."

"Oh. I was joking."

"How would I know that?"

He didn't apologize, only pursed his lips, appraising her. After a second, he said, "By the way, I like you in glasses."

She blushed. "Umm. Thank you." Hara pushed them up. "You must have noticed yesterday, my contacts were driving me crazy." There, now he knew, she was not just some weird blinker.

"All right. I get to ask you a question now."

"I'm an open book."

"Where are you from?"

"Where am I from? Come on, I thought you big-city folk were a little more cultured."

"I'm not sure—"

"I mean, does it matter? You have brown skin, do people ask where *you're* from? I grew up out in the sticks, eating peanut butter sandwiches and watching reality TV, just like most of America. Is that good enough?"

"Hara, I meant, where are you from, as in, where do you live?"

"Oh." She took a swig. "Just outside Portland, Oregon."

"I guess I hit a nerve. Not really an open book, are ya?"

She laughed. "You're right. I might have overreacted. A smidge."

"A skosh."

"A speck."

"A touch."

"A soupçon."

Hara and Derek turned to see who had added the last in the synonym list.

Gus, the blond point guard, grinned and tipped his drink at them. "You know. Soupçon. A touch or a drop," said Gus. At their silence, he said, "What? I like to do the crossword puzzle with my grandpa on Sundays."

Derek nodded as if unperturbed but Hara grappled with the shock trying to play out on her face. She didn't want to disrespect Gus. Not when he'd just revealed he was literate *and* good to his family, despite Hara's earlier impression of him. He wasn't who she thought he was.

Naomi, standing on the other side of him and having heard the exchange, mouthed *I told you so,* tilting her head to Gus, but then also to Derek.

Hara pondered that. Derek had opened up unexpectedly but she wasn't sure he'd actually revealed anything that made her alter her opinion.

One of the WAGs approached Naomi and said something to her, quietly. The young woman's dark skin turned ashen. She came closer to Hara, leaving Charles to talk with Gus. "Maybe it's time we go, huh?"

"You okay?" asked Hara.

"Just not wanting to get my ass beat. Tina didn't leave. She's waiting in the lobby for Charles. Maybe we could sneak past her?"

Derek put down his bottle. "I guess my man has a ride after all. You ladies need a ride?"

Hara was as eager as Naomi to shed the crush of people and the unrelenting beat of loud music. Her shoulders relaxed as she got her jacket and they made their way outside and waited for the valet, away from the fun and the dancing and the drinks. The mist blowing in from the harbor felt good on her hot face.

"Thank you for coming with me, Hara," said Naomi, head down, no longer the strong, confident woman from earlier. Rejection and conflict seemed to have made the young designer shrink into herself. Her red lipstick was suddenly stark and unsettling against her skin. It was hard to watch this transformation. Hara knew exactly how it felt to be publicly shamed and mocked.

"I'm glad I came." Hara put an arm around her new friend's shoulder and gave her a squeeze, not sure if it was a lie or not, especially when she shifted and caught sight of Derek. He was with the doorman a few feet away, signing an autograph and politely shaking his hand before walking over to them. The man was a seething mass of contradictions. Hara sighed. "But I'm ready to go, I guess."

"Maybe," said Derek, moving close, making her shiver. "If the valet ever gets here."

"Derek, I have to admit, I'm kind of surprised you don't have a car service, or even a driver."

"I like to be in charge of my own destiny. I don't want someone else driving me around. And I've never had much of a posse. I've got servants at home, if that's what I want. Most of those guys hanging around Charles and the others, they call themselves homeboys or crew and claim to be loyal, but they bail at the first sign of trouble. That is, if they're not the cause of the trouble."

"You're a real glass-half-empty kind of guy for someone who was born with a silver spoon and the skill to make it into the NBA."

Anger flitted across his face. "Maybe so. Or maybe I'm just realistic. Most people are not worth putting time into."

Hara stopped her tongue. He'd admitted it was hard for him to talk to people, but, seriously, couldn't he hear himself? The black SUV finally arrived. It was a quick trip to Naomi's door, and then only a few minutes more before they were at the O'Donnells'.

The ride was silent.

–*–

Derek didn't know what to think. Or what to feel.

The beautiful woman in the seat next to him had done something to him. Maybe she'd slipped a molly into his beer.

He couldn't remember the last time he'd spoken so openly. Not even with Charles. If he was going to be honest with himself, however, he'd have to admit it felt good. Damn good. And unless she was a fantastic actress, she'd really been listening to him, even seeming to find him interesting—not his fame or his money, but his true self. Sure, that could have been a facade, but it had felt real.

You know what else is real? She's a reporter, you idiot.

Derek hated that little son of a bitch in his head. He didn't want to believe he was just a story to her. She'd treated him like a human being. He liked it. But he knew he couldn't give in to this kind of truth-telling again. It was just too risky. Hara was a risk. A lovely, intelligent risk.

As they approached the O'Donnell residence, deep disappointment made his blood sluggish.

"Who's there?" said a tinny voice over the intercom at the outer gate. A camera swiveled onto them.

"It's Darcy."

The gates creaked open. Derek parked and turned off the car. He floundered silently behind the wheel for a second, dismayed that the evening was about to shut down and he'd probably never see her again. He didn't want to say the wrong thing.

The energy coming off Hara was confusing. She turned to him and bit her lip, her blue eyes searching his quizzically. He couldn't help her, though; he felt the same way, and her biting her lip in that tantalizing way was only serving to fog up his logical side.

"Thank you for the ride." As she spoke, she lifted her hand, possibly to touch the basketball player like she had earlier, at the bar. The place where she had clasped his arm in the bar was still warm. But, unfortunately, her hand dropped back to her lap this time. "It was really nice of you to go out of your way like this."

"I didn't. It's on my way."

"Oh. Okay, then. Well, good night." Hara started to open her door.

Derek shook himself into action. No matter what, he'd be courteous. He could at least do that for her. He swiftly opened his own door. "Wait."

He could see Hara pause and half frown, but he reached her side of the vehicle before she could protest. Derek opened her door and offered a gallant, dramatic sweep of his arm. Holding out a hand to help her out, he tried to pull it off as if he were always this smooth and debonair. *Talk about acting.*

"Thank you." After a second's hesitation, she brushed a dark lock of hair behind her ear and placed her long fingers in his. From her seat, she peered down at the ground. "It is quite a drop."

"Life is so much easier when you're not wearing high heels. Women can't even get in and out of cars." He heard it come out of his mouth before he could stop himself. Maybe one day he'd learn how to land a joke, but that moment was not now.

Hara looked at him for a second, a steeliness sliding over her features. "Maybe if guys didn't jack up their rigs to ridiculous heights just to drive down city streets, that wouldn't be true."

She tried taking her hand out of his.

Derek considered holding on but let go. "I'm not good at conversation. I'm sorry."

"So you've said."

"Let me help you down." Before Hara could argue, he reached slowly into the car and put his hand lightly on her hip, directing an arched eyebrow at her, seeking permission. He didn't want to offend her again. Nor did he want to get punched. She seemed like the type of girl who could take care of herself.

"Okay?" Derek asked, and then, suddenly, the sheer intensity of her sexiness hit him, simply from the feel of her hip bone and the trim waist under his palm. *Oh my God, please do not get an erection right now.* It was too late; his body wasn't listening to reason, only basic animal instinct.

Hara nodded and moved to the edge of the seat.

He inhaled sharply, struggling with desire as he grabbed her by the waist and gently set her on the ground. There was less than an inch between them.

Neither of them moved. Derek's long fingers remained wrapped around her, just below her rib cage, under her jacket; her breath was on his neck, driving him crazy. His mind skittered across all the logical courses of action he should be taking right now. But then Hara tilted up her head and all thought left; he was stunned by the intensity and shifting light in her eyes. Her clean, heady scent made him dizzy—that, and the fact that the blood had left his brain, settling much farther south. The air between their bodies heated up and then the space between them disappeared. His length was against her. He wasn't sure who closed the gap, but she did not seem to mind, pressing against him, creating a flash of lust in him that ran up his spine and set his nerves on fire.

Hara, her breathing ragged, put a hand on his chest and looked up at him, her mouth soft and waiting. She licked her lips and Derek nearly lost it. His hands on her waist tightened.

"Don't do that," he growled, one hand sliding to her lower back, pulling her closer, his length and his hardness fully against her . . .

The heavy front door of the O'Donnell residence creaked open.

The basketball player blinked, dropped his hands, and stepped back.

What am I doing?

–*–

Hara realized her hands were grabbing at air; she let them fall awkwardly back to her sides. The cold void where Derek had been just a second before made her shiver, a shock to her system. But that cold emptiness was the only evidence she had that the past few moments had actually happened, that she hadn't been dreaming again.

Not that she was 100 percent sure either way. Maybe not a dream. A mini seizure? Her mind whirled around and around. Had she just been about to make out with a famous athlete? With a guy who ran more hot and cold than a faucet?

She had felt his heart beat under his shirt, the hard pounding. She'd done that. Derek Darcy, a man who admittedly didn't like "most people," had physically responded to a girl like her. And it wasn't just his heartbeat that was hard. *Crazy.*

The logical side of her mind had been screaming at her, but her body had leapt into a tingling, hot place the second he laid a hand on her, and it was definitely not related to the heated seats in the SUV.

Derek!" Madeline called out from the door, a dark shape in the square of light. She stepped out quickly to greet them. Her words were directed at the ballplayer, as if Hara weren't there. "I am so glad you made it! I feel terrible I didn't get a chance to drop by the club tonight."

His tone was polite but Hara was close enough to see him frown. "You didn't miss much." Without looking at Hara, he started around to the driver's side. "Well, good night."

She stared after him. That was it? She pursed her lips and blew out her breath, frustrated. Once again, life had reminded her that professional athletes were not to be trusted. Certainly not with her emotions, anyway. She could not believe she had let down her defenses like that in the first place. What had she been thinking? Obviously nothing. *Lesson learned. Good riddance.*

But Madeline wasn't about to let him go so easily. Before he could get into his vehicle, the assistant called out, "Oh, Derek! Mr. O'Donnell has asked that you join us for a moment. He'd like you to come inside." Then, finally, she acknowledged Hara, her tone turning crisp. "Hara, I see you've made it safely back. Good."

Walking into the house, Hara could not remember a time she'd felt more awkward. Her movements were jerky, almost robotic, knowing Derek was right behind her. Luckily, the O'Donnells met them in the foyer and the attention shifted to their star rookie, not her. They did greet Hara quickly before turning to Derek, but she was not offended by their obvious lack of enthusiasm at her presence. She shifted from foot to foot like a schoolchild, wondering how long she had to stand there before it no longer seemed impolite for her to disappear.

"Mr. Darcy, how nice to see you. Quite a game tonight, dear," said Molly O'Donnell.

O'Donnell puffed on a pipe, his thumb hooked into his vest, doing his best to project a Victorian-era lord of the manor. "Boy, you had some bright moments. A lot to work on, but you'll get there."

"Thank you, sir. If you don't mind, I think I should be going," said Derek, but he was ignored.

"Nonsense. You're young, you'll live. I just need a few minutes of your time."

Madeline laid her hand on Derek's arm, while peering directly at Hara, her face devoid of warmth. "Is there anything you need for the night, Hara?"

All eyes turned to the young reporter. Hara bit her lip. "I'm good, thanks. Super-grateful for everything, but I just can't keep my eyes open. Good night."

No one tried to stop her.

Her first steps were slow; she was stupidly hoping Derek would call out to her, at least to offer a real "good night." The silence rang in her ears, pushing her faster up the stairs and down the maze-like hallways to her room.

Locking the door with a sigh, Hara shuffled into the bedroom. She kicked off her shoes and then her skirt before attacking the corset. Long, angry moments of struggling to get the laces loosened and the neck ruff unhooked left her on the verge of screaming in frustration. Finally, she wrenched the neck piece and the last closure came free, leaving her panting and drained, a hand to her throat.

She dropped onto the bed in her underwear. As images from the night, especially the last few minutes, tumbled around in a confused jumble, her face became hot again.

Hara sat up, her palms chilly against flushed cheeks. *I'm not ready to parse this.*

She changed into her old, comfortable pajamas and washed her face, moving on autopilot, choosing not to think, not yet. She picked up a book, hoping to live in another world for the next few hours, but her stomach let out a startlingly loud rumble, and then another as she tried to get comfortable on the bed. Groaning with frustration, Hara found she could no longer ignore her hunger. She'd meant to grab something at Tunnel, but then, well, the beautiful elite had surrounded her and she'd lost track of herself. But stomach pangs weren't going to allow her to stay in that alternate reality any longer.

She quietly crept into the hall, barefoot. O'Donnell and Madeline and Derek would be in the library or the living area, on the other side of the house, quite separate from the kitchen. She should be able to sneak into the pantry for some bread and peanut butter with no one knowing.

The wood floors were cold under her feet, yet she found herself dithering more than once to appreciate a lovely painting or sculpture. Hara was probably standing next to something famous, like a Picasso or Matisse. She had no idea. *I guess I really am a country bumpkin.*

Anything to keep the conflicting thoughts of Derek at bay, until she was ready.

The graphic sex painting didn't help matters. She hurried her steps.

Hara was halfway down the back stairs leading into the kitchen when she realized she could hear voices. *Damn.* Derek and the others were in there. Glancing down at her grungy pajamas, she grimaced. She would rather starve than have Derek see her this way. Or, worse, Madeline.

She'd backtracked only a few steps when Hara heard her name. She paused, wrestling with her code of ethics. Listen or not listen; what was the right thing to do? The first time she'd listened in on a conversation of Derek's, she'd hit her head on the door. The second time she'd eavesdropped on him, outside the library, she'd taken a big hit to her ego. Karma was surely telling her something.

Madeline's voice, with its overdone posh cadence, carried clearly up the staircase. "You have no idea who that girl is."

"I know she's a reporter. What do I care? I don't have anything to hide."

"But *she* does. You should steer clear of her."

Oh. My. God. What a classist bitch. There was no way she was leaving now.

"What are you talking about? She's totally normal. Way more normal than most of the people I've met lately."

"You're wrong," said O'Donnell. "She's only here because her father worked out a deal. He's in prison. I'd think you'd have recognized the name. Isari?"

"Are you talking about Thomas Isari? The bookie who ratted on all those athletes? Jesus."

The blood left Hara's head. She put her fingertips on the nearest wall, steadying herself, praying she did not faint. Or maybe she was asleep. Dreaming.

The hard, solid wall and the silky feel of the wallpaper stole that hope away.

"She's shifty, just like her father," said Madeline. "Thank God she's leaving tomorrow."

Derek was silent. No one spoke for a few seconds.

What did that mean? Her father had worked out a deal? He was locked up. He couldn't have had anything to do with this.

"We kept up our end of the bargain." This was the gentle, breathy voice of Mrs. O'Donnell. "We brought her in, a no-name hack, to talk to Butler. Now we're off the hook. We don't have to deal with her again."

"I don't understand."

O'Donnell interjected, "There's not much more to tell. Isari and his daughter gamed the system so she'd win that stupid contest. We kept her here, to keep an eye on her, having no idea she'd weasel her way into an invitation to your after-party. But now it's over. I'm sure you can see why it's a bad idea to be seen with her again, Darcy."

There was another pause. Hara had her head against the wall, trying to get her heart rate under control. Nothing made sense. Her dad set this up? *How?* She struggled to breathe normally. *Why?*

"Can I make you a martini?" Madeline asked, presumably

to Derek, her voice dropping into that smoky purr she must have thought was seductive. "We were going to go to the library to watch the game footage. Care to join us?"

"I don't think so. Thank you for your hospitality, but I better be going."

"You be careful out there, son. Need to protect my investment, don't I?"

"Yes, sir."

"If you need anything," Madeline jumped back in, "anything at all, you call. Anytime, day or night. You have my number, right?"

Hara fled.

CHAPTER 9

It was necessary to laugh,
when she would rather have cried.

—*Pride and Prejudice*

The sideways rain hit the windows, wide rivulets running down the plate glass in Logan Airport's Terminal C. The air, stifling, smelled of Dunkin' Donuts and french fries and body odor, somewhat reminiscent of the basketball stadium.

Hara crossed her arms and shifted on the hard chair, her feet propped up on her suitcase. She'd been in this seat for hours, listening to the never-ending rain. It was like being in Oregon, minus the clean air and decent airport.

Before taking up residence on the chair, she'd trudged through every airport shop, trying to kill off the stretch of infinite hours before her flight, moving slowly past Victoria's Secret nighties and Bose headphones and Boston Beer Works. Her brain throbbed, her stomach churned.

When she'd first arrived, she'd been in shock. The giant world clock at the entrance to the airport had not yet hit midnight when she'd walked through the front doors; her flight did not leave until the next night. Hara had found a bench across from the American Airlines counter, where a steady stream of people dropped off luggage and speed-walked back to their departure gates. Where else was she going to go in the middle of the night? Her credit cards were almost maxed, she couldn't afford a room. She could barely afford the taxi to the airport.

Hara was not ready to tell Carter, or her mother, about this massive cock-up, not yet, even if it meant sponge bathing in the airport bathroom.

Using her coat for a blanket and a sweatshirt for a pillow, she'd lain back on the bench and whispered passages from her favorite books to herself. She knew she looked crazy, but better that than having a nervous breakdown and sobbing it out.

When she allowed herself to think, she went right into dark and twisty.

He never believed I could do it.

He didn't give me the chance to prove that I could. He stole that from me.

Eventually, her brain stumbled into the blackest place.

Her father knew she was not a good enough writer for the big leagues. He'd been protecting Hara from the truth.

She'd been fooling herself.

Her dream of becoming someone bigger, better, than who she'd been back home, it was stupid. She was stupid. Hara should have realized time did not heal all wounds—that people in the sports world would put it together that she was the daughter of Thomas Isari. Derek had known exactly who the O'Donnells were talking about.

Hara screwed her eyes shut. There was nothing wrong with working for Carter's newspaper, where her past was no surprise to anyone. She'd have to cover city hall meetings and school board meetings and baby showers, but she could do write-ups on the high school games and cover the annual softball game between the police department and the fire department. It wouldn't kill her. She'd be fine.

Being a small person in a small town is fine.

The distraught young woman had waited in the ticketing lobby for hours, zombie-like, for the rest of the airport to open up, surprised when no one came to shoo her away. However, after trying to nap through boarding announcements, the squealing drag of wheeled suitcases, passengers bitching at the computers in the ticket-printing kiosks, crying babies, and the constant *swoosh-swoosh* of the automatic doors, all while making sure no one stole her suitcase, she realized nobody purposefully tried to spend a night in the airport. The worst was the oscillating air conditioner in the ceiling, shooting cold air out at a temperature meant to freeze beef and then shutting off just long enough for the corridor to heat back up to a clammy tropical jungle.

Still, better than being at the mansion of horrors.

So, Hara put her head down, shut her eyes, and bulldozed her way mentally through the misery and discomfort.

She never wanted to see any of those people ever again, wished she could erase the past few days. *And Daddy . . .* The pain she felt at his betrayal whipped through her, a fresh wound every time she thought of him. He'd let her think she'd made it this far on her own.

Finally, after the airport slowly shuffled to life and she'd been allowed through security and then visited every shop, some twice, she'd found her gate and settled in. The grim, dreary day slowly turned to night in the domestic concourse, with its banks of individual plastic chairs, the rain pounding the windows harder and harder, and a gusting wind occasionally bowing the glass.

Hara drank hot tea and watched the computerized arrival and departure board like it was a soap opera, getting tenser every time a flight changed from "on time" to "delayed."

A flash of purple and white light lit up the terminal; a jagged streak of lightning stretched across the twilit sky, from one end of the horizon to the other, scaring the bejesus out of Hara. But it was the cracking *boom* that made her shriek.

The old man next to Hara patted her leg. "Jumpin' Jehoshaphat, that lightning is right on top of us," he creaked, his eyes kind under bushy gray eyebrows. "I hope they got their lightnin' rods set tight."

Hara nodded in agreement. A lot of people were clustering at the windows, waiting for the next lightning bolt, excited by the violence of the storm. She was going to stay right where she was and avoid metal, the rubber soles of her Adidas planted on the ground.

Another blinding, massive bolt of lightning filled the sky, this time making the hair on her arms stand up. Another peal of thunder crashed overhead, shaking the building for what seemed like forever. Then the rain kicked the spray up a notch, as if someone were hosing down the windows.

More lightning. More thunder.

Rubbing the bristle on his chin, the old man said, "Ayuh. Mother Nature showin' off, then. Our first real nor'easter of the year. Looks to be a good un."

"I can't believe they fly planes in this."

"Reckon they thought the same thing." He got to his feet and nodded toward the board. He shuffled away, calling over his shoulder, "Good luck, miss. Be safe."

More than half the flights were now flipped to "delayed." A quarter read "canceled" in big red letters. Including her flight to Portland.

The airline personnel were crazed, unable to give her any help, unless she wanted a blanket and a sandwich for the night. There were no hotel vouchers available but they were bringing in cots. They weren't going to start rescheduling flights until tomorrow. They would gladly set up the automated system to text her when a flight to Portland was scheduled.

She took the sandwich.

The only phone number she had for anyone local was for Madeline. Big, hard no.

But she did know where Naomi lived. Kind of. She grimaced, looked around at the chaos, and decided it was time to test out the kindness of a stranger. Hopefully, Naomi was home. Hara could not take another night in this place.

–*–

The soon-to-be-ex-reporter hunched her shoulders and sprinted up to Naomi's brick building, trying to get out of the swirling rain and wind, puddles forming around her feet. Reaching over to ring the bell, she yelped in surprise when the entry door swung out, almost hitting her.

"What the—" Charles Butler quirked an eyebrow at her, a half smile on his lips. "What are you doin' here?"

"Um. Uh," she stuttered. *I'm guessing Tina would ask you the same question.* "My flight was canceled. I don't really know anyone but Naomi."

Her Uber driver sprang from the driver's seat of the Corolla behind her. "Hey! Butler! Man, this is awesome—"

"Ah, Jesus." Charles put a hand to his head, like he had a headache.

Rain dripped from Hara's bangs onto her glasses. "Can I come in?"

The apartment door at the top of the stairs popped open.

Naomi came running into the stairwell. "Baby, wait, don't go!" The girl stumbled to a stop halfway down the stairs when she saw Hara in the doorway. And the Uber driver beside her, his mouth hanging open.

"Well, shit." The young woman laughed, weakly, pulling down her camisole, as if she could morph it into a miniskirt.

"Hi," Hara said, her feet frozen. If her thighs were that thin, she'd hang out in her underwear, too.

Everyone's eyes shifted to the ballplayer. Charles laser-stared at the Uber driver until the kid hung his head and returned to his car.

The player chuckled. "Awk-ward," he said to Hara, then jumped up the steps to Naomi. "Sweet thang, you go on back inside. It's cold out here."

Hara felt a lump grow in her throat when she saw the big man put a soft hand on Naomi's cheek and peer into the girl's eyes.

Her thoughts shot immediately back to her father, reaching across the table to touch her cheek. She missed him, suddenly, briefly, until she was slammed flat again, remembering his disloyalty.

Charles twisted and swiftly bounded back down.

"Wait, Charles," Naomi called, a controlled pleading note creeping into her voice. "Please."

He didn't turn around, though, or say another word to her. Instead, he pushed past Hara, and went to the Corolla she'd arrived in. "Nice to see you again, Hara," he said over his shoulder. He pulled open the back door and said to the driver, "Can you take me to West Roxbury?"

With that, the famous athlete climbed into the Uber and was gone. Hara felt bad for the half-naked Naomi, left behind on the stairs, shivering, a light sheen of tears in her eyes.

The girl didn't seem embarrassed, though. She swiped at an eye and asked Hara, "What's going on? I thought you were leaving today?" Her cocoa skin broke out in ashen bumps as the wind gusted and pushed a spray of rain through the open door. "Come on, we'll talk inside."

Back in the small apartment, Naomi slid into a robe. "I'm going to make tea. Do you want some?"

"Do you have anything stronger?"

"I'm sorry, I don't. Hot chocolate is as good as it gets."

"I'll take it." They sat at the table, waiting for water to boil. Hara cleared her throat. "I interrupted something I shouldn't have. If you need to go, to talk to him, I can leave."

Naomi shook her head, her dark brown eyes welling again with unshed tears. But calmly, she said, "No. Tell me what's going on with you."

Hara told her about the canceled flight and her lack of funds. "Of course, if you let me crash here, I can send you some cash in a few weeks, when I get paid."

Naomi's mouth dropped open. "Is that how they do things in Oregon? My ma would kick my ass if I didn't take care of a guest. Whatever's mine is yours. It's still early, but when you're ready, the couch is comfy."

Relief swept through Hara. "To be honest, I think I'm ready to go to bed now." She pushed back from the table and stood. "I didn't get any sleep last night."

"Can I ask you a question first? Don't take this the wrong way, but how come you didn't just go back to the O'Donnells'?"

Hara burst into tears. She dropped onto the couch cushions.

"Oh. Oh no." Naomi sat next to her, drawing a soft blanket over them. "If you keep crying, I'm going to join you."

It took a while for Hara to fight back the boiling despair and tears long enough to get it out: how her father, a prisoner, had somehow set up the interview, yet let her believe she was here on her own merit, and how cruel the O'Donnells had been about her connection to her convict dad. And how Derek had first mocked her as a reporter, then later almost kissed her, then completely dismissed her without a word.

And, finally, she explained her fear that she'd made a huge mistake, letting her pride push her down the path to be a sportswriter, thinking not only that she was good enough but also that people wouldn't recognize her name—but now it was obvious she was going to have to be happy working at her local paper.

"I didn't deserve this chance."

"Damn. That's a lot to process. Let's go back to the beginning. How does your dad even know Mr. O'Donnell?"

"I have no idea." She could guess, though.

"And Derek Darcy. What an asshole." Naomi's lower lip stuck out and she crossed her arms. "Not all the players are like that, you know."

"Obviously not."

She gave Hara the side-eye. "You can't say anything about Charles being here. Swear it."

"You are my port in a storm! I am not going to turn on you. Besides, like I told Derek last night, I'm not interested in writing gossip." Hara sipped her drink morosely. She wasn't interested in writing anything anymore.

"It's not what you think. I'm no thot." The young woman next to her let out a long breath. "I wouldn't have an affair with another woman's man. He's left Tina, she just won't accept it. He can't afford a scene, though, so he's asked me to not tell anyone until it's sorted. Derek's his best friend and even he doesn't know about us. Yet." Her eyes were wet again. "Charles wants to be with me. He does."

Hara bit her tongue as long as she could. "I hope that's true. I like Charles. But if I've learned anything from Lifetime movies, it's that guys lie to their mistresses. I don't care how nice he seems."

"I'm not a mistress! He's a good guy. He just doesn't want to hurt her more than he has to. They've been dating off and on for years."

"I thought they were engaged."

"They were but Charles broke it off. And now she's threatening to go to the press and create a shitstorm if he doesn't come back to her. The organization has been pretty clear they don't want any drama. There's something in Charles's contract that he'll be docked, possibly benched, if he's involved in a scandal."

Scandal. Charles must have told Derek about Naomi, whether she knew it or not. Outside the library on the night of the party, they'd been talking about Charles needing to get ahead of some story. It had to be about Tina and Naomi. Hara frowned. If so, here she was, thinking she was going to break some big story, and it was just stupid, everyday relationship drama. Another sign Hara's journalistic instincts weren't as sharp as she'd believed.

After a few more minutes of hearing about the great Charles Butler, Hara nodded off, hours of misery having worn her down.

–*–

A loud crack of thunder woke her. Gasping awake, her back spasming with shock, she rolled off the couch, landing on a black shag rug. A gray pillow fell next to her head. *Not home.*

The wind howled and the bulleting *tra-tra-tra* of rain on the window was constant. Dim light seeped in through the blinds, offering signs of a grim morning.

There were no phone messages from the airlines. The day was beginning exactly the way it ended.

The thunder and lightning moved past quickly this time, however; after a few minutes, only distant rumbles could be heard. Though, she realized, some of the rumbling came from the noisy prep cooks downstairs, who ignored early-morning common decency. Hara could hear instrumental music, an odd mashup of flutes and techno. The cooks would sporadically bang pots and pans, possibly to drown out the sound of their own music. She couldn't believe Naomi slept through the cacophony.

After showering, Hara found that the thunderstorm was gone and the rain had ceased, though banks of black clouds blocked the morning sun. She was too anxious to sit around but didn't want to wake her benefactor. She decided to go for a walk. Being from Oregon, she wasn't afraid of a little rain.

Her mother had replied to her text from the night before, in which Hara told Willa the flight had been canceled, by asking if the friend she was staying with was handsome. That was it, no questions about why she wasn't with the O'Donnells or even if she was okay. Hara didn't reply.

It took her a few blocks to find the courage to call Carter. She'd have to be more forthright with her boss.

"I don't know what you're talking about, Hara. How could your dad have any sway over O'Donnell? You won a national contest," Carter said, as perplexed as she was. "Maybe you're blowing this out of proportion. Let's just get you on a plane and we'll talk about it when you get home. I'll call the airlines, see what I can do."

"Thank you." She hung up.

The rain had begun to pick back up.

Wiping droplets from her glasses, she suddenly realized where she was, recognizing the historic building in front of her.

Obviously, her heart hadn't caught up with her mind—her subconscious had led her steps to an address she knew by heart. Deep down, she'd known where she was headed all along, she'd just refused to consciously question it, not even when she'd strapped on her red satchel before leaving the house. Inside that satchel was her résumé and portfolio.

No. There's no way I'm doing it now. I'll stay home, write local stories. It was better than nothing and her dad was old news there.

The tall glass building sat on a foundation of old and stately brick and, according to a wall plaque, housed the offices of the *City Gazette*. One of the longest-running newspapers in the U.S., it had employed many famous journalists who had fought the good fight in Boston for its readers. She traced the engraved plaque, entranced, until the sky doubled down and let loose with some real rain.

Despite the deluge, she hesitated, trying to decide if she wanted to escape the weather in a place that symbolized her lost future . . . but then realized she sounded like an abused housewife on a made-for-TV special. *Get over yourself, Hara.* Despite the soul-scraping internal shift away from sportswriting as a career choice, she was still in awe of a place that had been one of the first to lead the charge for freedom of the press and upholding democracy. She was curious to see the guts of such a famous institution. And she wanted to get out of the rain.

The lobby boasted a massive, curving staircase that reminded her of the one from the movie *Titanic*. The first-floor bathrooms were more modern and, more importantly, warm, as she attempted to blot herself dry with paper towels and then the air blower. Her tennis shoes squelched when she walked and her jeans were unpleasantly damp against her legs.

As she emerged from the restroom, she heard her name.

"Hara?" It was Eddie, the redheaded beat reporter she'd met at the game.

"Oh, hi. Nice to see you."

"Yah, you, too." His smile faded and his eyes scrunched into suspicious slits. "You know, if you're here for an interview, don't bother gunning for my job. They love me here."

"I'm sure they do." So much to say to that. But how in the hell could he know she was thinking of applying? "My flight was canceled. Thought I'd check out the newsroom before I went home."

"Stahtin' with the hoppah, I see."

"Huh?"

"The hopper. The toilet."

"Well, my next stop is a little more exciting." She pointed at a large piece of equipment on display. "The old Linotype machine."

"I think we've got some stuffed carrier pigeons upstairs."

She laughed. "Any telegraph poles?"

"Oh, a whole string of them. Wanna see?"

Eddie led Hara to the elevators; they got off on the third floor. Over one of the entryways, she thrilled to see her favorite Walter Cronkite quote: *Freedom of the press is not just important to democracy, it is democracy.*

"This is sooo not like the newsroom back home." Despite herself, she was inspired.

"I know, right? It's pretty damn nice, compared to our old offices." They walked into a well-lit, open space, with wide aisles and enormous windows, surrounded by glassed-in offices and conference rooms. Dozens of large, ceiling-mounted TVs peppered the huge room, so the staff could watch for breaking news and website analytics. One of the big news stories was, of course, the weather and the delayed flights.

"Goin' to the game tonight?" Eddie asked.

"I'm hoping I can still get on a flight out. Besides, I wasn't invited."

"Invited? You're press. Don't you have your press pass?"

"Yes . . ." She tried to remember where she'd last seen it. "I guess. But like I said, I hope to be crammed into a tight space at thirty thousand feet."

He shrugged. "Fine. You think you can get Butler to give me five minutes tonight?"

"Ha! You think I have power over Charles?"

"You call him Charles. I've been on this beat for five years but he's never hung out with me at Tunnel. I'm not on his radar."

"You know about the club?"

"The Boston Gossip Bitches—they were at Tunnel. They took pictures and posted them on their blog."

Hara was surprised. "I can't imagine I created much of a stir."

"You didn't. I mean, you're hot and all, but those gals were going for pics of Tina and Charles fighting. They weren't sorry."

"Dammit."

"What? That your friend was raked, or that you were scooped?"

"Don't be a dick. Unless an athlete has gone totally off the rails or done something illegal, I've never written about anything other than their ability. I hate exploiting drama around private lives."

"Fair enough. Though my boss would tell you it sells copies."

"Every boss says that."

"So, you're not here to try out as a gossip columnist. That's great, I guess. But what *are* you doin'?"

"That is an excellent question."

He straightened his tie, clearing his throat in an exaggerated manner. "If you're still around tonight, you can be my date."

"Uhhh."

"I'm going to pretend I'm not offended. I'm talking about the game, ijit."

She wouldn't accept a million dollars if it meant seeing Derek or O'Donnell again.

Then, through the haze of angst and anger she'd been packing around since yesterday, she saw another truth:

This was the job she'd chosen.

Was she going to give up just because her heart was betrayed and her ego had been kicked?

After working for years toward this goal, and putting up with years of shit, you're just going to roll over, Hara Isari?

Maybe she wasn't a great writer. Maybe she wasn't even that good. But she could still learn.

Was she really giving up because someone else didn't believe in her?

When had she become a quitter?

An image of a dimly lit staircase in a condemned tenement popped into her head. It was from her favorite poem by Langston Hughes, in which a parent tells a kid not to sit down when things get hard. He'd said that life could be like a scary set of stairs, but to keep climbing even when dealing with splinters or burned-out light bulbs.

If she had to get encouragement from a literary parent versus a real parent, so be it.

Fine. If she was stuck in Boston, Hara would take that as a sign from the universe. She would write a freaking phenomenal story. The haters could go screw themselves.

"Sure. If I don't get a flight out, I'll let you know. Can I get a tour first?"

Eddie took her around to the writers, editors, designers, photographers, and graphic specialists. They ended in the sports department. The small crew happily shared war stories; they also spent quality time poking at Eddie. It wasn't until their editor showed up that they quieted down.

"Hara Isari. Saw your article on Butler come across the wire this morning. How'd you manage it?"

"Yeah? It's out on the wire already?" She smiled, her heart trilling at proof she had managed the feat and now her words were in the hands of readers across the nation. Even if she got the interview because of her father, she'd done the work.

But then the implication of the man's question set in. Was he asking how Thomas Isari's daughter managed to get a job in sports? Or was he scoffing at the writing? Beating back the rising distress and disillusionment vying for space with her tentative, newly rebuilt self-worth, she said calmly, blithely, "Good luck got me here, I guess."

Inwardly, she cringed. *Totally just sold myself out.*

"Seems to me our Eddie either needs to grow tits or work a little harder for his good luck."

Nice. Top-down sexism. If she did stick with sportswriting, she'd only have more of this to look forward to . . . Hara decided it was time to go with a bolder response, cupped her hands under her breasts, and said with a smirk, "I'm pretty sure these little guys didn't get me in the door." Then to Eddie, she said, "But maybe your boobs are bigger than mine. Break 'em out, let's see how that works for you."

"Hey, I didn't say it!" he sputtered in protest. "Besides, you don't have to patronize me. I'm with those guys week in and week out; I'm not worried about covering the team. I'm not writing fluffy features, I'm writing real stories."

Hara's lips twisted in fury. He'd gone right for the nads and, in his condescension, didn't even know it.

Before she could say anything, the editor snorted. "Eddie, take it down a notch," said the asshole who'd thrown the grenade in the first place. "Everyone, get back to work." The man wandered off.

"Yeah, Eddie," Hara blazed, "fuck right off."

The bullish behavior over the past few minutes had moved Hara from depressed to straight anger. Finally. She could do anything when she was mad enough. She'd just forgotten that. Her courage rose with every attempt to intimidate her.

The male reporter had the sense to dip his head, sheepish. "Yeah. I crossed a line. Sorry. It's just a blow, you know? They've shut me out. And then you come along . . ."

"I get it." She tucked her hair behind an ear, to see him clearly. "You're not going to like this, either: I want to submit a résumé." She tugged out the folder with her papers from her bag. "I promise, I'm not trying to take your job, but I do want *a* job. The universe continues to put opportunities in front of me"—he didn't need to know that her father had kick-started the universe's plan—"and I have got to jump on and ride it out."

Eddie stroked his beard. "I figured." After a second, he

shrugged. "You gotta start somewhere, I guess. I'd just appreciate it if you don't show me up."

"No promises." Her phone beeped. It was a text from Carter. He could get her on a flight later that afternoon or tomorrow. Which would she like?

Hara slid her phone back into her jacket. "Damn."

"I take it you're here another night." He sat on a desk. "Let me make it up to ya. Buy you a bag of arena kettle corn."

The universe kept giving her the choice to move forward. She'd said she wouldn't ignore it. When life got hard, she couldn't just sit down.

"I guess so." She pushed up her glasses. "I'll meet you there. In press row."

On the way out, she stopped in the human resources office. Handing over an application and her portfolio took willpower and a stern warning to her limbs about shaking in public, but she did it.

CHAPTER 10

An unhappy alternative . . .

—*Pride and Prejudice*

Hara poked Naomi's buzzer but no one answered. She tried a few times, standing in a heavy drizzle, and was just about to find a quiet, dry corner in the restaurant, when the door finally buzzed open.

Reaching the apartment, Hara found Naomi waiting for her, appearing an altogether different creature than she had the night before, with dark circles under her eyes, gray skin around her lips, her posture bowed. Even her hair drooped.

"You look terrible."

"Thanks. Want some brunch?" The girl poured cereal into two bowls and placed them on the tiny Ikea table. She seemed to float across the floor, weightless, to retrieve a carton of milk from the refrigerator.

"Seriously, you okay?" Hara frowned.

In reply, Naomi, who had unscrewed the milk container

and sniffed it, suddenly recoiled, gagged, and sprinted for the bathroom.

That wasn't good. "Naomi?" Hara knocked on the bathroom door. She could hear quiet retching sounds. "Can I get you anything?"

The toilet flushed and Naomi emerged, shaking slightly.

Hara handed her a glass of water. "How long have you known?"

"I found out yesterday. I should have guessed sooner. Mornings aren't treating me so well." Naomi sat at the table, hunched into herself. She pushed the bowl of dry cereal away.

"I can tell." They sat quietly for a moment. Finally, Hara said, "You can't be too far along."

"No bump yet." Naomi placed her slender hands over her stomach. "I'm guessing I'm about four to five weeks, maybe even six."

"Charles? Did you tell him?"

"Yes. Last night. He left right after I told him." She groaned and put a hand over her eyes. "I am a freaking cliché. He probably thinks this is on purpose, so I can ride his gravy train."

"What do you want to do?"

"I have no idea." Naomi wiped a hand across her mouth. "What do you think? What would you do in my situation?"

"Above my pay grade." *Run away, girl, be free,* thought Hara. Derek had been the perfect reminder—professional athletes were treated like gods, and too many came to believe they *were* gods. And, obviously, a good chunk of them didn't know what "monogamous" meant. Or what it meant to be a good partner. Who needed that turmoil?

"The only thing I know," said Naomi, "is that I don't want Charles to someday turn his back on me, accuse me of snagging a money source. I love him. I need him to respect me."

Hara nodded. "Love" seemed a little much, but who was she to judge? "I get that. Respect means everything to me."

They were quiet a minute more. The rain had picked up again, creating moving shadows in the dim room and a soft, liquid background music.

"Anyway," Naomi said. "What's your plan? What did the airlines say?"

"My editor got me on a flight out tomorrow. I know you said I could stay here, but I swear, if this is too much, I don't have to."

"Please. I'm fine with it. You should go to the game tonight."

"I think I've talked myself into it." She could focus on the failings of the Fishers' second-year rookie, write a hit piece. That would be fun. "Are you going?"

"Nah. I don't want to get jumped by Tina. The memo regarding their breakup hasn't quite sunk in; like I said, she's threatening to feed the press some story to make Charles look bad if he walks away. I can't even begin to imagine her level of crazy if she finds out I'm pregnant." She folded her arms. "I'm not tryin' to dim the woman's light, I got mad respect for her. She just need to see, she and Charles dead."

Uh huh, thought Hara. What was in that bowl of cereal? Powdered delusion?

"Besides, he was pretty mad at me for jumpin' him at Tunnel." The girl's lower lip quivered slightly. "I just wanted to spend time with him out in the open. But the organization will punish him if he is caught up in a scandal. I'll let him take care of the Tina problem."

Hara gazed at her, unsure of what to say. She wanted to ask how the girl let herself get pregnant if that wasn't what she wanted, but again, who was Hara to judge? To be sanctimonious? She'd have to pay to get pregnant, at this point.

"Whatever," Naomi said. "I have bigger—or littler—things to worry about right now. I'm going to take a bath, pretend everything's normal."

Hara changed into dry, warm clothes and sat down with her computer. Her next steps were murky.

Her phone rang.

It was Telmate. Her heart lurched. She wasn't sure she was ready to talk to her father. But she couldn't help herself. After accepting the call, she said, "Hi, Daddy."

There was a rustling on the other end of the phone, a cough. Then, "Baby girl! Just checking in. How was the trip? Are you home?"

"No, my flight was delayed because of rain and lightning. I've got a ticket for tomorrow."

"Shit." There was a pause. When he spoke again, his voice seemed far away. "Are you back at O'Donnell's house?"

"No." She took a deep breath. "He is a righteous son of a bitch. But it's you who I'm really mad at! How could you?" The last came out in a wail.

"Hara—"

"I know what you did. You made me look weak. And stupid! I thought you of all people believed I could do this. And now I'm questioning myself, ready to give up, because, like always, you had to lie and cheat and ruin my freaking life."

He fell into a coughing fit. Finally, his voice cracking, he said, "What are you talking about?"

"What am I talking about?! Goddamn it, you let me come out here thinking O'Donnell picked me because of my writing, when you were the one who reached out to him . . . You think this is how I want to succeed? Huh? I'm not like you. I actually try at life."

I guess I'm going to let that sanctimonious flag fly, after all.

More coughing.

"Jesus. Get some cold medicine, you sound terrible. Why did O'Donnell do this, anyway? He owe you some gambling debt from the good old days?"

His voice was barely audible. "Something like that."

"That's just fantastic. He's a crook, too. Freaking fantastic."

"You're blowing this out of proportion. I got you a chance, you took it, and now you're going to start getting some notice from the big dogs." Thomas was breathing heavily but kept going. "Hara, be pissed if you want, but don't think I regret it for one second. I'm stuck in this shithole while you're out there; this was the only way I could help. For the love of God, do not fuck this up just because you're mad."

"I've been getting by without your help for ten years." Hara hung up on him.

She instantly regretted it.

He might not be a famous poet like Langston Hughes, nor was he creating beautifully worded analogies about dark staircases and life, but he was her parent. And he *was* offering the same kind of advice, albeit less lyrical. More, his particular set of hard life "stairs" were covered in urine and blood, and guys with shivs waited in the shadows, yet he kept going.

She didn't like what he'd done, or how he'd done it, but she understood why. He wanted her to keep climbing, make sure she didn't get stuck like he had.

But he should have known she was not like him. She was not a cheat.

Naomi appeared in front of her, wrapped in a towel. "I'm sorry, I didn't mean to eavesdrop. Hard not to, in my tiny palace, even with the water running." She had the laminated press pass in her hand. "You left this in the bathroom. No matter how you got here, you're here."

The pass dangled between them. Hara finally took it. "I want to go, to be all tough and say screw it, I'm going to get something out of this while I'm here. And Derek can go to hell."

"You mean O'Donnell?"

"Yeah. Him, too." She sank onto the sofa, her chin in her hand, her voice softer. "But another part of me is so embarrassed. O'Donnell thinks I'm some kind of blackmailing fraud, and so does Derek. I'm sure he'll say something to Charles. I cannot bear it, them thinking of me that way. I want to explode with shame. Having to see them will send me into seizures."

"Or you could cover the game, get your stories out there, keep working on your craft. Prove them wrong over time. Success is the best revenge, right?"

"I know. I agree. I am going to go, do what I can, use the opportunity to work on my portfolio." But what if she really didn't have the talent? She didn't know anymore. "It's so not fair. I've always worked my ass off. And I've always tried to follow the rules, to do things ethically, so no one could put me in the same category as my father." She shook her head and repeated what was looping in her head: "It's so not fair."

"Quite a pair, ain't we?" Naomi folded her arms. "But you still goin', even if I have to drag you."

Hara, on the verge of tears, laughed instead. The girl in front of her weighed all of 120 pounds, and most of that was hair. "I thought you weren't going to the game."

Naomi shrugged. "Nah, boo, not unless you make me." She turned to go back into the bathroom. "No offense, but I could use some alone time."

—*—

The Fishers' empty training room smelled of Lysol, rubber, and old sweat. Derek's breath swooshed out as he pushed up the weight bar, though the load was light.

"Whatcha doin', Darcy? I don't want you hurting yourself right before the game," said the coach.

The young player hefted the bar onto the stand and slid out from under it, then stood. "I'm being careful, promise. Just wanted to get my warm-up started."

"That's not—" the coach started to say, but then O'Donnell stepped into the room and cut him off.

"Happy to see it, m' boy." He slapped Derek on his bare shoulder, leaving a red mark.

Derek kept his face blank but karma had his back: O'Donnell realized he had sweat on his hand and mewled in displeasure. The owner swiped his palm back and forth on his pants, almost hard enough to create a friction fire. *A liar's pants actually catching fire—that would be something to see.*

Derek could not get over the fact that this supposed leader of the community knew about the college rules that Charles's family had broken and completely looked the other way. It's not that he wanted to see Charles in trouble, but right was right. His best friend and his boss were . . .

Not your problem, remember? No distractions. He just needed to get out on that court and focus.

Besides, what was he going to do? Rat out Ms. Butler so she lost her house? And if the association found out, O'Donnell would have to kick Charles out. He'd suffer, the team would suffer, and then Derek would suffer. *Get off your fucking high horse, man!*

He wiped the sweat off his face as his teammates began to file in; the coach and owner moved around the room, talking to players. But O'Donnell returned, alone, a minute later. His old-man eyebrows writhed like caterpillars over his squinty eyes.

"Darcy, I spoke with Charles. It sounds like you and I need to have a little chat. Meet me in the owner's suite after the game."

He marched away before Derek could respond.

What had Charles done?

–*–

Hara called Carter, checking in and telling him about the opportunity to go to another game. He encouraged her to go, and even offered to send a car to pick her up. She texted her mother, saying she'd be home tomorrow and she was going to another game that night. *That should hold Mom over.* She'd think Hara was hooking up with athletes. The reporter could only imagine what Willa would do if she knew about Derek Darcy kissing her. Well, almost kissing her. *Bastard.*

An hour later, raindrops splattered off the sidewalk and the long hood of a stretch limousine pulling up to the building. Only her boss would call a limo service.

She hadn't been paying attention to the weather, though she should have. The rain had ramped back up, creating fast-moving streams in the gutters and pooling on the roads. Hara had pushed off her flight until tomorrow. What if she got stuck again? If she had to, she'd call Carter, get an advance on her next paycheck. She was getting out of this town, whether it was by train, bus, automobile, electric scooter, rowboat, whatever it took. Once she was done sucking the marrow out of game two, she wanted to go home, sleep in her own bed, decompress, gather her wits, and reconnoiter. Replan her future.

Hurrying to the limousine, she stepped in a puddle, her mules instantly soaked.

"Mother—"

The driver had come running to help her into the vehicle, but a gust of wind took his cap. He chased the hat into the building's doorway and pinned it against the wall. She'd just gotten her car door open when another gust tugged on it, almost pulling the metal slab away from her.

His hat tucked inside his coat, the muscular driver grabbed the door. She thought she heard him apologize, but her hood rustled in the wind, brushing against her ears as she scuttled like a crab into the cavernous back of the limo.

Removing her hood, Hara sat on the edge of a velvet bench seat and brushed large droplets from her face and fog from her glasses, then struggled to shed her wet raincoat, tight over her kimono-esque blazer. Finally, she managed to wrestle out of it and spread it on the seat next to her. Squinting into the gloom, Hara felt like she was in a cave, spelunking in luxury.

She settled in, smoothing down her short bangs, trying to psyche herself up for the night ahead. She wore tight black jeans and her black blazer, with a light blue camisole that made her eye color pop but wasn't super-exciting, fashion-wise. Naomi had talked her into borrowing dangling gold earrings and a gold necklace, which stood out with her hair pulled back into a bun. The red mules looked fine but unfortunately now felt gummy and damp under her bare toes. *Thank God I wasn't wearing the Louboutins.* If she'd stepped into a puddle with those on, she'd have to sell a kidney to replace them. Hara slid off her shoes and dragged her feet over the carpet, trying to dry them. Her toes felt good, sinking into the thick woolen fibers.

"Ma'am? There's a champagne split on ice back there, if you like," the driver said over the intercom.

"It's like you know me." Hara gave him a thumbs-up through the partition window.

She was going to cover the game and she was going to write a story that would go viral, dammit. It would be good enough to prove her father wrong. But Hara was not offering herself up as fodder to the O'Donnell contingent again.

As they drew up to the main entrance of the arena, people stopped and stared. She chugged the last half of her glass of the sparkly wine. "Crap." She should have had him drop her off down the block. The crowd waiting to get into the stadium probably thought she was someone famous. But before she could dwell on it, the door next to her popped open. "Miss," said the driver, holding out a hand to help her out of the car.

Hara swallowed. Then she grabbed her stuff, tucked loose tendrils behind her ears, and laid her hand in the chauffeur's with a languid movement, pretending she was an actress in a PBS miniseries. She played the queen, of course.

She emerged gracefully from the car, adjusted the sleeves on her blazer, and stood tall. "Please don't wait for me. I'll call for a ride when I'm done here." Hara then glided into the arena, nose in the air. Passersby said nothing, just watched her, wondering who she was.

Life was so much easier when you could pretend to be someone else.

CHAPTER 11

I am only resolved to act in that manner, which will, in my own opinion, constitute my happiness . . .

—*Pride and Prejudice*

The warning buzzer sounded. The game was going to start in a minute. She was still trying to decide if it was lucky or not that Eddie really had saved her a seat.

"You should take your notes verbally, like me," said the "seasoned" reporter, now her self-appointed mentor. He'd been offering a litany of suggestions since she sat down. "Here, give me your phone, I'll download a dictation app for you."

"No, it's okay. I like to write out my notes, I'm fine." She had a couple of dictation and transcribing apps but she hadn't wanted to spill out her thoughts about the game audibly, not when the other, more experienced reporters might hear her. And judge her.

"Let me show you some of my favorite shorthand symbols, then . . ."

Hara ignored his mansplaining, watching instead as Kitty Morretti stood on the sidelines by the players' bench, talking to Gus, occasionally tossing back her head with a laugh and softly touching his arm. He definitely was into it. They seemed cozy. She was sure hundreds of jealous women in the stands were currently plotting the demise of the heiress.

Gus was called away, leaving Kitty alone. She glanced around, clearly uncomfortable. When her eyes lit on Hara a dozen feet away, relief passed over her features and she started in her direction.

Hara realized the heiress was exhibiting social anxiety, just like everybody else. Hara liked her even more than she had at the club.

The reporters immediately around Hara quieted down as Kitty approached, staring straight at Hara. Hara twisted, sure there was someone behind her waving to Kitty, but no one seemed to be paying attention. Turning forward, she saw that Kitty was directly in front of her.

"Hey," said the beautiful young woman, swinging her hair back over her shoulder, her Italian lilt adding to her allure. "You're the reporter working with Charles, right? What are you doing down here? Come on up. There is a fantastic view from the owners' box, it smells nice, and there's free booze."

"Oh, hi!" Hara had to gather her wits. *Do not geek out.* Of course a famous person was talking to her. And inviting her upstairs. She was Hara Isari. "I don't know . . . are . . . is Mr. O'Donnell up there?"

Kitty scrunched her forehead, thinking. "I don't think so."

"How about Madeline?" Hara mock shivered. "We do not get along."

Leaning close, Kitty grinned and whispered, "That scary *puttana* is definitely not up there. You're safe." Her lilting voice went back to its normal volume. "Come, I'll get you through security."

"And you're sure no one will care?"

"My *famiglia* owns this property. You're my guest." She shrugged elegantly. "Besides, the owners brought you in, they know who you are. Are you coming?"

O'Donnell would not be thrilled to see her. She definitely did not want to see him. However, if he wasn't there . . . Hara jumped up, grabbed her damp rain jacket and satchel. Kitty had mentioned free booze. She could take notes from the upper decks just as easily as down here. And she wouldn't have to worry about ducking every time Derek came close to the sidelines. Was there a journalist on earth who would turn the offer down? Eddie sure wouldn't.

She wavered for just a second longer, trying to decide if she was an asshole for leaving Eddie, especially since he was the one who originally talked her into coming to the game. Kitty sauntered off with a motion for her to follow.

The Boston reporter stared at Hara with his bulging eyes. "No. No way. Was that Kitty Morretti?" He slapped his forehead, a move straight out of a cartoon. "You show up from out of nowhere and you keep getting these breaks. I don't get it. I won't make the boobs joke again, but, seriously, how are you making this happen?"

That was an excellent question. "Maybe, Eddie, because I know how to talk to people without insulting them." He did make it awfully easy to leave him behind.

Hara, following Kitty, kept her shoulders back and strutted off the court as if she ran the joint. The whole fake-it-until-you-make-it thing was really starting to pay off. She focused only straight ahead, however, with no desire to see who might be close by. Or if Derek was watching her from the clutch of players by the bench. Ignorance was bliss. *I'm just going to live out my favorite clichés.*

At the private elevator, Kitty gave the security guard a code and they were whisked upward at an incredible rate. The elevator door slid open only seconds later and directly in front of them was a perky concierge with a clipboard, asking Hara for her name and identification. Kitty intervened, thankfully, leaving Hara to take in the sights. Behind the concierge was the opening to the owners' suite, a long, low-ceilinged lounge with a panoramic view of the arena floor.

The room hummed with energy and women's laughter, backed by a quiet hip-hop soundtrack. The mood was upbeat. Hara was sure that would change if the boys fell behind. Nobody liked their team to lose, but if your income was based on performance, it had to be tough to be a player's partner, powerless to help.

A sleek walnut and black leather bar extended almost the length of the back wall, lined with padded leather stools—seats filled with the lovely women of basketball. A bartender in a bow tie shook two cocktails. A waiter circled the room offering finger foods. Wall shelves labored under the weight of dozens of high-end bottles of booze and a range of decent wines. Hara found it amusing the organization had Boston's Samuel Adams beer on tap right next to a display of spendy Cristal champagne bottles.

Maybe twenty-five people milled about, a mostly female crowd, though there were a few young men from the posses, everyone talking and getting food and drinks and finding seats. A few relaxed in the theater chairs in front of the arena window, a long row of swiveling black leather recliners with heavy walnut trays and cupholders. The lounge also offered bistro seating, as well as gatherings of small sofas and armchairs. Five large TVs with muted volume were located around the room. One, tucked back in a corner, was set up for gaming; a couple of teenagers played Fortnite, cursing into their headsets. Other TVs showed games being played around the country, as well as commentators on the floor of the Fishers' game about to start.

At one end of the room, a den with a rolling screen door provided semi-private seating, including a desk with a couple of computers. Two old men were huddled back there, bent over the gray luminescent screens. They had to be owners.

The smell of pulled pork and intoxicating spices filled her nostrils. At the end of the bar, a server refilled chafing dishes and cold plates. She salivated at the cheese trays and charcuterie boards and meat sliders and assorted fruits. Why would anyone ever leave this room? There was a chocolate fountain and a soft-serve ice cream machine as well.

Hara watched Kitty cross the space to talk to an African-American woman in her early thirties with shiny, dark brown curls reaching her tiny waist. The young heiress beckoned her over.

"Tina, you remember Hara? The reporter from Portland?"

Hara did a double take. Charles's fiancée-slash-not-fiancée had been sporting black dreads last time they met. The current style had to be a wig, but if so, this was an impressive piece. The thick, dark curls, highlighted with streaks of red, were shiny and healthy and absolutely natural looking. With dramatic wing-tipped eyeliner and Versace from head to toe, Tina made Hara think of a tiny Beyoncé. Like a little kid, Hara blurted, "Wow. You are beautiful."

Tina's face had been tight but she gave Hara a full smile, showing off blinding white teeth. "Aren't you sweet?"

"Rarely." Hara forced herself to smile back. *I'm sorry,*

Naomi, I don't mean to be nice to your nemesis. "Sometimes it just slips out, when I'm not paying attention."

"Poo," Tina said. "I don't believe it. You don't have no hard edge on ya."

Was she saying Hara was fat?

Tina continued, "Now, we do need to get one thing clear. There's to be no reporting on what you hear up here, okay? This is where the ladies come to get away from reporters. You got that?"

"Yep. Conversations are off the record. Promise. Unless someone wants to talk to me on the record."

"They don't."

A glass shattered over by the bar, quieting the room. A young woman apologized loudly and profusely while a group of five or six women tut-tutted.

"Oh gosh! I'm sorry. I'm so sorry. Here . . ." The girl wobbled off her stool.

Tina rolled her eyes. "Excuse me." She moved briskly to the bar. "Sit down!" she said to the stumbling girl. "Button yourself up. Drink some water." To the bartender, she said, "Jimmy, she cut off. We not having a scene today, Zia, you hear me?"

The girl nodded weakly, sitting down without an argument. The rest of the room returned to normal. Kitty leaned into Hara and whispered, "OG rules the roost."

Hara nodded. She was terrified for Naomi. This was the wrong woman to mess with.

A woman dressed in a pink Juicy Couture tracksuit with high heels and big hoop earrings interrupted the party. "Hey!" she said loudly. "Look at this." She pointed to one of the muted TVs.

Two desk reporters wearing concerned expressions silently

dialogued about the breaking news. The captions ran in Helvetica across the bottom of the screen:

> . . . The early-season nor'easter has swung back over the Boston area and is, unfortunately, increasing in strength. An incoming king tide is already causing minor flooding in low-lying areas, and waters are expected to rise overnight. More intense rain showers are on the way, and the wind gusts may reach 60 mph in some areas.

"Winter hasn't even started yet and already we're gobsmacked. This sucks." The lady in pink sniffed. "I hate this weather."

The talk shifted to favorite vacation spots to escape Boston winters, from sunny Malibu to the Caribbean. Hara momentarily felt superior—this bout of rain would barely register as a storm with an Oregonian, and sixty-mile-an-hour gusts on the north coast made for good kite-flying weather.

Flooding, though? Hara was used to flooding in her hometown and knew what to expect, but here? She shifted in discomfort, assessing the faces around her. Were they worried about the storm? Should she be? She grimaced. There was nothing to be done about it at the moment. "Kitty, when they talk about flooding around here, how bad does it get?"

The heiress waved a hand, dismissive. "They'll block off the streets that have low spots. They make it sound like a big deal, but it's not."

The starting buzzer rang and the teams assembled on the court, ready for the jump shot.

Hara dug out her notepad and stepped up to the window overlooking the gym floor. "This is an amazing view. Wow. Thank you," she said to Kitty. The box jutted out over the floor just enough that Hara felt like she was floating directly above the court. The windows were so clean it was hard to tell there was anything between them and the air the peons below were breathing.

Hara took a seat at the end of the row trying to be unobtrusive and turned her attention to the game, now with a bird's-eye view. Another little gift from the universe. As long as she kept moving forward, as long as she worked to stay on this wave—and ignored the negative crap—maybe there really was a chance she could make it in the big leagues.

Charles and the lead opposing player swiped at the ball, and it was Derek who recovered it. The ball went to the Fishers and the clock started. The game was on.

"Do you see that? Gus moves like Apollo." Kitty settled into the chair next to her, champagne in hand. She leaned forward and placed her chin in her other hand. "He is haawt." She gave Hara a quick glance. "I saw you talking to Derek at the club. He is the finest of the fine."

"Uh huh." He was. She flashed on him pressing up against her outside the O'Donnells', and then her dream, his strong fingers stroking her . . . Oh, he was fine, all right. *Dickhead.*

As Hara followed the action on the court and took notes, the women around her got louder. While there was a lot of shouting at the players on the court, and at the refs, there were also plenty of side conversations centered around gossip, especially a rejected engagement, and a woman worried that her son was gay and her husband wouldn't take it well, and someone else complained about balancing the multiple babies and their mamas attached to her man.

Hara had thought these women wearing expensive clothes and jewelry, most of them wealthy and spending their time in trendy restaurants and penthouses, would have different conversations than the rest of America. But no.

"Why didn't you invite Katya to your boutique opening? You hurt her feelings."

"Why should I be nice to that ho? She hits on Steven every time I leave the room. Besides, her weave stinks. She needs to wash, the nasty bitch."

"Why you always gotta get so shady? Can't you go one day without insulting somebody? It don't always have to be messy round you."

"What are you talking about? She's not here."

The basketball wives and girlfriends were dealing with as much daily drama over personality conflicts and mundane bullshit as everybody else. One big difference from the people in Hara's small world, however, was that these women rarely put up with shit for long, especially if they felt disrespected. Many of them had poured a lot of time and effort and self-sacrifice into maintaining their ballplayers' careers and finances, and they were willing to throw down to protect themselves and their families. Their men were warriors on the court, but these ladies battled it out in high heels in the back rooms, doing their part in making sure status quo remained status quo.

As the game progressed, both Charles and Derek were shining stars, pure grace on the court. O'Donnell had not shown up in the suite, much to Hara's relief, but the other owners in attendance were vocal in support of their rookie, happy to see him slinging hash now that he was finally off the bench.

Hara wrote down everything they said. Who was she to look a gift owner in the mouth? Tina had only made her promise to not say anything about the WAGs.

The halftime buzzer rang. The game had been going at a breakneck pace, and ended with a lobbed shot to tie it.

Thank God she hadn't decided to fly out that day. This was a great game to cover.

She stared at her notes, surprised at her feelings. Earlier, she'd been wallowing in self-pity, but now that she was embracing this time and doing what she loved, she felt good again. She would continue to prove herself. No one else was going to do it for her and that was okay.

The women and men in the suite turned their attention to food, drinks, and the weather. The news stations reported scattered road detours and unrelenting rain.

Kitty's phone rang. She argued in Italian for a few minutes and then hung up. "*Bella,* I am sorry to abandon you, my father says I must go."

Hara, bewildered, asked, "Your father?"

"*Si*. He says my driver is waiting for me and that I am to come straight home. He fears I will be trapped here." She snorted. "If the players are trapped here, I'm not sure I'd mind." The heiress wrapped herself in a Burberry cloak. "You can come home with me. Or would you stay?"

Once again, Hara wanted to ask Kitty just how old she was, but bit her tongue. She'd never had a dad around to make decisions for her. But, if she were worth millions and millions of dollars, Hara probably would have someone paying close attention to her, too. She looked back down at her notes. Would she give up on this story? Or see it through? "I . . . I guess I'll stay. I'm sure I can get an Uber, or even walk if I have to. Naomi's is only a few blocks away, I'm sure it'll be fine."

"*Ciao,* then."

At the end of the third quarter, Hara shivered, a chill running up her back. She glanced away from the game, checking out the room behind her. And froze, a deer in the headlights.

Madeline and O'Donnell had come in and were now

talking to the men who were part of the owners' cooperative. She shrank down into the seat but before she could turn away, Madeline glanced up and locked eyes with her. The assistant's mouth shaped a surprised O, which would have been funny if Hara didn't feel so much anger crawling up out of her stomach, a feeling that increased exponentially as the assistant approached and then stood over her.

"What are you doing here?" Madeline asked with a constipated grimace. "I thought you'd flown home."

"Umm." *You are a hateful woman.* "Flight was canceled due to weather. I've been staying with a friend."

"No offense, but how did you get in here?"

No offense. Right. Hara sat up straight, tapped her shoe with her middle finger. "I walked in. The planes aren't working, but my feet are."

"I'm sorry, you are going to have to leave."

"I—"

Tina surprised them both from a few seats down, yawning loudly and stretching her arms out dramatically. Then she said, "Unclench your pearls, Madeline. She's fine. I invited her."

"Ah, Tina." Madeline crossed her arms and smirked. "From what I hear, you might not be the best person to be handing out passes to our VIP room. Didn't Charles dump you?"

Tina tossed her hair and hooted, but then leaned back, stretching her legs out in front of her. The WAGs around Tina angled in, but she just said, casually, "You are treading on some thin ice, little miss secretary." She twiddled her fingers lazily in the air by her head. "Buh-bye."

Madeline rolled her eyes and stomped off in three-inch heels, rejoining the owners. She whispered something to O'Donnell. They both stared at Hara for a second then went back to their nation-building conversation.

"Anybody who is not a friend to Madeline is a friend of mine," Tina said loudly to Hara, uncaring that the assistant could hear her. A number of other women chimed in, grumbling in agreement, though most of them wisely kept their comments out of earshot.

Hara nodded her thanks.

The next hour was stressful. As Madeline stared daggers at Hara's back, the game remained tight, back and forth. In the last portion of the fourth quarter, the Fishers were up, but only by two points. Tempers ran high. Hara had stopped writing down most of what the owners had to say, it not being fit for public consumption.

Then, with only three minutes left, Charles did something shocking.

The floor general shoved his own teammate out of the way to get to the ball. Derek had just rebounded the ball and was stepping back for a shot when Charles used one hand to push him to the side, hard, and plucked the ball from his hands before driving back to the basket, swarmed by the opposition. The foul whistle blew.

Hara thought maybe Charles was called for jumping his own man, but instead, the foul was called on the other team. *How did the refs not see that?* Maybe they couldn't believe it, either. Charles, who should have been penalized, instead set up at the free-throw line while Derek slowly took his place at the bottom of the key, glowering; Hara could feel the heat on the top floor.

"Whoa. That was crazy," the woman in Juicy pink said.

Tina snorted. "What? You mean big Charles hogging the ball? Not surprising."

Everyone around them grew quiet.

"Come on. It's no shocker Charles got a problem with loyalty. When shit gets real, it's all about him." Tina sucked her teeth. "That's why he needs me, to keep him focused."

Hara took Tina's critique with a grain of salt. His move on Derek looked purposeful, but there had to be more to the story. She didn't believe Charles would do something like that unless there was a good reason.

The six-foot-seven point guard wiped the sweat from his forehead and toed the line at the top of the key, his arm going up for a shot when, suddenly, the lights flickered.

Then, the lights went out.

A silence descended with the darkness.

CHAPTER 12

Do not give way to useless alarm . . .

—*Pride and Prejudice*

The dark, heavy air crashed in on her. Screams from below broke the initial hush and swelled. Women and men in the room with Hara yelped and cursed in alarm. She sucked the cloying blackness into her lungs, and let out a distressed grunt.

What if this was a terrorist attack? Her mind went into gibberish mode as she clenched the armrest of her chair. Should she get under it? Would she fit? She felt her hair turning white.

Hara forced her head back and breathed in deep. Breathed out. Taking another shaky breath, she realized the power outage was most likely due to the big storm. *No more catastrophizing, Hara Isari.*

"What the fuck?" shouted a teenage boy behind her. "I lost my last life!"

A sound like a cackle burst from Hara's throat. She cut

off the weird, nervous laugh before it could grow and become unstoppable.

She hated the dark. And it wasn't just that she was blind—it was also that the radios and the fans and the clocks and air-conditioning and everything else electrical had shut down, creating a void, a lack of background noise that would normally be humming behind the muffled shouts and screams from below.

Was this what it was like for her daddy? Lying on his bunk at night?

The arena was in blackness at most for fifteen seconds before generators kicked in. A fifteen-second eternity. An orange glow illuminated the stadium stairwells and the doorways, and a few emergency lights cast a weak light from overhead. The huge stadium remained mostly in shadows but at least people could see now. She and others let out loud sighs. *Thank God.*

–*–

Derek, standing at the edge of the key, pressed his eyes shut and clenched his fists, trying to control his rage while listening to Charles dribble on the free-throw line, preparing himself for the shot.

What the hell? Charles totally dicked me on purpose.

There was a collective gasp from thousands of people around them. His eyes popped open. He found himself in a shocking blackness, thick like soup, with some parts consisting of a darker, shifting blackness that made the hair on the back of his neck stand up.

What in the hell? he thought again, much more adamantly this time.

Derek felt the Chicago point guard next to him twist around, a sweaty arm brushing against him. "Dude, what is this?" the player growled. The other guys on the court were muttering and cursing.

"I don't know, man. I don't like it." Seconds ticked by. *Should I just be standing here?* He felt stupid, unable to make a decision.

The generators whirred to life and emergency lights clicked on. Relief shot into his veins. But then the security guards flooded into the arena and the relief turned to ice. Some of the guards circled around him and the others on the floor, while others were lining up at the team benches. No one had guns drawn, but their hands were on their belts.

I mean, seriously—what in the hell!

–*–

Hara almost whooped when the generator lights kicked in, but she clamped her lips shut in time. Upstairs and down, people were standing up in their seats, staring around with wide eyes, trying to decide what to do. That included Hara. She peered down into the gloomy arena and then back around the suite. *What is this? What am I supposed to be doing?*

The owners were on their cell phones, trying to reach maintenance or anybody with a clue of what was happening. After a minute, O'Donnell broke from the pack, pushed open the doors, and went to the elevator, stabbing at the flat buttons in the dark wall panel.

"Sir. Sir! You can't take the elevator." The concierge hurried after him and pulled on his sleeve. "You'll have to take the stairs."

"Fuck me."

He came back in. Jerking a thumb toward an emergency exit door on the other side of the room, he and two other men pushed rudely through a milling clot of women and strode out, presumably to fix the issue.

"Ladies and gentlemen," the massive loudspeaker in the middle of the arena blared, loud even through the glass encasing their suite. "We apologize for the disturbance." The announcer sounded as bewildered as everyone else in the audience looked, thousands of faces lifted to the speakers in the ceiling. The majority of the fans quieted and sat back down, hunched in their seats, wanting to hear what answers the voice of God could provide.

Madeline went to the bay windows and slid open one of the panels. They could hear the arena noises clearer now, the mass shuffling and cursing.

A mechanical squeal shrilled and rebounded off the walls. "Ahh!" yelled sixteen thousand people, clapping their hands over their collective ears, including Hara.

"Sorry, sorry!" said the frantic announcer. "Er, it looks like we had a power outage."

Simultaneously, at least a hundred class clowns from around the arena shouted out, "No shit!"

Ripples of laughter followed. The merriment probably would have lasted longer, had not even more security begun to funnel out onto the court and take up position by the player benches and along the wall under the basket where Charles and the others were clustered.

The women around her, dressed in Gucci and Prada and anxiety, pressed close enough to the box windows to leave nose prints. And boob prints. There was a lot of nervous sweating happening in this room. "What's goin' on? What's with the security? Why are they circling the wagons?"

Fans who had sat down popped back up, wondering the same thing. Even though there were a few minutes left in the game, some ticket holders began streaming out the exits. The rumbling from the crowd grew louder.

"One minute, please!" said the announcer. "We should be able to resume play in just one minute."

It had gone quiet in the owners' box, with the ladies talk-whispering, watching their men closely. The intercom and radio link that had provided the live feed to what was happening on the Fishers' bench no longer worked. Everyone watched as Tina barged up to the only admin left in the room.

"What's going on, Madeline?"

The executive assistant, normally pale, glowed in the dim light. She cleared her throat. "I don't know why the power is out."

"I am talking about the freaking gun show down there! What are they doing?"

"Oh. Oh, that. The organization is just making sure our assets are safe, just in case. There's nothing wrong. Company policy. If they were in immediate danger, the players would have been removed from the court already." Madeline left the windows, headed toward the bar. "Jimmy, I could use a shot of tequila."

Tina glared daggers at the assistant and then huddled with her girls.

I am pretty sure this has never happened before. Hara breathed in, out. If nothing else, the event would make an interesting story. That is, if someone could get the lights back on.

She still had cell service, though, and her data.

Googling "Boston power outage," she came across a live stream from a local news station. "Boston is experiencing record flooding in the North End and the downtown waterfront.

With a now-twelve-foot high tide in the harbor, and over four inches of rain in the last two hours, we are experiencing a three-foot storm surge."

Others clustered around her. She turned it up.

"Higher than expected winds and floodwaters have caused sporadic power outages around the city, and the waters have reached the Rose Kennedy Greenway, a rarity in Boston. The Aquarium T stop is closed due to high water and several buildings have been compromised along Atlantic Avenue and Commercial Street, with significant water intrusions. Causeway Street, near the arena, is closed. The police are urging residents to shelter in place and stay off the roads.

"Stay tuned. We'll be back with more on what is quickly becoming the storm of the century."

"Jesus." Tina frowned. "That's why the power is out? The flooding is right here!"

The WAGs were agitated all over again.

Hara, on the other hand, immediately felt the tight grip of terror loosen, her cognitive powers gelling back into shape. She had proof now. No zombies, no men with guns. Flooding was slow; she had time to think and deal with it. Not to mention, every time the news stations at home used the term "storm of the century," the hyperbole was laughable. She was sure it was the same in Boston.

One of the women kicked off her high heels, picked them up along with her purse. "I gotta get my driver. We outta here. Who's with me? I've got room." Barefoot, the player's girlfriend moved quickly to the door and down the stairs. Others followed. Most of them kept on their shoes.

What should she do?

There was another short, high-pitched squeal overhead. "Okay, folks . . ." A well-modulated, car-salesman voice rolled out of the speaker system, replacing the squeaky, stressed-out announcer from moments before. "We're going to have to call it a night. We are calling the game as it stands."

"Boooo. Boooo. Booooooo."

"The Fishers organization apologizes, but this is for your own safety. We are being asked to evacuate the building. As you leave, be aware there are rising floodwaters on neighboring streets between us and the harbor. It is in everybody's best interest to vacate the premises quickly but calmly. Calmly! Please follow the exit signs. Check the website for compensation tomorrow. Drive carefully, folks."

Hara gathered up her notes and her jacket. She longingly eyed the bottles of liquor behind the bar, but Madeline was chatting with the bartender, and much of the room had cleared out. Better to slide out, unnoticed. She'd call Naomi from downstairs.

In the stairwell, the backup lights were out in some places, only dim flickers in others. Hara's flashlight phone app provided plenty of light to see the stairs in front of her, but seemed to make the darkness at the back of the deep shadows move with her. She could hear others in the private stairwell, below and above her, yet she had an overpowering sense of isolation, felt surrounded by danger. She forced herself to keep moving. The skin on the back of her neck crawled. Every scary movie she'd ever watched had prepared her for this moment; she checked behind her every other second, sure that Chucky or the girl from *The Ring* were inching up on her. She wanted to conquer the dark stairwell with bravery, like in the Langston Hughes poem, but symbolic courage and persistence were a hell of a lot easier than facing literal terror. She almost peed her pants when someone opened a door a few floors up. She could hear heavy footsteps on the stairs above her.

Despite going down instead of up, she was sweaty and twitchy by the time she reached the double doors on the bottom level.

Two security guards let her out but Hara immediately wished she could turn tail and go back upstairs. The barely lit causeway, jammed with thousands of ticket holders trying to exit the arena at the same time, smelled like an overcrowded zoo. The scene was chaos.

Namaste, namaste, namaste, she chanted in her head, trying to control her anxiety in the dim, stuffy corridor.

Then, Derek Darcy jogged up to the security guards next to her.

"O'Donnell told me to meet him after the game. Is he still in the owners' box?" he barked at the guards.

Hara blinked, tried to step back, but there was a wall behind her. She edged slowly sideways, not wanting to attract attention.

"Nope," said a door guard. "He beat feet right after the lights went out."

Three team assistants were behind the ballplayer, providing a barrier between him and the shuffling throng of ticket holders. In the low flickering light, wearing a beanie cap, quilted jacket, and sweats over his uniform, Derek went unnoticed by the bystanders. Why would a player be out here, with the hoi polloi?

His eyes widened when he caught sight of Hara. "I thought you left." Then, "I'm looking for Charles, too. Is he up there? Is Tina?"

"Um. No. Tina left before I did. I haven't seen Charles. But I did see him push you at the end of the game. That was—"

"Hey!" It was Eddie, his eyes bugging out, his hair looking extra red in the gloom. He skidded to a stop next to her, not realizing he was about to get taken out by an amped-up security guard.

"It's okay, I know him," Hara told the guards and assistants, hoping they cared what the random girl talking to their player had to say on the matter.

Eddie, still impervious to the people closing in around him, said, "I'm glad I found you! Friggin' pissa out there. Let me give you a ride. You can crash at my place."

"Hara, you need a ride?" Derek asked, looming over her, his eyebrows knitted together.

"I—"

"Oh geez. Darcy." The red-bearded man blushed. "I mean, Mr. Darcy. I'm sorry, I didn't see you there."

Most nonobservant reporter ever.

Darcy threw his chin at the reporter but said to Hara, "I've got my SUV. I can get you where you need to go."

Hara swallowed, her throat clicking with dryness.

Then her phone vibrated with a message. She read it and frowned. "That's not good." She looked up at Derek, who folded his arms impatiently. "It's Naomi. The girl you saved from Tina at the bar? You gave her a ride home"—just before he'd almost kissed Hara and then blew her off—"I'm staying with her, but she has no power, and I guess her place is full of smoke, thanks to a small fire in the restaurant below her."

"You're not at O'Donnell's? Never mind. Come on." Derek grabbed her hand and pulled her down the causeway, Eddie and the team assistants jogging alongside.

"Hey! Hey, let go of me!"

He stopped. "We need to leave if we're going to go get Naomi."

"Use your words, man." She tugged her hand free.

"Do you, or do you not, want to go to Naomi's?"

"Well, yes . . ."

Eddie puffed up, stroking his beard nervously. "Don't do that! I've got a fireplace, you'll be warm and safe—"

"Can your car drive through high water?"

"No."

She turned to Derek, grimacing. Before she spoke, she had to swallow again, trying to clear the gigantic, dry slice of pride caught halfway down her throat. "I'm sorry I mocked your jacked-up SUV. Would you maybe be willing to get Naomi and take her somewhere?"

After Derek nodded, she turned and patted the redheaded reporter on the shoulder. "Thanks, Eddie. I know you're trying to help. But Derek has an SUV." Plus, she didn't really know Eddie; maybe he was a serial killer aiming to stock his freezer. Better the devil you know.

"Let's go!" Derek started moving again. "I want nothing more than to spend my evening, driving through water-covered roads and ferrying you about."

"You offered! Never mind, then." She planted her feet. *Serial killer it is.*

The basketball player didn't turn around, just kept walking. One of the assistants looked back to see if she was following, raised a quizzical eyebrow.

"I will say it again," Eddie, next to her, stage-whispered. "How is it you know these fuckin' guys? I mean, Darcy is your chauffeur?"

Hara shrugged and said goodbye. She could feel Eddie's stare crawl across her back.

"Jerk," she grumbled, reluctantly trying to catch up to Derek's receding figure. Once again, though, she shoved her ego down. She was a total masochist, obviously. He could help her, and Naomi, so she supposed she could put up with Derek's arrogance for a while longer. Who else was she going to call? Madeline?

She was at Derek's side by the time they reached an entrance leading into the private, enclosed garage where he had parked his car. He told the assistants they could go. There were no more crowds, not in the garage, so they left.

Climbing into his vehicle, Hara said, "I don't know why you are doing this, but thank you."

He frowned at her. "Who wouldn't help someone in trouble? What kind of asshole do you think I am?"

She didn't answer.

CHAPTER 13

It rained hard.

—*Pride and Prejudice*

Two guards manually tugged open the electric garage doors. Rain sprayed the front of the car, making Hara jump. The guards moved back and waved them through. The driveway sloped down steeply onto one of the main roads in front of the arena.

"You've got your seat belt on?" Derek asked.

So thoughtful. I promise not to sue you if we get in an accident.

Hara peered through the night, only their headlights to guide them. They could see streetlights and buildings lit up one street over, but this street was dark. "Maybe it's not as bad as they've . . ."

They reached street level and pulled out. A sheet of water sprayed up from under the tires. The front tires skidded for half a second, until the back wheels hit the flat road and grounded the vehicle.

"This should be interesting."

Derek didn't reply. He concentrated on the crowded road, blurred by the streaming rain and windshield wipers.

A gust of wind rocked the SUV, making both of them jump. There was no talking for the next few minutes, as Derek maneuvered through the traffic coming out of the coliseum, directed by traffic cops in fluorescent yellow at the dark intersections, water dripping heavily off the lips of their police hats.

Traffic thinned out quickly, once they got on the blocks closer to Naomi's side of the harbor. Water sprayed up in sheets from their tires—something that was once fun to do with mud puddles was now terrifying. The floodwater looked only a couple of inches deep, but Hara knew from past experience, and plenty of hurricane footage, that looks could be deceiving.

As they finally reached Naomi's building, Hara sucked in her breath.

The Chinese restaurant was closed, and from the outside looked fine, though it was hard to tell in the dark. It was the amount of water on the street in front of it that was so disturbing.

Water sloshed up against the bricks at the base of the structure, hiding the sidewalks; white foam splashed back from the tires of parked cars. Outside the tight circle of headlights, the pitch-black buildings loomed along a street that seemed to be moving. Hara started to open her door, eager to get her belongings and get far away from here.

"Wait."

Seriously? Hara arched an eyebrow at him and opened the door anyway, slowly and with panache. Rain ran down inside the vehicle. And onto her pants.

He smirked. "Why do you always have so much attitude?"

"You're an ass."

He lost the smile. "What is it with you? You think you'd be more grateful. I'm just trying to do the right thing here. Maybe you should try it."

"What!" She'd almost forgotten, after all that had happened in the past hour: Derek thought she was a conniver.

They'd almost kissed, then he'd pushed her away without a word, watched her leave without even a goodbye. Then, he'd listened to O'Donnell's story about her in the kitchen and believed every word of it. She wiped at the water on her pants. "Forget it. Let's just get this over with."

He sighed, handed her a flashlight from the center console, and opened his door, glancing back over his shoulder. "You're welcome for the ride." He slammed his door before she could respond.

Hara didn't want to, but she laughed. He'd gotten himself the last word.

She jumped onto the sidewalk and almost lost her balance, one foot sucked out from under her. Grabbing onto the door just in time, she got herself back upright. The wind worked tendrils loose from her bun and lashed them against her face.

"I tried to tell you," said Derek, there to steady her. She stiffened under his touch, but he didn't seem to notice. Did he not remember the last time he helped her out of a car?

Hara had been prepared to get her feet wet, which was inevitable, and not even the first time that day. A half inch of water wasn't enough to do anything but ruin her shoes. Or so she thought. But it wasn't just a puddle she'd stepped into, it was a shallow, fast-moving stream.

Her next steps were balanced and strong and she was able

to stand on her own. "I don't need your help," Hara said, loud enough to be heard over Mother Nature.

He backed away, hands in the air. "Fine."

Water, rushing and slapping, ran over her feet, and wind gusts pushed and pulled at her and rattled windows and fire escapes. It was more frightening than she expected. Following Derek, she was almost knocked off her feet by an especially hard gust.

Without thinking, she grabbed the back of his coat, but he didn't say anything. Didn't even look around, thankfully, as they buzzed Naomi's door and waited, bent against the wind. Her pride stung but better that than getting knocked down.

"You'd think these tall buildings would serve as a wind block."

Derek buzzed again and then glanced around. "I think, instead, the placement of the buildings has created a wind tunnel through here."

"Lucky us." Hara saw a light bobbing in the window on the floor above. Naomi's frightened face appeared, highlighted creepily by a flashlight. Hara shined her own flashlight under her chin and grinned. The light upstairs diminished.

Naomi had the door open for them in record time. "Derek *Darcy*? Is that you? And Hara? Are you here to rescue me?" She stepped back so they could come into the alcove, out of the deluge. "Where's Charles?"

"Charles?" Derek said, stomping his feet and shaking out his coat. "He's not here." He narrowed his eyes suspiciously. "Why would he be?"

Hara slowly took off her fogged glasses and put them in her pocket. They'd been useless in the weather anyway. *So. Derek really doesn't know about Naomi.* What had he been talking about after the interview, then, telling Charles to come clean? Hara wanted to punch her fist in the air and yell, "I knew it!" She'd been right in the first place; there was a story she was missing.

Naomi colored, realizing her error. "Oh, nothing, no, I figured you guys were always together," she finished lamely.

"Uh huh," Derek said. He sniffed. "I can smell the smoke. I assume it's much worse on your floor. More importantly, the water is rising. You should hurry, if you want to bring anything with you." He prodded Hara from behind. "You, too."

"Touch me again and I'm going to rip your finger off."

–*–

Derek waited in the SUV. It took less than five minutes for the young women to reconvene at the bottom of the staircase, Hara having quickly exchanged her blazer for a sweatshirt and her mules for tennis shoes. She didn't have rubber boots, and Naomi's shoes didn't fit, so sneakers would have to do.

"Be careful." Hara put a hand on the other girl's wrist as Naomi reached for the doorknob. The wind howled and the rain hammered down, even worse than it had when Hara first arrived.

Naomi nodded, put down her overnight bag, turned the knob, and slowly opened the door.

An intense blast of wind grabbed the textured metal slab in Naomi's hands, tugging it outward. Hara watched, helplessly, as the slightly built girl held on to the doorknob, a shocked look on her face, before she was snatched off her feet and yanked outside.

"Naomi!" Hara screamed. "Let go!" But it was too late for that.

She jumped out after Naomi, who'd toppled headfirst down the cement stairs, while the door banged loosely behind her, against the side of the building. Hara was almost blown away herself, buffeted back and forth by the wind, but, keeping low, she was able to withstand the gusts and make it down the stairs to Naomi.

The girl lay facedown on the sidewalk. Water sluiced around her head, her face.

Hara jumped to her side, her mind trying to keep a grip on logic. She crouched low and lifted Naomi's head clear of the water, praying she wasn't harming the girl further. *Please don't be a paraplegic, please don't be a paraplegic.*

Hara's jeans and sneakers were soaked; she knelt, making sure she was planted firmly enough not to get knocked over by the rushing water, and rolled Naomi onto her back, her friend's head propped on Hara's leg. With rain pelting Naomi's closed eyelids and slack face, Hara burst into tears. A huge lump protruded from the middle of the girl's forehead. "Naomi! Wake up!" About to shake her, Hara pulled herself together. *Be gentle. Think.*

"Is she breathing?" yelled Derek, crouching next to Hara, swaying in the wind, his face ashen.

Hara nodded, pointed to the girl's rising and falling chest.

"I am so sorry." The wind carried away his words, making it hard to hear, but his copper eyes darkened, churned with emotion. "I should have come back for you." His mouth turned down as he looked at Hara, worry and regret etched into his features. "Are you hurt?"

Hara wasn't sure, but she thought his voice had cracked.

She shook her head, long, sopping strands of hair swinging slowly with the motion. Her hair had come undone. So had she.

His face turned stern as he gently slid his hands under Naomi. "We need to get her to a hospital." The basketball player picked up the unconscious girl effortlessly. Water ran off her limp body as if she were a fountain.

"Hold on to me, Hara."

The sound of her name on his lips made her shiver. *Jesus, what is wrong with me?* Hara desperately wanted to wrap herself around Derek's back, wind her arms around his stomach, let him protect her. Instead, she held on to the back of his coat again. Derek opened the front passenger door, gently slid Naomi into the seat, and buckled her in.

An odd whistling and clanging sound pierced the wind. Clutching even harder onto Derek's coat, Hara whipped her head around, and gasped. A stop sign had been shorn free from its post and flew toward them, spinning, occasionally bouncing off the ground, like a feather on a windy beach. Except this was a large, metal projectile.

She only had a second to act. Derek, leaning into the cab of the SUV, fiddling with Naomi's seat belt, had no idea they were about to get smacked by a sharp-edged flying object. Hara shoved him, hard. He fell into the vehicle, lying across the unconscious girl in the passenger seat.

"What—"

"Stay there!" Hara screamed. "Don't stand up!" She grabbed the handle of the back seat door, praying it was unlocked. She wrenched it open and crouched down next to Derek's legs. Water washed over her feet, splashing her ankles and knees. "Don't move!"

The stop sign hit Hara's impromptu shield with an awful shriek of metal, then popped up and over the door. Hara could see it flying for a few dozen feet, until its weight pulled it back to earth. She heard it continue on, clanging against the ground every few seconds.

"Was that . . . ?" Derek, wide-eyed, stared at her over his shoulder, his body still bent over Naomi.

"I know, right?" Her voice shook. Hara peeked around the door before standing up. Besides small pieces of litter swirling around, the coast looked clear. For now.

Derek closed the front passenger door and they stood facing each other. Again. By a car. Derek wrapped his fingers around her upper forearms and peered down at her. "Thank you. Are you okay?"

She nodded, her hair clinging to her face. She'd give anything to be away from here, and yet . . . "We should go before a yield sign comes looking for its brother."

Derek's warm, strong hands slid away; raindrops took their place. Hara climbed into the back seat, glad for the protection.

Then she tensed. Instead of running around to the driver's side, the ballplayer bent his long frame into the wind and jogged back inside Naomi's building. The loose door still flapped in the wind; it had already taken out one of their party.

Minutes later, Derek emerged from the black entryway with two suitcases.

He went back for our stuff?

Hara's stomach was a writhing knot of worry and frustration at the unnecessary, unwise gesture, watching as he braced against the wind and scanned for flying objects. But she was also extremely moved by his thoughtfulness. He hadn't needed to come at all, yet here he was, being brave and solicitous.

Derek opened the back hatch, tossed in the luggage, and slammed it shut, making Hara jump. But not Naomi. "Please wake up," Hara begged her, reaching through the seats to throw a jacket over her soaked and unconscious friend. "I've got you, I promise."

CHAPTER 14

Adieu to disappointment and spleen.

—*Pride and Prejudice*

Derek clambered in and slammed his door. His chest hurt from breathing so hard. And from fear.

It was hard to see the young girl lying limp in the passenger seat next to him, held in place by a seat belt, her head flopped to the side. He shifted around to Hara, half expecting her to be in tears again. Instead, she stared at him intently, clear-eyed. Energy seemed to crackle off her. With wind-blown hair and a high flush on her cheeks, her eyes such a sharp, deep blue . . . she was a mess and she was beautiful.

"Weren't you wearing glasses? Did you lose them?"

The reporter touched her cheekbone then dug around in her pocket. "That explains why I can barely see. I forgot I took them off." She pulled out her hand, empty. "Dang it. They must have fallen out."

"We'll have to deal with it later. Let's get to the hospital." He faced forward, put on his seat belt, then watched in the rearview mirror as Hara tucked her long hair behind her ears and stared out the window. He was once again struck by her allure. *Stop being weird,* he thought to himself, *we gotta get outta here.* "It'll take a couple of minutes, but at least we'll be heading away from the flooding this time."

Derek realized he'd been stupid driving over here in the first place. He glanced into the rearview mirror again, this time checking the empty streets for traffic. A wave of guilt swept through him; Naomi would have been safer staying inside. And he'd put Hara in danger.

Her attention was focused on Naomi, though occasionally shifting to the terrifying scenes outside. Gritting his teeth, Derek turned the wipers up as high as they'd go and slowly pulled out onto the street.

Leaving the stadium, he'd felt relatively safe in his SUV, assuming high clearance and four-wheel drive made him impervious to the storm. But water was powerful and sneaky. At the very least, he should have thought about the dips in the road, where the water could go from one or two inches to a foot deep. The dark, rippling surface gave no clues as to the depths below.

They'd been lucky on the way to the apartment. But leaving . . . not so much.

A hundred yards from Naomi's building, the front tires were suddenly off solid ground. Derek could feel the front half of the Mercedes lighten, a floaty sensation tweaking his senses. After a second of weightless panic, the back wheels grabbed. He jammed the SUV into reverse and stepped on the gas, slow but steady, trying for grip. The tires spun for a moment and then gripped the pavement, hauling them backward.

Let's try this again. This time, he put a wide berth between him and the side of the street where it seemed the lowest point. Though he couldn't always see it, riding the center line seemed a safer bet, especially with no other vehicles on the road.

Hara didn't say anything, only stared out the window, bent forward so as to keep a hand on Naomi's shoulder. He wanted to pull over, get centered. Instead, he forced his foot down on the gas pedal. Slowly. Slowly. But moving forward.

Two blocks from Naomi's, they could see rescue rigs and the Boston Fire Department headed down multiple side streets. At one intersection, they could see a car three or four blocks away, down a slope and closer to the harbor, caught in a slow but forceful current. Water was halfway up the doors. There were people inside. Firefighters were in boats, struggling to get to them.

"Oh my God," Hara said from the back seat, barely audible.

"Don't worry," Derek said. "I'm being careful." And he was doing enough worrying for the both of them.

A second later, she said, "Look at that."

She pointed at a waterfall rushing down a set of stairs leading into a building's basement. Derek tried squinting into the dark opening. Should he stop? What if people were down there? But Naomi was beside him, hurt. She was his immediate concern.

When the blacktop was finally visible again, Derek flexed his hands, bringing color back into his white knuckles, and loosened his grip on the steering wheel. The rain continued to be heavy and wind gusts buffeted the vehicle, but Derek was able to get them to Mass General with no further incident. The hospital building was a beacon of light, the emergency bay signs a welcoming bright blue.

They had power. He could see emergency workers bustling

in and out of the doors. The pain in his chest eased, just a little.

–*–

Hara's internal threat level dropped from bloodred to light orange as she watched doctors check Naomi's pulse and other vitals, place a brace around her neck, and then carefully lay the unconscious girl on a wheeled stretcher. They'd made it out of the flood zone and Naomi was being cared for by professionals. They'd heard water in her lungs, but they would run all the necessary tests, do the necessary procedures, give her some really good drugs . . .

"Wait!" Hara shouted after the doctors, who were moving swiftly through the double doors.

"Miss, you can wait in the waiting room. We'll come find you when we know something." They went inside.

"No! Stop." Hara sprinted after them, trying not to slip on the tiles in her wet sneakers. "She's pregnant."

Maneuvering down a crowded hallway, they slowed but didn't stop. "How long?" said a doctor.

"I'm not exactly sure, but I think she said it's been five or six weeks."

One of the nurses exchanged a glance with the doctor. "At least she's still early."

Hara frowned. "She wants this baby. You'll try to save it, right?"

"Of course."

And then they were gone. She leaned against the wall, drained of energy.

"Did you just say she's pregnant?" Derek, having caught

up to her in the hall, folded his arms, his face scandalized. "Naomi's pregnant. Yet she's been trying to get with Charles?"

It took Hara a second to process his comment, which seemed to come from left field. "Wow. Feminism incarnate, right here, in the flesh."

"Give me a break." He made a disparaging noise. "Jersey chaser, nothing new."

"Nice. Also, super-empathetic for the girl who just got knocked out."

"Honestly, this mess is why I don't trust anyone. Period." Derek's copper eyes were dark, scanning Hara up and down.

"Are you referring to me now? Thanks." Hara put her hands on her hips. "You know, for a Pepperdine guy, you're awfully dumb. Who do you think the father is?" Hara dropped her voice, trying to get control. "He was with her last night, you know. Not for the first time. She says she loves him."

"Come on, don't try to pin this on Charles." He jammed his hands into his pockets. "He and Tina might have problems, but they were together up until last week. And they're together now. I know my boy, and he wouldn't do this to her. There are less than five people on this planet I like and trust and he is one of them." His voice had begun to sound less confident, but then he ended strong: "Naomi is not."

"Naomi and Charles are not who you think they are. Neither am I."

"Really? You're the one who's got them wrong. And you—you're not a reporter, doing whatever it takes to get a story?"

Hara rocked back. "Believe what you want. You're going to anyway."

"Why would I believe any differently? I know how you got the interview. I know you're only still in Boston to sniff out a story on Charles. You don't care about Naomi."

"You are so far off base." *Of course he brought up the interview.* She started for the outer doors. "Just give me my suitcase and go. Just freaking go."

"What are you going to do?"

"Well, because I'm a normal human being, I'm going to call her family and then I'm going to stay here until I know Naomi is okay."

–*–

The phone went to voicemail three times in an hour before Charles finally picked up.

"Derek, now is not a good time."

"Hold up," Derek spit out, barely able to talk he was so angry. "Your side piece is in the hospital. She was knocked unconscious and breathed in water. She's not okay. And the baby. She might lose it." He paused, waited for some reaction. When there was none, he said, "Charles? Did you know she's pregnant?"

"Uh huh."

"Uh huh? That's all you're going to say?" The rookie leaned against a wall in the hospital lobby, drawing his beanie lower, flipping up the collar on his wet puffy coat.

"Listen, I gotta go. Tina has me looking for candles and flashlights."

"Dude! Even if you're not the daddy, you were just with this girl. You don't want to be here for her?"

The phone clicked off. Derek slowly put it in his pocket, reining in his anger, fighting for impassivity, for distance. His new mantra: *This is not my concern. This is not my concern.*

But rage blew past his walls. Dammit. Hara was right. His teammate was not who Derek thought he was.

He paced back and forth. Where was the hardworking, loyal friend he'd known his whole life? Derek stopped and almost slapped himself. Thinking back on Naomi, he realized he should have withheld judgment until he'd had more information. Charles was in the wrong.

And, right now, Derek was responsible for the unconscious girl. He'd let her come out of her building door without him, knowing how stormy it was. Regardless of her relationship status with Charles, he had to do what was right. Derek jogged back to the waiting room.

And Hara . . . he had no idea what to think about her. She was otherworldly, beautiful. She'd probably saved him from decapitation. She seemed sharp as hell. But she was so damn contrary. And there was no way to forget it was her dad who almost ruined the professional world of sports.

O'Donnell had been right—he should probably stay away.

He'd forgotten about his boss. With any luck, the old man had forgotten about him.

A doctor came into the waiting room the same time Derek did, calling out, "Family of Naomi Austen? Anyone here with Naomi Austen?" When no one replied, Derek guessed her family wasn't there yet and so raised his hand. But where was Hara? After a quick scan of the room, he spotted her sleeping shape in a row of chairs by the wall.

Hovering over Hara, he paused for a second, her gorgeous face peaceful, open in her deep sleep, as she lay stretched out across chairs, heat rising through her wet clothes. "Hara?" he whispered.

"Hmmm?" she said, not awake, not moving, except a flutter of her long, sinewy fingers curled under her cheek.

Oh my God, you're adorable, he almost said out loud. Biting his lip, instead he said, "Hara, the doctor is here. He wants to talk about Naomi."

–*–

Hara stared at her fingernails, not sure what to do.

Next to her, Derek was also quiet, his long legs stretched out in front of him.

The doctor had explained that Naomi was conscious and seemed to be mentally fine, but her lungs were filled with fluid. They had her on IV antibiotics and other medications, including meds that made her sleep. They didn't want her to have visitors until the next day. Thankfully, Naomi's father had arrived and he'd been taken back to her room, so she wasn't alone.

The biggest threat was to the baby. They wanted to monitor Naomi, make sure she was stable enough to keep the fetus. It was far too early to hear a heartbeat or see anything with an ultrasound, but she wasn't bleeding, so that was a good sign.

"She's young and strong, so hopefully she'll be okay," the doctor had said. "But this kind of trauma to the mother can bring on miscarriages, especially when the fetus is so new." On that note, he'd left.

Yikes. Don't sugarcoat it.

"Hara?" Derek's voice was quiet.

"Yes?" She didn't look up. Everything was fuzzy anyway, beyond a five-foot border, thanks to her missing glasses.

"Your clothes are wet and you're shivering. Why don't you come home with me? I have a guest room with its own bathroom. You can take a bath, get warmed up. I'm only about fifteen minutes from here, but nowhere near any flooding."

Hara put her fingertips to her temples and rubbed. Did a professional basketball player just invite her back to his house? She felt like she was Dorothy, fresh off the tornado in Oz. "I—I don't know."

"I can take you back to the O'Donnells' place."

"No!"

His eyebrows lifted in surprise. "Ohhhkay."

"I don't trust them."

His eyebrows came down and knit together. "That is the second time today I've heard that about Connor."

Hara shrugged. "I'm not surprised. He's not a good guy."

"Well, we can get into that later. For now, you need a place to stay and I have an empty room. You're safe, I promise."

Hara wanted to joke about that, something about how Naomi would beg to differ, but insulting him wasn't in her best interest. He didn't seem to have much of a sense of humor, but he did have a house with a roof and a bed. "Here you are again, going out of your way for me." She sighed. "I know it seems like I'm not appreciative—I am—it's just that I'm too tired to get into arguments."

"Lady, you think you're tired? I played a long, hard game and then immediately jumped into my vehicle and drove through a flood. I'm wiped. I can definitely use ten hours of sleep. And a hot shower."

"That's true, you do need a shower." She smiled, to let him know she was kidding. "Hope you have a lot of hot water because, I have to agree, a bath sounds fantastic and I've got fairly limited options." She squeezed water from the cuffs of her sweatshirt. "Do you think I could also wash these clothes?"

"Of course." He scratched his forehead, just below the beanie. "I cannot wait to take this disgusting hat off." Instead, he tugged the stocking cap down tighter over his ears, which

Hara knew he was wearing to keep people from recognizing him. When he pinched the hat, gray water droplets burst from the knit and ran down his temples.

"Oh my God," Hara said, "we're soaked in nasty floodwater. I've probably got hepatitis and Ebola."

"Let's get out of here before they decide to put you in isolation."

Isolation. That made her think of her father. Hara pictured Thomas in his cell, worrying about her. If her father had access to the news, then he would know that the arena lost power during the game and Boston was flooded, but he wouldn't be able to find out anything more. He might be a jerk, but he was her jerk, and she didn't like to think about him worrying about her. She'd already texted Carter and her mother, to let them know she was safe.

Hara gathered her satchel and jacket, Derek grabbed her suitcase—the one he'd brought in not too long ago, after she'd told him to screw off—and they made their way out to the entrance. Derek brought the SUV up to the front doors, one more sign of polite kindness. Whatever he was thinking, or whatever his motives, she was grateful she didn't have to walk out into the rain and wind again. Oregonian or not, she was way over this storm.

They sat in silence as he drove, but it felt more peaceful than last time. He clearly wasn't a talker, and for now, she was okay with that.

After what seemed like forever, Derek said, "We'll be there in a few minutes. Are you hungry? Do you want me to stop? If you can wait, and you're not picky, I do have stuff to make sandwiches at my place."

"If it's okay with you, I would rather not stop anywhere. Let's just go home." She clicked her teeth. "I mean, your home.

Ha. I would love to be at home, my home, though I don't know why. My mom is sweet but she would just drive me crazy."

"You live at home?" Before she could answer, he must have noticed her face and said hastily, "I don't mean that as an insult. Personally, I'd slit my wrists if I had to be back at my parents' house, but that's just me."

"Oh, I wasn't kidding about my mother. She's unbearable sometimes. I'm only back at home until I can find a job with a city paper."

"Sportswriting."

"That's the dream." Though the dream had been foggy lately.

They pulled up into a massive portico that fronted a glass and steel high-rise. A valet met them, opening Hara's door. She expected to get the stink eye, considering the state of her clothes and hair, but the man in gray livery was nonchalant. "Madame? Sir? I'll have your things sent up to the penthouse, Mr. Darcy, if you would like to go straightaway."

He reached for Hara's satchel, but she politely declined. No way was she giving up her notes and her laptop, even for five minutes.

She was exhausted, incapable of fully appreciating the modern beauty of the lobby and even the elevator. Stepping from the lift directly into Derek's foyer, she found herself in awe at the fact that he had his own elevator. *Imagine.* Yet, the apartment was gorgeous and spacious and welcoming, but not opulent. Derek's style was minimalistic but with comforting touches.

He pointed her in the direction of a guest suite, a large room with a window seat, a four-poster queen bed, and a sunken tub in the bathroom. She immediately started the water, added liberal helpings of bath salts from a nearby shelf, and stripped out of her clothes. There was a bathrobe hanging behind the door. The bamboo material was plush; it was like putting on a robe at an expensive spa.

"Derek, what should I do with these dirty clothes?" she called into the hallway, cracking the door only wide enough to allow her voice out. Instead of yelling back, however, he appeared in front of her. Somehow, she had managed to be wearing a famous athlete's bathrobe and he was just on the other side of the door.

"There's actually a mini washer and dryer in a closet in the bathroom. By the way," he said, holding up her suitcase so she could see it, "the doorman brought your clothes." He set it on the floor in the hall and then held something up to the narrow opening. "He also found these on the back seat."

"My glasses!" She clapped in delight and, not thinking, opened the door. As she reached for them, her bathrobe gaped open.

Most of her breasts were exposed. Hara was afraid to look at him as the heat rose from the skin on her chest and she drew the bathrobe tight again. "Th-thank-k you." She felt not only exposed but vulnerable. At the same time, she didn't want Derek to leave. Why was she always so conflicted with this guy?

He picked up her suitcase, pretending nothing had happened. "Do you want this?"

"Sure." She didn't want to let go of the bathrobe again. "Do you mind just sliding it in here?"

She shuffled back to let the door open farther. With his eyes averted, he bent forward and set the suitcase inside the room, but then startled her when he straightened and inhaled deeply. She took another step back. "I know, I smell a little ripe—"

He chuckled, a rare event, and finally looked at her. "Not

unless your body odor smells like lavender and vanilla. I'm guessing you found the bath salts. I love that smell."

She laughed. "You use bath salts?"

"I'm a complicated man, Hara."

"A complicated, floral-scented man."

"Maybe not right now."

"Luckily, I'm not close enough to tell."

He made a funny, tiny hop toward her. "How about now?"

"Whew. You're not wrong. You are the one who is ripe."

He ducked his head, blushing, backing out into the hall. "All right. I'm going to take a shower."

"I was only kidding—"

"I know. But it's time to get cleaned up, and then I'll make us something to eat. Deal?"

–*–

Emerging warm and clean, a glow on her caramel skin, her hair smelling like soap and flowers, Hara slid back into the plush bathrobe, decadently soft on her silky arms and legs. She brushed out her long hair, and then used a hair dryer to get rid of some of the dampness.

Putting her glasses on, she was surprised they were no worse for the wear. One problem averted. She opened up her suitcase and dug around for a pair of underwear. She dropped a faded blue pair back into the case. Not that anyone would see her panties, unless she, too, ended up in the hospital. Yet, without thinking about it too deeply, she chose a pink lacy pair, the least embarrassing, just in case someone "accidentally" saw them.

An email notification chimed on her phone and showed an unread message from the Salem prison. Her father was allowed access to a computer once a week, if he had money in his account for sending a message; the computer was set up with a program specifically designed to monitor prisoner emails.

Hey baby girl,

I heard there was a big storm tonight. The guards have been talking about a power outage during the game. I'm not sure if you were there. I'm hoping you are home and safe. Write me back, let me know. Don't stay mad. I only want what's best for you. I needed to help. Not because I think you can't do it on your own, but because it's the only thing I can do for my child. If you are still there, be careful. Better yet, come home. I mean it. Do not get close to O'Donnell, you can't trust him.

I love you.
—Daddy

Hara read it again and then closed out her email without replying. Bitterness churned in her stomach. Obviously she couldn't trust O'Donnell, not if he was willing to do back-alley deals with a convict. Her father. She loved her father and knew he loved her. She even understood his logic. That didn't mean she had to forgive him. But she didn't want him to have a stress heart attack, either. She opened the email back up and replied:

I'm fine. Don't worry about me.

—Hara

Derek called, "Hara! Let's eat!"

The appealingly low timbre of his voice was not to be ignored. When she paused to think about it, she was surprised she'd so easily given in to staying at Derek's for the night. She barely knew him. Yet, after all they'd gone through in the past few hours, Hara felt like she knew enough.

She had to accept that she'd been partially wrong about her initial impression. He was wealthy, but he was not entitled or without compassion, not like she'd thought. His demeanor could be dour, but that didn't mean he was heartless. Derek had helped both Hara and Naomi when he didn't have to, even putting himself in danger to do so. He was judgmental and standoffish, but if given the chance, he was kind, in his own way, and he was loyal to the people around him.

Hara started to take off her robe in order to get dressed, but her arms and torso broke into goose bumps. She shivered, hard, then decided she was fine, wrapped up in the thick cocoon. She rewrapped it around her, making sure it would stay securely in place, and tightened the sash. "Coming!"

She sat at the long kitchen bar. Derek, his hair damp, and dressed now in loose Adidas joggers and a clingy T-shirt, took ingredients out of the refrigerator.

"I can make a mean roasted chicken panini. Interested?"

"You cook?"

"My parents have a full waitstaff. I do not want that. I do not need that. So. Panini?"

"Yes, sure, that sounds great. I get not wanting to follow in your parents' footsteps—though your parents' footprints are from handcrafted Italian loafers, while mine are from rubber boots and Croc knockoffs. But are you not close at all to them?"

"I see them every once in a while. Which is too much time, especially with my father."

"I'd give anything to be able to have my father around again." Hara immediately regretted her words. She did not want to have a conversation about Thomas Isari, the reason several of Derek's peers were in jail. No need to remind Derek her father was a felon. "But let's talk about something else. Maybe we should call the hospital, check on Naomi."

She called Mass General while he sautéed chicken pieces and onions, then made the sandwiches. It was nice, him gliding around the kitchen, being domestic. A famous basketball player, making her a meal. On hold, waiting for the nurse, Hara quietly watched him. Admired him. It was funny how even just cooking, he moved with graceful strength. His face remained calm, emotionless. She noticed the cute dimple in his square chin, and it made his countenance seem less stern.

The food was ready by the time the nurse got back on the phone, stating that Naomi remained the same; she was sleeping comfortably but the fluid in her lungs was still a concern.

"Thank you." Hara hung up, wanting to feel relieved but, instead, felt increasingly anxious.

Derek handed her a loaded plate, garnished with sliced apple and Brie. *Oh, he's so fancy. I like it.* She took a bite, and then another. It was delicious, seasoned by burned adrenaline and fatigue.

He said, "I hope Naomi is going to be okay. You did a great job tonight, keeping it together. It was tough, seeing her like that."

"At first I thought she was dead. There is no way I could have kept it together if that had been true." She paused as he handed her a glass of red wine. After taking a drink, she said slowly, "My grandpa died the same day my dad was sentenced. Not long after that, my grandmother's dementia spiraled and she was moved to an old folks' home." She took another drink.

"Even my mom changed, became distant. All these people, gone. It's not like Naomi and I are longtime besties—but it was still terrifying to see how close she was to being a goner, too."

Derek leaned against the counter, listening, eating his sandwich. He swallowed and said, "For the record, I would have lost my shit if Naomi was dead, or even if she was screaming in pain. I hate it when people suffer. But especially this time, when I could have prevented it."

"You are not the reason Naomi was hurt. It was a combination of circumstances. We could have waited a few more minutes and you would have come in. Or, frankly, Naomi and I could have hunkered down at her place for the night and let you go on your merry way."

"I would never have left you there."

"Are you like this with everybody?"

"What? Responsible? Yes."

They ate quietly for a few minutes more.

Slowly, hesitantly, Derek broke the easy silence, saying, "You can tell me if this is too personal, but that night at the club, you thought I was asking you a racist question . . . but why does it bother you if someone wants to know your heritage?"

"Because my cultural background does not define me. Don't get me wrong—I'm not ashamed at all. It's just that my family is diverse, obviously, but they did very little to create cultural roots in me. My mother is African American and Daddy is Japanese American, but no one in my family has ever tried to share what it means to be a part of either of those races. I didn't realize I was missing out on learning about who I am, about my roots, until I was in middle school. And that was only because it finally dawned on me that my first name is Japanese and not from the Greek goddess Hera. No one ever talked to me about it."

"Do you ever embrace your Asian heritage? Now, as an adult?"

She shook her head slowly. "I want to, but my grandparents were put into an internment camp and came out two years later determined to prove they were Americans. They spoke only English, scrubbed anything Asian from the home, made sure my father had no accent, played football, and ate steak and potatoes. He used to joke that they wouldn't even let him play chess—it was too Asian. Growing up, I never saw a kimono or ate sushi, nothing."

"What about your mother's family?"

"None left, except her. My mom was just like every other mom. I was just another Pacific Northwest farm kid. She grew up in that town, too. About the only black family history I get from her has to do with how to deal with racism. And the only bit of Japan my grandparents maintained had to do with gardening and caring for the apple orchard. My father grew up knowing next to nothing about being Japanese. He promised to take me to Japan one day, but, well, that didn't pan out, for obvious reasons."

"It must have been hard, growing up in a small town with your dad in prison."

"You have no idea." She took a long drink of her wine. "I learned to just keep my head down and work, knowing eventually I'd be out in the bigger world, away from all that. I don't plan on being back for long. Besides, though it might not seem like it sometimes, I try to make it a habit to find something positive and live in the moment when I can."

"I have to ask, and I don't want to start an argument, but if you are so dead set on not being like your dad, why did you let him rig the contest with O'Donnell?"

Time came to a crashing halt. The air in front of her swam.

He remained leaning against the counter, and yet Derek suddenly felt too close.

Hara drained her glass. "I know you won't believe me, but I had no idea. Not until the night after the first game, when I heard O'Donnell talking about it. I thought I was here because I deserved it. Because I earned it. If I could rip out my heart and show you the truth, I would. It's crushing me, making me doubt myself." Hara gnashed her teeth. "I could kill Daddy for doing that to me."

He tipped his head to the side, a range of emotions scuttling across his face.

"You believed them, Derek. I know you did. I hope you don't still believe them. You've been so hot and cold, you can't blame me when I come off as defensive."

"Listen, Hara, like I said at the bar, I'm not that great in social settings. I'm awkward and serious and if I try to say something funny, it comes out wrong." Derek put the remains of his sandwich down and folded his arms. "But it's true, I did believe Madeline and O'Donnell. I am sorry about that now. They were very convincing, and I hadn't really spent time with you, gotten to know you."

"Yet, you almost kissed me."

"There is that."

"Yeah, that." Why was she bringing this up? The conversation so far hadn't been mortifying enough?

"Well, I don't have any regrets. Except maybe that Madeline interrupted me." He dragged his gaze to hers. Hara's heart leapt at his words, whether or not it was wise. He continued, "I mean it. I didn't know how to react, either to the kiss or their accusations, and I'm sorry if I hurt you."

"Well." She picked up her empty glass of wine and glared at it reproachfully. "I should probably drink some water." Before he could do anything more for her, Hara slid off the bar stool and went to the cupboard for a glass.

She could sense Derek move behind her. Even without contact, she could feel the heat and energy he radiated. Not thinking, she stepped back, into him. Touching him was better.

Both of his arms went around her, pulling her back into him, closer, his cheek pressed to the side of her head, his breath trickling warmly into her ear. He nuzzled the hair at her temple.

Hara's heart pounded hard enough she was sure he could hear it. This was so far outside of her normal pattern with men, but she wanted it. One more gift the universe was offering, if she wasn't too afraid to take it. She wanted him, now. She was breathless. Terrified, exhilarated, confused, and aroused. Hara made herself turn to face him.

One arm remained wrapped around her, the other reached over and gently removed her glasses. Then, slowly, he bent and kissed her. His full lips caressed hers, his copper eyes open and intent on her. Inquisitive. Making sure she was okay. His enticing offer of intimacy was sealed by his respect.

She opened her mouth slightly and ran the tip of her tongue just inside his bottom lip. He responded by pressing her mouth open and sliding his tongue inside hungrily.

Passion torched through Hara, burned away any misgivings, any thought of complications and conflicts. The heat in her stomach spread, warming her in every corner and crevice. Their bodies slammed together, the friction intense.

She bent her head back as he kissed down her neck, arching her body into his. Her hands reached up, moved over the hard muscles of his chest, the rounded pecs under his thin T-shirt fitting perfectly into her shallow palms. *So firm. So strong. So . . .*

Hara lost her words then, as Derek pushed her robe down, revealing the top of her breast, his lips now tracing her collarbone with an occasional flick of his tongue. Hara moaned. Her nipples were erect, rubbing against the material, crying out for Derek to release them. He heeded the call, slowly, moving his lips down to just above the hem of the robe, then pushed it down with a light fingertip. His hand went to her breast, holding her up as he took her fully into his mouth, gently flicking and sucking. His other hand slid inside her robe and cupped her ass. He squeezed, and pulled her even tighter to him. She ground against him, moaning.

She was bare to the waist. He undid the sash and slid two fingers between her legs, stroking over her panties. It was unbearable.

"Please, Derek."

He eased the pink lace over her hips, letting it drop to the floor. "Yes?" he asked.

"Yes. Yes."

Derek swiftly picked her up and sat her on the counter, kissing and sucking on her nipples. "You are exquisite," he groaned against her skin.

He continued downward, soft butterfly kisses moving up her thigh, driving her mad. By the time his hot breath was directly on her, she was writhing, saying, "Yes, please, Derek. Please, Derek!"

As his tongue lightly touched her, and then plunged, she cried out. He groaned, vibrating against her as she pushed closer, closer. When his tongue slowed and flattened and teased, she thought she would explode. "Wait! Wait!" she cried out, holding his head. "I want you inside me."

As he stood, Hara wrapped her legs around his waist. Derek picked her up like she was nothing and carried her to the bedroom. She wanted so badly the deeper connection to this man she had once thought was beyond her reach. Within seconds, she had her wish.

His sculptured body slowly lowered on top of her, hard and ready. Then, Derek surprised her by rolling them over, so that she was on top. His face was flushed and soft but his eyes burned like sparking metal in a forge. "I want you to be in control," he whispered. Then he put a hand to her cheek, running a thumb over her cheekbone. "I want you to be happy." He moved his hand down to the curve of her breast.

Hara, looking down at him, almost burst into tears. The gentle affection was as alluring as his physical strength and overcharged masculinity. She had never imagined she could feel so safe, so desired, and so turned on at the same time—especially not by a man who had to have had hundreds of one-night stands. But she was in control and she liked it. If nothing else, she'd be walking away with a memory that would keep her warm for years.

Hara knelt over him, slowly settled herself onto him, just barely, not sure how she was able to keep her movements slow and controlled. He groaned and started to thrust, but she put her hand on his chest. "Shhh. Slow, slow."

She pulled back up but immediately slid back down, just a little farther, slowly. Derek watched her, helped her, his strong hands on her hips. Her insides were pulsing; he grew harder, bigger, and she couldn't hold off any longer, sliding all the way down, crazed with satisfaction, filled like never before. There was no emptiness. She moved, gripping him as she came up, grinding and crying out as she came down.

"Hara! I can't wait . . ."

She accommodated him, meeting each thrust. Her world had shrunk to this one location, this one act, this one moment.

She needed nothing but him, wanted nothing but this. They twisted and moaned and sucked and plunged until both of them shattered into a million little pieces.

Hara broke and came apart multiple times over the next few hours, each moment its own while they were together.

CHAPTER 15

The loss of virtue in a female is irretrievable; . . . one false step involves her in endless ruin; . . . her reputation is no less brittle than it is beautiful . . .

—*Pride and Prejudice*

Derek was full, satiated . . . joyful. It had been a long time.

Light from the hallway fell across Hara's narrow back, a darkly golden trail for him to trace with a fingertip, from between her shoulder blades down to that slight incline just before it turned into the tight mound of buttock. The luscious young woman slept on her stomach, her head tucked into the crook of her petite elbow, her long black hair twisted into a loose rope. Her back rose and fell at a comforting pace.

The first tinges of morning light were beginning to creep into the room. He'd told Hara he wanted her to be happy, but the truth was he needed her to be happy with him. He needed to know that the kind, beautiful, intelligent woman he'd stumbled into didn't find him boring, or worthy only because of status or money. He wanted Hara to like him.

It was crazy.

The girl next to him emitted a kittenish noise. His heart

expanded; he pictured the Grinch's heart, as affection and sex made Derek's heart grow three sizes.

Why this girl? Why was she so special?

The heart wants what the heart wants, I suppose. But she was worth it. Hara *was* something special, and there was no need to define it.

Derek was surprised at the depth of his response to Hara, a girl he barely knew, and a reporter. He'd known so many users, so many weak-willed leeches. So many rich weasels and abusers. So many adulators, cheaters, and hard-hearted scam artists. Hara claimed to have been innocent of her father's mischief, unaware of the rigged contest, and he believed her. Or, he wanted to believe her. She came off as honest and down to earth, but so did most people, until they didn't. He had a hard time believing in people in general.

Hara wasn't just words—that was one thing. She'd saved him from the road sign, and kept Naomi from drowning in floodwater. Then, she'd been willing to sleep at the hospital, to be with the girl until her family got there. So, she could be brave and giving. He'd seen it.

I don't know why I'm winding myself up here. He'd just given her a place to sleep for the night, not a commitment ring.

He'd also believed that Charles was brave, if not giving. Now it seemed his best friend—only real friend—was as hinky as the rest of humanity. How could Charles have let his mom take that money and then never say anything? If he'd just been honest early on, it could have all been fixed and Charles's career wouldn't be in jeopardy. Now . . . if it got out, it would hurt Charles's mom, and Charles. And the team.

It was breaking the rules, and it felt so wrong to Derek to take advantage of a system put in place to protect people. He'd like to think the people in charge were upholding those rules, but, no. O'Donnell was just like Derek's father, paying attention only to the laws that fed his greed.

Why was he thinking about this right now?

Hara made that same, small kittenish noise again, wriggling against him. He spooned up against her, glad for the warmth. He grew hard, pressed to her rounded bottom, his chest against her lean back, his hand lightly on her breast, but he didn't want to wake her just yet. She needed rest, after a stressful evening and then a long night of athletic wear and tear.

The cell on the bedside table chirped, making him jump, but Hara's breath remained slow and sweet.

Derek patted around in the gloom until he found the phone and silenced it. He squinted through heavy eyes at the screen: O'Donnell. Just then a text came through, O'Donnell telling him to come to the residence as soon as possible—they needed to talk. He put the phone back down, sighing. As soon as possible? It was only six in the morning. *This can definitely wait until later.*

Hara flopped onto him, one arm draped across his stomach, her face on his chest. "Mmmm." She was sleeping, he was pretty sure.

Her warmth erased any thought of O'Donnell.

Smiling, he stayed still, absorbing the peace and quiet happiness of this moment. He hadn't had a woman in his bed for a long, long time. Despite the perception that athletes were dogs, he was not much of a one-night-stand guy. Thinking back, he realized his last long-term relationship had ended almost two years ago, when he was still at Pepperdine. He didn't like entanglements or drama. He didn't like most people.

He drowsed off, dreams flitting on the edge of consciousness.

Then the phone rang again. It could have been five minutes, or five hours.

Groping for the cell, he silenced the chirp, and cursed under his breath. It was Charles calling this time. What could he possibly want this early? But then Derek felt a rush of cold prickles. What if something had gone wrong with Naomi? Maybe they needed him.

Derek sat up, pushing off the bed quietly. He glanced down at Hara to make sure she was still asleep; the contented half smile on her face, her hand curled under her cheek—she was out. The basketball player picked up his briefs and tugged them on in the hallway, as he answered the phone. "Charles? You okay? Everything all right?"

"No, man. Shit is comin' apart. Can you come over here?"

Derek could hear ESPN in the background. "Where's 'here'? Is this about Naomi?"

"O'Donnell found out she's pregnant. He said he's sending someone to take care of it. What does that mean?"

"Jesus, you're gettin' too wound up. He's not the Mafia. He's not sending someone in for a hit."

"You don't know him, Derek. I'm worried about her."

"So worried that you're with Naomi right now?"

"Well, no. No, I didn't—Tina be stickin' to me like glue! This is different, man. I don't want this to blow up into a big deal."

"Sounds like O'Donnell feels the same way. What, you think he's going to pay her off somehow? Why even bother?"

"I don't know what he'll do. But he doesn't want my name in the papers at all, not if he isn't controlling it. He doesn't want reporters checking up on me."

"You gotta do something about this bribe money with your mom, Charles! If you don't, O'Donnell will always have a hold on you. This kind of shit will always be happening. Well, not this exactly—hopefully you're going to get a damn vasectomy."

"Enough lecture," Charles hissed in his ear. "Can you just swing by the hospital, check on Naomi? Tell her to be careful of O'Donnell. I feel like shit, man."

"You should. You definitely should." He hung up on Charles.

Derek had wanted this season to be a fresh start. It appeared now that plan was all going to hell. Who would he be without Charles there to back him up? Nobody. He'd be back on the bench.

Within seconds, a text came through: *I know you are pissed, but someone need to make sure she okay. I can't.*

Derek snorted and replied, *You can't because your girlfriend will find out about your pregnant mistress. Classy AF.*

"Derek?"

The sleepy voice came from his bedroom. "Right here." He went back in the room, hoping to slide back under the sheets and press against her naked body.

Instead, Hara stood next to the bed, pulling on a T-shirt over her lacy pink panties.

He immediately reacted to her and there was no hiding it. "Come back to bed, baby. It's still early."

"I heard you talking about Naomi. She okay?" Hara held onto the hem of the white T-shirt, her black hair cascading around her, her blue eyes vivid even in the dim light.

Derek shut his eyes for a moment, tried to sear this image into his brain. An image to come back to later and think about when he was alone. She wasn't getting back into bed; he sensed the good times were over. "I'm not sure."

"Okay. But what was that other stuff you were talking about? It was Charles, right? He hasn't been to the hospital, has he?"

Suddenly, his hackles went up. Hara the reporter. Here she was, asking questions.

Hara must have noticed his expression. "Hey, I wasn't trying to eavesdrop. But you were only a few feet away." She tilted her head to the side and tucked long strands behind her ears, her expression sad. "My impression of Charles is a cocky, womanizing athlete with a good heart. I usually stand by my first opinions. I think I'm a pretty good judge of character. Am I wrong, though, Derek? Am I wrong about Charles?"

"Let's make some coffee." Derek tossed her a robe and put on one himself, not answering her question. He didn't know the answer, not anymore.

Following him into the hall, she kept going, the sleep now gone from her voice. "You were talking to him about money—"

"Hara!" he said sharply over his shoulder. "You are talking about things you know nothing about."

"You're right. I know he's your friend. But if you're covering something up for him, then you . . ."

Derek was glad she didn't finish her sentence. He wasn't covering. He'd just found out, for God's sake. He would do the right thing; he just didn't know what that was yet.

"Ballplayers." She sat on the same stool as the night before and sighed heavily. "They're paid millions of dollars and the one thing that is asked of them is that they spend their time playing a game, and then, in their off time, that they be role models for the young people who idolize them. You're given fame and glory and riches. Why take more?"

Derek bristled. Who was she to question him or his boy? "In this instance, you have it wrong," he said stiffly. "This is off the record, but I want to make sure you have all the facts, that you do not blow this into something bigger than it is. Charles grew up poor, and when he was still in high school, living in a run-down house with his single mother, she took money from a college recruiter, not knowing that broke association rules, and not telling Charles. She did not break any law—she thought she was doing what everyone else did, and didn't consider it a bribe since Charles already had decided to go to school there."

"Do you believe that? That Charles didn't know? How is that even possible? And you really believe this woman was so naive that she thought people were dropping free money at her feet? That college just bought her kid."

"Ms. Butler is a good woman. She and Charles have been my family." Derek felt his heart crack. Hara was the exact wrong person to share all this with, but he had no one else. Something was breaking inside of him. "I have never trusted anyone else. This whole shady deal bothers the shit out of me. I want to believe in them. I actually do think his ma just wanted to provide for her son. Charles . . . I don't know. Two days ago, I would have said, Oh hell, no, that boy wouldn't let that pass. But now . . . now."

"I saw him block you in the locker room interview, and then, in the last game, he pushed you away. Maybe he's not one hundred."

"I don't know why he did that. I tried to find him, to talk to him after the game, but I never saw him. I was also looking for O'Donnell, though, since he wanted to see *me*. God knows why. But then crazy town happened and here we are."

"Here we are."

"Hara, I wish to hell you hadn't heard me say anything." Derek wanted to kick himself unconscious. How could he have been so stupid? "I know this is a story for you. An up-and-coming reporter, you could make your name on this. But can you just wait?"

"I like Charles. He's been good to me. I am well aware I do not have the full picture. On the other hand, this is so much bigger than Charles. Bribery is national news, and bribing college athletes' families has *national* impact. We need to trust that coaches are doing what's best for student athletes, not buying them off and then using them like poker chips, controlling their career choices because they feel like they own them." She blew out her breath angrily. "Besides, someone else is bound to find out. Like I said, I like Charles, I want to hear his side, but some other reporter is going to find out and bring a whole different spin and repercussions. Better to be in front of it than behind it."

"That's what I told him. But I'm hoping you'll hold off. Let Charles do the right thing. Let him come forward. It's what's best for everybody."

"I don't know."

"Can you give him a few days, at least?" Derek pleaded, hating himself for it. "Let me talk to him."

They both backed down, quietly drank their coffee. The space between them felt gray and dirty and infinite. He wanted to pick her up and carry her back to the bedroom, to make her forget everything she'd heard. Her smell and her touch could take him away, too, make him forget everything. Derek started to stretch out his hand to her, to bridge the space, but she pushed back from the table, unaware or uninterested.

"I promise, Derek, I won't do anything rash, or without talking to you." Standing, she put down her coffee cup. "First things first. I'm going to head over to the hospital and check on Naomi. Do you want to come with me?"

"No, O'Donnell's been trying to get ahold of me. He wants me to go over to his house to talk to him. I better figure out what is up with him."

"But we're okay, right?"

"Everything's fine, Hara. You're just doing what you think you need to do. So am I." *But I can't say I trust you. I don't trust anybody.*

–*–

Hara pulled her hood up and sprinted to the Uber waiting for her on the corner, the rain only a light drizzle and bearable without the howling winds from last night. Her suitcase banged against her leg; she'd brought it and her satchel, not sure where she was going to end up that night.

Was she going to fly home? Get a hotel? Sneak back into Derek's bed?

Clicking on her seat belt, she stared at her hands, disoriented. Unsure. A kaleidoscope of images cascaded through her mind as the Boston streets, covered in storm debris and standing puddles, flashed in front of her eyes. Her body was heading toward the hospital but her mind was jumping around through space and time, from being on top of Derek, filled with his heat and desire, to standing outside O'Donnell's kitchen as the old bastard talked about her father, her insides empty and cold.

How was this fair? Life had taken a major turn for the mind-blowing great, but there always had to be a freaking complication.

She could ignore the story. Hara could pretend she didn't know anything and see where this thing with Derek might go. She could leave for home on a good note and maybe see him again, maybe not, but they'd part on decent, if not affectionate, terms. Friends with possible benefits.

Maintain a relationship that wasn't a relationship and had no guarantee or likeliness of being a relationship.

Or, Hara could be a journalist and report what she knew. It wouldn't hurt to wait a few days, not just because she hoped Charles would do the right thing, but also because she needed time to corroborate and research before she committed anything to print. She couldn't just write something this big based on an overhead conversation and hearsay. She had to research the hell out of this before she made any decisions.

And what about Derek? She'd think about that later.

The automatic doors of Massachusetts General Hospital rolled open with a whoosh of air, blowing her hair across her face and filling her nostrils with the tingle of astringent. This time, she noticed the fall decorations, the wreaths and garlands of twigs and orange and green leaves hung with gold ribbon. She imagined they were there to soften the impact of standing in a building filled with tragedy and pain. The decorations were actually very pretty.

She felt bad that Naomi lay in a bed upstairs, suffering with fear over the future, while Charles was probably at some spa, getting a massage and a happy ending.

Whoa there, Hara Isari. Take a step back. She was just pissed because she might have been wrong about him. She needed to keep an open mind, to find out what was true or not, and why he'd done the things he'd done. Hara had to remove herself from the story. That's what good journalists did.

Hara stopped at the information desk, festooned with more fall foliage and manned by two old women who had withered down to the same height and had their perms done by the same beautician.

"Hi, can you please tell me what room Naomi . . . Naomi. Oh, geez. I forget her last name."

"I won't bother asking if you're family, then," said one of the women, not unkindly. "I can't find who you are looking for with only a first name. But here"—she pushed a ceramic pumpkin bowl across the counter—"take a piece of candy."

Hara took a cellophane-wrapped hard candy—the same butterscotch candies her grandma kept in the pocket of her housecoat—and thanked the woman. She found a seat in the corner, needing a place to sit while she came up with a plan. How could it be that she still didn't have anyone's cell number? Except Naomi's, and she wasn't answering. Then brilliance struck. Sucking on her candy, she called Naomi's number again and listened more closely to the message.

"Hello, dahlings! You've reached Naomi Martin's voicemail because she's too lazy to answer. Leave a message, or don't, it's up to you."

Boom. Naomi Martin. One problem down, about twenty more to go.

A voice from behind her made Hara freeze.

"It's done. She gets it. We don't have to worry about Naomi."

The recognizable voice was close, but on the other side of a potted plant. Peeking around the dusty fake ficus tree, Hara saw Madeline Bingley blaze past the little old ladies' information desk, her resting bitch face on full wattage as she spoke into a cell phone.

Hara waited a few minutes in the lobby chairs, making sure the coast was clear. After getting Naomi's room number, she hurried to the elevator, her suitcase bumping along behind. As she entered the small, sparse room, the young woman in the bed fluttered her eyes and then opened them.

"'Sup, Hara." Naomi's voice was weak, scratchy, her face a deep ash, her corkscrew spirals creating a wide halo against her pillow. Without makeup, and a hospital gown in place of sophisticated clothing, her youth was apparent. So was her weary sadness.

"I'm sorry to see you this way." Hara went to her and lightly put a hand on Naomi's arm, avoiding the IV. "I won't ask how you feel. But can I bring you anything?"

"No, my dad is coming back later." She cleared her throat. "They're keeping me another night; they can't seem to get the fluid out of my lungs."

"I have a weird question to ask, but was O'Donnell's assistant just here?"

Naomi closed her eyes. Her face seemed to sink in on itself.

"What's going on, Naomi? Spill it."

"I can't."

"Why?"

"I . . . I signed something. I can't talk about it."

"That sounds bad."

"The most I will say is that on the windowsill over there is an appointment card. I have a doctor's appointment in the building next door. Take that as you will."

Hara groaned. There was no denying what her friend meant. An abortion. Hara's father had said not to trust O'Donnell, but this seemed like so much unnecessarily cruel meddling. "Did you make the appointment? Is that what you want?"

She shook her head. "I don't know. I'm so confused. I just don't know." Thin tears spilled over her lower lashes, ran down into her ears. "I guess I do. But I don't like having the decision made for me."

"What happens if you don't go?"

"My life changes, doesn't it?" She reached out her hand. "Hara, please, don't say anything to anybody, okay? Can I trust you?"

"Of course." Charles had gotten a woman other than his

girlfriend pregnant, and now she was being guilted into an abortion, his career hanging over her head. That wasn't news. It was just goddamn sad.

A deep voice interrupted them. "Naomi?"

Hara swung around. A towering man in a hoodie, the thick cotton drawn low over his forehead, filled the doorway. He might have appeared menacing if his face, what was visible, hadn't been so hangdog.

"Charles." Naomi's voice was small but tinged with joy.

The basketball player squeezed past Hara and sat on the edge of the bed, putting a hand on Naomi's.

What have you done here, you son of a bitch? A wave of rage swept through Hara but evaporated quickly. Naomi was a big girl. She'd gone into this with open eyes. And Charles? He was here. They could work it out together. The ballplayer had other, bigger problems.

"I'm gonna go. Naomi, you call me if you need me. Please. I'll be here." But would she be here? She had a flight out that afternoon. Heading back to the lobby, she wasn't sure where to go.

She could go home or she could take advantage of the opportunity in front of her, a story to look into, a real story. Hara just wished it didn't involve Charles. Maybe she'd end up not running it, she decided, but there was no reason to walk away just yet. One or two more days in Boston wasn't going to kill her.

She wasn't sure where she stood with Derek. She'd like to find out, to see him again, sooner than later, but she wasn't going to ask to stay there. Too soon. Too needy.

Unfortunately, Naomi's power was out, and the roads on that side of town were still dealing with water and damage. She could go back to O'Donnell's, but she'd rather die.

Carter.

"All right! A story!" her boss sang into the phone twenty minutes later. "I canceled your plane ticket and got you a room. You are going to love it, less than half a mile from the hospital where your friend is."

"Thanks."

"Just wait until you see the place."

"You didn't have to go to so much trouble."

"Oh, I had to. I've always wanted to stay there. It's called the Liberty." Carter hooted with laughter, making her think that he'd had more Irish than coffee that morning. "It used to be the old Charles Street Jail! The hotel bar is the Alibi, used to be the drunk tank. So clever! There's an Italian restaurant called Scampo—which means 'escape'—in the section where guards transported prisoners from the paddy wagons to their cells. Seriously. I might fly out and join you."

"Wha—"

"Honey, don't you worry, this is a luxury hotel in the Beacon Hill neighborhood. The renovations cost over $150 million. I wouldn't stick you in a dump. But I'm sure there are ghosts. I mean interesting ghosts, not just old pickpockets. There was a captured German U-boat captain being held there who broke a pair of sunglasses into shards and slit—"

"Gross."

"I'm just sayin', there are bars over the windows in some places. This'll be an experience you can write about. Might as well get as many articles out of this trip as possible."

"Speaking of," she said, "I need to get out my notes from last night's game and the crazy power outage. I know other reporters have already beaten me to the punch, but I can send off a game review by tonight, if that's okay. I should go."

"Wait. Don't hang up on me yet. First of all, I put money in your bank account to cover the food and travel. And, second, I've got to know . . . you said this girl's apartment didn't have heat or electricity and the roads were flooded. You didn't go back there, did you? Where did you stay? The airport again?"

Hara opened and closed her mouth. There was so much building inside her. Without using names, she'd already told him about Naomi's accident, and she'd told him about "a player" whose family had taken money from a college to secure placement. But she wanted to tell him more, to tell him all the details and how she felt about them, what the people were like here. She wanted to tell him about Derek, the good and the bad, and how attracted she was to the ballplayer, and how confused . . .

"Another friend let me stay. I'll tell you more later, okay? Right now, I just want to get started. If the information checks out and we do end up printing it, the story could be huge, Carter."

She shut her eyes. Her daddy had nothing to do with this story. *If this happens, it's because of me.*

CHAPTER 16

> There is, I believe, in every disposition a tendency to some particular evil—a natural defect, which not even the best education can overcome.
>
> —*Pride and Prejudice*

Derek rolled up to the gate in front of the O'Donnell residence, said his name into the speaker, and felt the grinding creak of the gate in his joints. He didn't drive forward right away, staring across the brick roundabout in front of the historical residence. There was storm debris and standing water on the road, and quite a bit of water in the driveway.

Why was he there? It couldn't be good.

He was greeted at the front door by O'Donnell himself, his fine white hair sprayed up into a wave. "Thanks for coming. Let's go into my study. Do you want any coffee or tea, anything sent over from the kitchen?"

"No, I'm good, thanks." Derek followed him into his study and took a chair. His gaze landed on a group of three paintings on the wall behind O'Donnell's desk. The player froze in shock. It was hard not to stare. He wanted to turn away but couldn't.

Each painting was a different sexualized scene, all sadomasochistic acts set in nature. In one, a man was tied to a massive oak tree and a creature with the body of a man and the head of a goat was ramming a big horn into the captive. The captive's face was twisted in pleasure.

I cannot fucking unsee this. He tore his gaze away before he could decipher what was going on in the other paintings, though he had the impression they were even more violent and disturbing. *Lawd, am I in a murder room?* Was he about to get fucked up by Bubba? There was no plastic tarp on the floor under his feet, though, and the freaky old man was sitting down on the other side of his massive desk. Derek moved to the edge of his seat, just in case, ready to spring up and ninja his way out, if need be.

He had to get it together. Refocusing on the unblemished nature outside the window, the player took a breath and centered himself. Calmly, in a civilized tone, he asked, "How did your place do with the flooding?"

"The river is right up to the back patios, but supposedly it will be receding in the next twenty-four hours. The gardens are under half a foot of water, so I'm sure they've been destroyed. The buildings have all been built up but if the water continues to rise, we're going to have to deal with damp and mold in the substructures for years. Very disheartening, to say the least."

"It sounds like you've been lucky so far. No real damage. I saw some pretty terrible destruction in certain neighborhoods last night."

"This is a beautifully maintained historical site. Some of *those* places could stand to be refurbished or even demolished. But this place, well, if something happens here, it will be a travesty."

How was it that he and Derek's father weren't best friends? The only difference between them was skin color. Though his father didn't spend too much time embracing his cultural heritage. Gobs of money had made him blind to his own skin, not to mention to the black community, and he definitely turned up his nose at those in poverty. His mother was the same way, though less aggressive, simply floating along in her little bubble made of Waterford crystal, never dealing with real-world problems. Or people.

O'Donnell picked up an unlit pipe from his desk and put the stem in his mouth, sucking on it. He said to Derek, "You know, Charles is worried about you."

Derek coughed, caught by surprise.

"Me!"

"He says you're struggling in your role as a support player. That you are taking a lot of unnecessary chances on the court, trying to assert your dominance. We just don't need that, Mr. Darcy. We *need* a team player."

"Charles told you I'm not a team player?" The blood had left Derek's head, leaving him fuzzy-headed and bone cold.

"Not in those words, no. But that you are trying too hard to make a name for yourself."

His lips were numb, tingling, from the loss of blood. "No, he didn't."

O'Donnell didn't answer, just tipped his head to the side, eyes half shut, and sucked on his pipe.

The phallic nature of his boss's oral fixation did not elude Derek. He stifled a disgusted shiver and said, "Sir, you've seen me play. You brought me on, and you kept me on last year when I couldn't play. I'm not a ball hog, but I do take the shot if I've got it. I don't know what this is about, but I am a team player. Ask the coach. I always have been."

"Boy, the coach and I have talked about it. I need you to just back down a bit, stop pressing so hard. Get the ball to Charles."

"I—"

"Exactly. *I, I, I.* Play for your team. Not yourself. Now, be a good boy and do as I say. Share the ball. That is what is best for the Fishers."

Derek put his head in his hands, a pickax tapping on his center lobe. After a second, he pushed up from the chair. "Is that all? May I go?"

"You are acting like I have stolen your favorite toy." His boss put down his pipe and came out from behind his desk. "I'm not punishing you, Mr. Darcy. I'm just, you know, guiding you. I only want what is best for the team and for you." The old man clapped Derek on the shoulder, suddenly jovial. "So. I'll see you at the game tomorrow."

Seeing himself out, Derek could not clear the buzzing fog that had filled his brain. This didn't make sense at all. Charles was trying to push Derek into the corner? Why? Why would he do that? They'd always worked together, supported each other, been the perfect partners out there. It's why Derek had wanted to be on his team in the first place. Charles had wanted that, too.

What had changed?

—*—

"Yes, Mother, I have been talking to the players, meeting plenty of interesting people." Hara pressed a hand to her forehead, which did nothing to alleviate her headache.

"Men. Hara, I want you to be mingling with men. I'm sorry your new friend got hurt, but you need to stay focused on the goal."

"Since my interview made it onto the AP wire and I've covered two games, one from the owners' box, I'd say I met my goal." She had no intention of telling her mother that it had been her father who arranged for her to win the contest. No reason to give her even more fodder in her fight against her being a sportswriter. Hara was going to write this new story, all on her own.

"You—"

"I know what you meant. That I'm supposed to be flaunting my goods in front of wealthy men, trying to get their attention." *Derek seemed pretty taken with my goods, taking me for a good, long time . . .* "You don't have to worry, I've met plenty of men and I've been pleasant."

"Oh? Do tell."

Hara sighed. There was also no way she was going to tell her mother about hanging out with some of the team members at the nightclub, and definitely not about spending the night with Derek. Not yet, anyway. "I don't have time to gossip right now, but I promise to tell you all about it when I get home."

"When will that be, exactly? Don't get me wrong, I'm thrilled you've been able to spend more time over there, with the right kind of people. But I do want to know you're safe. You are safe, right, Hara?"

"Carter has me set up in an incredible hotel." She smirked. An incredible hotel that used to be a jail and was filled with the ghosts of murderers. "I should be done with my story in the next few days."

They hung up and Hara unpacked her few belongings into the closet, next to a hotel bathrobe. She stroked a sleeve, smiling. *Ah, memories.*

When her car had first pulled up in front of the Liberty, she'd been afraid to get out. The hotel's stone complex, built in 1851 as a jail, now looked like a posh castle with floor-to-ceiling windows and soft lighting. The lobby had three lovely balconies encircling the room. Those balconies had been the guard catwalks, back in the day, and were now sprinkled with small gathering areas, where couples shared secrets, and businesspeople drank martinis and stretched their legs.

The four stories of open brick wall were broken up by cream panels, murals of stylized trees reaching from floor to the very, very high ceiling. What should have been cold and hard had been transformed into an elegant, warm space. The staff at the highly polished teak front desk were kind and attentive though she was dressed in jeans and a sweater—as opposed to everyone else in the lobby, who were in a contest for best dressed.

Her hotel room was ready, so they were able to let her in early. The amazing room boasted huge windows and plenty of natural light, hardwood floors, thick area rugs, a fully outfitted bar, and a rich leather headboard and matching chair set.

She texted pictures to Carter, making sure to include the oil paintings in her room that were of famous Boston locations and looked to be original, though they were almost outdone by the fifty-five-inch flat-screen television and elaborate gaming console. A little something for everyone.

After a quick Internet search, she was surprised, and slightly disturbed, at how easy it was to find the address for Ms. Butler. Privacy just did not exist anymore.

Two hours later, Hara walked the streets close to the Butler house, wanting to get a feel for the neighborhood, grateful for a break in the cloud coverage that offered weak sunshine with a light breeze. It was nice not to have to deal with constantly wiping raindrops off her glasses.

There didn't appear to be river flooding here, but storm

drains were stopped up and the gutters were overflowing. Locals were out, in storm cleanup mode. The wind had done a lot of damage to these row houses—limbs, garbage, and roofing shingles littered yards and the sides of the road, and dozens of downed trees were resting on houses or cars, or sticking through broken windows. A yellow and red plastic play structure was wedged high in an old elm tree. There was a collection of five or six garbage cans rolling around in one driveway.

Coming around a corner, she squealed in horror.

A leg sat in a pile of leaves over an impacted grate, a shallow gutter stream gently bumping it, making the appendage shift and quiver.

Hara didn't want to but her eyes looked again, without her brain's permission.

After a second, she let out a breathless laugh. It was the leg to a mannequin. Hard plastic, the toes represented by one solid wedge shape. She took a picture on her phone of the surreal scene and texted it to Carter. *Art everywhere, boss.*

Eventually she found her way to Ms. Butler's address. The home was the same style and size as the other houses on the street, but the new siding and windows and roof stood out, as did the wide veranda. The front walk area was landscaped, while the other homes had patches of mud or moss and chain-link fences. The street was lined with old Jeeps and run-down Honda sedans but there was a black Mercedes in the driveway.

The differences didn't prove anything. Her son was making millions. If anything, it was crazy that she still lived in this neighborhood and she only had one car.

Hara went to the front door but hesitated before ringing the bell. What exactly was she supposed to say? *Hey, did you take a bribe a few years ago?*

The woman must have seen her through the side window. She opened the door before Hara had a chance to push the doorbell. "Yes? May I help you?"

"Hello. Are you Ms. Butler, the mother of Charles Butler?"

The older woman's face remained impassive, but her high cheekbones and the shape of her nose and mouth were the same as the famous ballplayer's.

"Um, hi, my name is Hara Isari. I'm a reporter out of Portland." Hara held up her press pass, which any third grader with a printer could have made. "I interviewed your son a couple of nights ago and thought I might do a follow-up piece. Would you be willing to answer some questions?"

"No. Honey, I ain't tryin' to be rude, but my boy has told me not to talk to reporters."

"Oh. Well. He's already sat down with me. Are you sure you can't take a second . . ." The woman crossed her arms and shook her head. Hara hadn't expected to be shut down quite so quickly. "Do you mind if I leave a card, in case you change your mind?" The young reporter pushed a card at the woman before she could answer.

Closing her fingers around the business card, Ms. Butler said, "You go on along now, you hear? Don't make me feel bad." She didn't wait for Hara to respond; instead, Charles Butler's mother slowly but firmly closed the door in Hara's face.

Next stop, library archives, to find any old articles that might have featured Charles back when he was a high school phenom.

Later, she'd dig up Butler's high school coaches, to see what they had to say. She was going to have to interview college coaches and managers, too, but those questions were going to have to be carefully curated, if she had any chance at all of getting them to talk to her.

Maybe she would eat first. A straight caffeine diet was not doing her any favors, even if Hara's mother would beg to differ. Despite being closed out by Ms. Butler, and starving to death, she was excited about this chance to redeem herself, to really do something important. To prove she didn't need her daddy to shape her world.

—*—

"Ms. Isari? We have a message for you. It was just dropped off," said the clerk at the hotel's front desk, catching her attention.

Maybe it was Derek. A thrill went through her. She'd sent him a text hours ago, trying to sound casual, telling him where she was staying but with no pressure for him to get back to her.

That's what she'd written, anyway, but it was a lie. She did not feel casual. He hadn't responded and it was making her stomach clench and her insecurities go into overdrive, mostly along the lines of who was she to think Derek Darcy was going to do anything more than get a piece of ass and then move on to the next woman? Hara had given him the freaking milk—he wasn't going for the cow, especially not when he could easily get himself a unicorn.

Breaking the seal on the heavy cream envelope bearing her name, she found a single sheet of paper.

Ms. Isari,

The organization paid your way to Boston and gave you an exclusive interview. I would appreciate your abeyance of our agreement and that you do not go outside the club. Mr. Butler's family and friends wish to maintain their privacy. I've been informed the storm caused you to miss your return flight. Contact my assistant Madeline Bingley immediately if you are in need of a replacement airline ticket, or if my office can be of further service. Thank you for your respect and restraint in these matters.

—C. O'Donnell

Well, that was fast.

How in the hell did Connor O'Donnell find out where she was staying? The only people she'd told in Boston were Derek and Naomi. Ms. Butler had obviously informed her son of Hara's visit. Would the player be that put out over Hara talking to his mother? O'Donnell certainly was enflamed. Why would the owner care so much? And who was it that ratted out her location, Naomi or Derek?

She didn't feel very good. This was already going off the rails and she'd been investigating for maybe six hours.

Her excitement waned. *Abeyance. Who freakin' says "abeyance"?*

–*–

Derek stood in his bedroom, his nose buried in her bathrobe, inhaling her scent, wondering what he should do next. She'd texted where she was, but should he go? Or at least call?

In the beginning, he'd had nothing but contempt for Hara, believing her to be an inept reporter and just another good-looking young woman in a push-up bra wanting to hook up with one of the big boys. Derek had no more faith in her being a good human than any other person he'd ever interacted with. *But.* But there was something about her that was different from other people. She was so much more. She was beautiful, obviously—a dusky-skinned goddess with translucent eyes and that long, silky hair he could run his fingers through all night. And her smell. *Mmm.* So heavenly. But it was her spark—her kind and charismatic soul—that made the blue of her eyes so piercing. Something deep in him had been triggered, a desire to be close to someone else. To let someone in. To be loved.

He wasn't thrilled she was a reporter; that for sure was confusing, knowing Hara's job was to report on his every move. To *judge* and report.

True, she had found out about Ms. Butler's bad move and had agreed to not run a story. Not yet, anyway. He wasn't 100 percent on trusting her, but . . . 80 percent? He really needed someone to talk to right now, about O'Donnell. Was 80 percent good enough?

His doorbell rang, and then there was a loud banging. Someone was in his foyer, pummeling his front door. *What the fuck?* Was the doorman asleep at the switch?

The security camera revealed his teammate pounding on the thick wood with one meaty hand, a case of beer in the other. Derek swung open the door and Charles stumbled in, drunk. It was only five in the afternoon.

"The doorman just let you up here, without asking or even giving me a warning. That guy is so fired."

"Dude. He's a fan. He's seen me here before." Charles swayed on his feet. "I brought beer."

They did need to talk. Beer was never a bad thing. "Do you want me to put those in the refrigerator?"

"No. I plan on drinking them."

Derek helped himself to a bottle from the case, which only

had a few left. *Bad sign*. They cracked their drinks open at the same time, gulping in unison. Finally, Derek swiped at his mouth, put down the bottle. "Bro, you got some explainin' to do." He sat down at the kitchen table.

Charles hung his head, dropped into a chair. "I know."

"O'Donnell is losing it, man. He told me I had to lay off. To not play so hard." Derek jumped back up and started pacing. "To feed you the ball and not take so many shots. He said *you*"—he jammed a finger in his teammate's face—"started the convo, Charles. That you told him I was hurting the team."

Charles huffed. "That fuckin' guy. Not me. He is the one trying to control you. Just like he's controlling me. Even Naomi. Do you know what he did to her? I was stupid enough to tell him she was pregnant, thinking maybe he'd get off my back, feel sorry for me. Nope. He sent his bitch to take a bite outta my woman. Tried to make her have an abortion."

"How can he *make* her do that?"

"He's a straight-up bully. He had Madeline tell Naomi that her next stop was Tina's house, to tell her about the affair. Then Madeline told her I'd be fined most of a year's pay if the papers made a big deal out of this. Maybe kick me off the team. They got her set up with an appointment, even though she still hurtin' from last night." He clasped his head in his hands, turning in a slow circle. "I told Naomi to do it, it would solve everything, but you should have seen her face. I had to go and told her I wouldn't be able to see her anymore, at least not until everything settled down, and the bitch threw a glass at my head."

Derek just stood quietly, listening, trying to process the craziness.

"And that stupid reporter! She's trying to find a story. First she's sticking her nose in Naomi's business, getting her all wound up—"

"That's not exactly what happened." Derek sat back down.

"—and then she went to Ma's house! I was good to her, why she gotta play me? Little uppity thing, she don't know who she messin' with."

Derek's heart dropped. Hara wasn't dicking around. "You gonna give her a beatdown before she finds out about your mom, is that it?"

"Me?! Hell no. O'Donnell is the one she's gotta watch out for." Charles slammed his bottle on the table, waved his hands around wildly. "Everything is shit."

"It's only going to get worse if you don't take care of things. And the consequences are bigger than you. You know that, right?"

"What can I do about it? Turn Ma in? She still doesn't get it. But only a few people know, and I'm just lookin' at it like no harm, no foul, at this point. O'Donnell will chase the reporter off; he can't afford to have her around." He slumped. "Like I said, O'Donnell has turned everything to shit. He's ruined my life. My woman. My game."

"Bit of a stretch, eh, Chuck?" Derek was done listening. "First of all, just tell Naomi she can do what she wants to do, and that you'll support her. They aren't going to fire you. How many guys in the last five years had girlfriends get pregnant—ten? More? Second of all, if it does become some crazy big story, you can pay the fine. You can afford it." Derek leaned back and put his hands behind his head, trying to project calmness. "I mean, the man can't ruin your game. You're lit. You're always lit."

"Doesn't matter." Charles gulped down the rest of his beer. "Naomi won't talk to me. She gonna do what she wants. Fine. So there's all that." His eyes were swimming as he leaned forward. "I never ask you for no favors, man, not even when we was kids and you was gettin' dropped off by your chauffeur and I was ridin' the bus for an hour." Without making eye contact, he opened another beer. "My life would be a lot easier if you could just do what O'Donnell asks. Dial it back a little."

Derek tried to understand what he was hearing. "Dial back what—my game? Seriously? You did talk to him, then. Dude, I just don't get it. I'm playin' my balls off, but we are better together than apart." Derek slammed his beer down on the table. "That's how we've always been. You helped get me onto this team. You're my friend. Why are you trying to get me kicked out now?"

"No, no, no. My brother, I don't want to lose you. I just want you—*need* you—to calm down, stop going for the gold on your own."

Derek was done with this shit. "You're drunk. Go home."

"Listen. This isn't about you. O'Donnell needs to see *I'm* in charge on the floor. Otherwise . . . well, otherwise I'm in trouble." He put up his hand to ward off Derek's baffled response. "No offense, but that's all I can tell you. I need you to trust me."

"No offense, but how do I trust you? I did trust you, up until a few days ago. Then I find out you're cheating on Tina and your mom took money and you didn't do anything about it. And I just can't get over that O'Donnell knew!" He spit out his words.

Charles reeled back dramatically, as if Derek had slapped him. "Of course O'Donnell knows, he always knows. That guy is the devil."

"What are you talking about? He found out about the college money and he brought you onto the team anyway. He protected you."

"He didn't do it to protect me. He did it so he can hold me

hostage, so he can make money. I do what he says or he hurts Ma and takes away my contract. He's so far up my ass I'm gonna be in the shit forever. Or I'm gonna be in jail."

"Jail! You are not making sense."

He swayed in his seat. "You ain't makin' sense."

"Nice."

They drank quietly for a minute. Derek stared at Charles across the table. His teammate, a guy he thought he knew.

The man's eyelids were drooping like those of a small child in a high chair, drunk on milk. Eventually, his eyes shut and stayed shut and he dropped his head back, snoring.

Derek pried the beer from Charles's hands, looking down at him ruefully. *I'd think the big fella was cute if I wasn't so pissed at him right now.* He half walked, half dragged Charles back to his room and dumped him on the bed. Removed his sneakers and threw a blanket over him. His friend might be fucking up at life, but Derek couldn't just kick him out. Not like this. Instead, he put a bottle of water and some aspirin next to the bed and left him to sleep it off.

Derek's phone rang. It was Hara. His heart thumped. Perfect timing. She might be wrong for him, but she was only here for a little while. Parts of her were very right.

"Hey. I'm in your lobby," she said in her naturally sultry voice. "Can I come up? I'm not a stalker, I promise. But I need to talk to you about O'Donnell."

CHAPTER 17

They parted at last with mutual civility, and possibly a mutual desire of never meeting again.

—*Pride and Prejudice*

The doorman smiled at Hara as he put her on Derek's elevator and pressed the appropriate button. "Mr. Darcy must be having a party tonight."

Before she could ask what he meant, the door closed. Her nose wrinkled; beer tinged the air. Stepping into Derek's private foyer and knocking on his door, Hara prayed she wasn't actually walking into a party. *Oh God.* What if he had a girl in there? She should have thought this out.

She was close to backpedaling into the elevator when the door opened. A blast of male energy poured over her, a sexual heat emanating from the man in front of her. "Hi."

Hara ducked her head shyly. Studying the floor, she expected the soundtrack to *Sixteen Candles* to start playing. She hadn't felt this awkward since middle school.

"Hara?" He put a light finger under her chin, pulling her face up. "Are you mad at me?"

"No." Her pulse raced. She could feel it in her throat. "Are you mad at me?"

He put his hands on her hips and his face close to hers, his breath on her cheek. Derek's lips hovered but did not touch. "Can I kiss you?" he whispered.

Hara met his mouth hungrily, her tongue sliding across his. The passion they'd shared the night before had not been spent, merely banked, the hot embers jumping now to full flame. Both his hands went into her hair, holding the back of her head. She meshed against him but, after a second, forced some light between their bodies, her hands on his chest no longer caressing, now pressing him away, just a little. "Hi," she said.

"Hi," he replied, flashing his white teeth in an honest smile. "Glad to see you."

She grinned back. Derek Darcy really did like her. "You, too."

There was a loud snort from down the hall. From Derek's bedroom. There was another snort, which then fell into a full-blown snore.

She took a step back and cocked an eyebrow at Derek. Hara was fairly sure that was not a girl. "The doorman said you were having a party."

"That's Charles." Derek smirked. "He's passed out. I put him on my bed."

She felt her face flush, relieved Derek hadn't been with someone else. "Does Charles know that I know about his mom?"

"Skipping the small talk, then." He sighed, motioned her to follow him to the kitchen table, which held a number of empty beer bottles. "He knows that you went to see her, that you are at least looking for a story beyond your interview with him. He's pretty mad. But the real problem is that I think Charles told O'Donnell about it. He's the one I worry about. I should never have told you. I probably shouldn't ask, it's none of my business, but did she say anything?"

"She didn't talk to me."

"I don't know about you digging into this story, Hara."

My friend, there's only so many people who are going to make decisions for me. No matter how great you are in bed, you are not one of them. Nor is O'Donnell. She shuddered. She did not want to think about that creepy bastard in bed.

"I told you," she said, aloof. "I'll research it, but I'm not going to print anything unless it's substantial and corroborated. I've still got plenty of people to talk to."

"I know what you said. But I'm worried about you, at this point, as well as Charles. He said O'Donnell is involved. And he's angry."

"Funny you should say that." Hara took the letter from her pocket and gave it to him. "This came to my hotel."

As Derek read the letter, his face remained emotionless. But when he handed it back to Hara, his eyes were stormy. "Not tough to read between the lines here."

Hara, trying to remain emotionless herself and not come off as defensive, said, "Did you tell him where I'm staying?"

"No!" he said quickly, then dropped his voice. "I saw O'Donnell this morning. He didn't ask about you."

Naomi had to have told Charles, then. But why would Charles tell O'Donnell? Why did he care? She knew sports reporting would have its downfalls, but having guys actively working against her didn't feel good. Then again, now that Charles knew she'd gone to his mom, he must think she was actively working against *him.* Hara guessed the goodwill was gone. She couldn't be a reporter and be everyone's friend.

Derek continued, "I don't like him, Hara. Maybe you should get some distance from the O'Donnells."

Her stomach twisted. Something else occurred to her. "You know what? I shouldn't be here. I don't want to get you in trouble, too. They've already warned you away from me once, that night in their kitchen."

"I may be a rule follower, but I'm not going to be their lap dog. If O'Donnell was playing by the rules, he wouldn't be worried about you. He certainly wouldn't be chasing you away, or giving me lectures."

"He lectured you? What do you mean?"

A grimace turned down his lips. "O'Donnell is going to bench me again unless I start being a 'team player.' He says my job is to feed the ball to Charles. That's it." He rubbed his forehead, like he had a headache. "You might be right. It might be best that you aren't here. I can't be talking to you about team business like this."

"You just said—"

"I am an idiot." He sighed. "And you are a reporter. I love Charles, I love my team, I want to be loyal. It's a big deal to me that I prove myself this season. I don't think you're a bad person, but it is your job to uncover dirt and tell the world. You could conceivably ruin this season for my team."

Yep, she couldn't be everyone's friend. And this guy was all about himself. "I'm not a 'gotcha' reporter!" She stood up, fiercely holding back tears. "You know that!"

"I'm just trying to get a handle on things, that's all. Come on, I'll give you a ride back to your hotel."

"No need." She hated roller coasters, and this was the worst. Her pulse raced again, this time out of frustration and anxiety. And rejection.

A cell phone rang, breaking the tension.

It was on the kitchen island, next to Derek. "That's Charles's phone." He peered at the screen. "Naomi is calling, should I answer it?"

"Yes!"

He pushed the button. "Hello?" He paused. "No, this is Derek Darcy." Pause. "I know, this is his phone but he's not available right now. Can I give him a message?" Another pause; this time he frowned. "You're sure? Is there anything I can do?" He stared at Hara, concern etched on his face. "Okay, yes, I understand. I'll tell him." He hung up.

"What's wrong?"

"That was Naomi's father. I guess Naomi told him Charles was her boyfriend, and he thought Charles might want to know . . ." He cleared his throat. "Naomi miscarried. They've had to sedate her."

After having everyone up in her business, the decision had been made for Naomi anyway. Poor girl.

"I'm going over there." Hara put her coat on. "Should we wake Charles? He'll want to see her, right?"

"Good question." Derek shrugged. "Where's he stand with this girl? He just told Naomi he wasn't going to see her anymore. Maybe the best thing for her is if he stays away."

"He's your friend." Hara thought she knew what Naomi would want, but what did she need?

"He did this. He's made all these messes and he's not cleaning up any of them." Derek stopped and folded his arms. "Besides, he's too drunk."

She picked up her satchel, made sure she had her phone. "Well, I'm gonna go. And I know you're worried, but I'm not going to print a word about any of this. It's personal and painful and the public doesn't need to see this side of their favorite Fisher. More so, Naomi deserves privacy."

Derek nodded and then picked up keys off the counter. "Fine. I'll drive. No need to wait for a car to get here."

The first few minutes of the ride were quiet, slightly tense.

Derek finally broke the silence. "Why does life have to be so messy? People are so goddamn irritating. Charles, Naomi, Tina, that whole thing—irritating. So unnecessary. And O'Donnell. I really hate that guy."

"Your biggest defect is that you hate *everybody*." She was only half teasing him.

Derek raised an eyebrow at her, then turned back to driving. "And yours is that you willfully misunderstand people. You decide whether or not you like them in the first five minutes, and then despite evidence to the contrary, you stick with it."

"You are challenging me about not giving someone a chance? That's rich."

They rolled into the hospital's parking garage, and the tension was broken by the excited lot attendant when he realized who he was handing a ticket stub to. "Mr. Darcy! Oh my gosh! Will you sign this?"

Derek was sweet, taking the time to write a message to the man's son. But as they drove through the enormous lot, Hara couldn't let it go. "That other 'Mr. Darcy,' the one who was kind to a stranger—you should let that guy out more often."

"I gave *you* a chance. I'm glad I did, Hara. I don't regret having met you." Parking, the ballplayer turned to her and said, "Do you think I should come up? Probably not, huh?"

"It's nice of you to offer. I'm not sure she'll want to see either of us. I'm going to pop in, give her a hug, see if she needs anything, and then stay only if she wants company."

Derek got out of the SUV, tugging on a baseball cap. Pulling the brim low, he said, "I'll walk you into the lobby."

Hara didn't argue. It was dark and she didn't want to walk through the garage by herself. *Ha! That's not really it, is it?* she chided herself. No. She wanted to eke out as many minutes with this complicated man as she could, make the stroll through the dark lot count. When they parted ways here, it would probably be for good.

She wanted to work things out, to find a way she and Derek could bypass the issues, just be together, just for this short time, even if it was unrealistic that the famous athlete would ever want to be with someone like her long-term. But, in reality, he had too many problems with his teammate, and something going on with the team owner, and he had his own goals. For obvious reasons, he saw her, a reporter, as a liability. And, frankly, yeah, Derek was getting in *her* way, making her care about Charles more than she should, when maybe he didn't deserve it. Hara frowned. Too much of who he was most of the time—well, it *was* the wrong Mr. Darcy.

She wanted to figure out what she wanted. What was best for her. Not Derek, and certainly not Charles.

If she had to pick her career, make it front and center, wasn't that the sane choice to make? The one night with Derek had been fun but it was clearly going nowhere, fast.

He took her hand, swinging it as they walked under the buzzing fluorescent lamps.

Her heart clenched. He seemed to be just as conflicted as she was.

"Is this okay?" he asked, his face sincere.

Her heart melted, whether she wanted it to or not. He was always asking permission before touching her. Like he respected her. Hell, like he wanted to touch her. Her, Hara Isari.

Derek Darcy. She just couldn't figure him out.

He left her at the front entrance, with a soft kiss on the cheek.

"Goodbye."

–*–

A low light filtered out from Naomi's room, through a cracked door. The hallway on this floor was silent and empty, except for soft beeps and whirs from the surrounding rooms and a few nurses down at the entry desk. Hara knocked softly.

No one answered. She pushed open the door and poked her head through. The bed was empty, the blankets tossed back. She almost withdrew when a weird, heavy smell hit her in the face. Hara held her breath.

What is that?

The bathroom door was shut. Naomi was either in there or they'd taken her for tests.

To give Naomi privacy, Hara waited in the hall for a few minutes, but no nurses came by. Impatient, she decided it would be okay to knock on the bathroom door. As she walked back into the room and around the bed, though, her foot slipped on something wet.

Looking down, Hara's vision wavered and the room spun in a lazy circle. "Na—Naomi?" she whisper-screamed.

She'd stepped in a pool of blood seeping out from under the bathroom door.

CHAPTER 18

> You may well warn me against such an evil. Human nature is so prone to fall into it!
>
> —*Pride and Prejudice*

The doctors pumped nearly half a gallon of blood into Naomi before they were sure they had her back.

"This girl wasn't messing around," one of the nurses said to Hara, coming out of the room after changing the bandages on Naomi's wrists. "She lost almost forty percent of her blood. She'd turned off her monitors, so if you hadn't gone in there when you did, she would only have lasted maybe a minute longer. Maybe."

Hara hadn't been allowed back in the room, but they'd let her sit in the hall. She was too freaked out to make it any farther than the narrow, hard bench a few feet from Naomi's door. Hara couldn't remember how to use her legs, much less figure out what she should do next.

The sight of Naomi, slight and childlike and curled up in a fetal position on the white tiles, would likely stay with her forever. The copious amounts of dark red blood pooling around her, even in her hair, and the slackness of her petite features . . .

Hara wanted to dislodge the slideshow of horror via whatever means necessary. Heavy drinking, lobotomy, whatever.

The girl had people in her life who loved her. Why would Naomi try to kill herself? She'd only known for a short time she was pregnant, and she hadn't even been sure she wanted it. A miscarriage was definitely an occasion to be sad and confused, depressed, but to want to end it all? Naomi was so young and talented and beautiful. She could have more babies, when she was ready. Why throw in the towel for good?

It blew her mind. Naomi had seemed like a girl who walked in and took what she wanted.

Having a relationship with a professional athlete was just too dangerous for normal people.

Hara suddenly, desperately, wanted to talk to her father. He was her touchstone, the man who listened to her, encouraged her, consoled her. He was also out of reach, as usual. When it came to emergencies, he wasn't there, hadn't been since she was a child. And Hara had never learned to rely on her mother, not unless she wanted to be treated like an incapable imbecile who needed her decisions made for her.

She yearned to have a partner to lean on in times like these. Hara almost broke down and called Derek, but restrained herself. She could not push a relationship into existence after a one-night stand.

So, do what you always do, Hara Isari. Fight your way through this. Buck up. It's Naomi who is suffering, not you. What needs to happen next? Let's get going!

Naomi's dad was on his way, so Naomi wouldn't be alone. But how about Charles? Should he be there? Or not?

She'd go back to her hotel, Hara decided. Focus on her

job. She needed to work on the story about the arena's power outage and the flood, write it up as a feature this time, since a simple recap wouldn't do a day after the game. Then she could try to find contacts from Charles's past. Tomorrow, there was an early game, the last before the team went on the road. She'd go, sit in the press row with Eddie, and see if he knew anything about Butler's time in high school and college—without tipping him off, of course. Shouldn't be hard to keep Eddie in the dark; the guy was a worker bee but didn't have the sharpest stinger.

Hara messaged for an Uber. Then, unable to stop herself any longer, she texted Derek. *Bad news. Naomi tried to kill herself. It was awful. She's stable but you should tell Charles. I'll be at the hotel tonight, if you want to talk. Or maybe I'll see you at the game tomorrow. Good luck.*

Hitting *send,* she prayed she didn't sound desperate. Only open to possibilities.

–*–

Derek was just walking into his apartment when his cell pinged. Reading the text, he cringed and slid the phone into his pocket. He'd call Hara later, make sure she was all right, but first he had to deal with Charles. Even through a shut door, Derek could hear him snoring.

Before he made it down the hall, Charles's phone rang, still on the kitchen counter. Derek jogged over, saw it was O'Donnell. His hand hovered, undecided, until the ringing stopped. But then it immediately started up again. His boss again.

"Hello, sir, this is Derek. Charles can't come to the phone right now."

"Unacceptable. You go get him. Now."

"To be honest, he's sleeping."

"Are you telling me you two are a couple?" The old man then made a slurping noise that made every hair on Derek's body stand up. "By God, that makes sense. Maybe it was you that got this Naomi girl pregnant, during a three—"

"No." Derek was too shocked by this crazy leap to say more. O'Donnell's lascivious tone was worse than the implication. The paintings behind the owner's desk obviously represented a frame of mind. Derek finally kicked out some words: "Besides, you'll be happy to hear Naomi isn't pregnant anymore. She miscarried." He couldn't keep the bitterness out of his voice.

"One less abortion to worry about, then—"

Derek cut him off. "However, she did try to kill herself. Sliced her wrists. Pretty bad." He didn't know why he was telling O'Donnell, except maybe to pry some empathy from the old bastard.

"But she didn't die? Too bad. One less whore on Butler's scoreboard wouldn't be a bad thing. He's got enough problems."

"You don't mean that." Derek shouldn't have been shocked but he was.

"Son, I did not get to where I am by being softhearted. Now, don't take this the wrong way, but you and your teammates are commodities. I protect my commodities."

He couldn't believe what he was hearing. "We are also human beings. Naomi is a human being."

"Fine, fine. Whatever you say. Get Charles up, tell him to call me. I need to talk to him before the game, make sure he stays away from that reporter Isari. She's become a problem, obsessed with Butler. If she tries to come to the next game, I might have to do something about it. Let me know if you run into her, Mr. Darcy."

He wanted off the phone, desperately. "Yes, sir."

"And you're ready to be a team player tomorrow? Support Charles? If not, you've got a knack for riding the bench."

"Yes, sir." Derek spoke like a robot.

"Good night, then."

"Good night, sir," he said automatically. He swayed on his feet in his apartment, though his mind whirled and stormed, far away. *What in the fuck? I mean, what in the fuck? Am I stuck in a bad cable movie?*

Had O'Donnell just threatened Hara?

Derek tried to wake Charles, to get him up so he could go to Naomi. The big drunk only groaned, rolled over, and fell into a deeper stupor. He didn't bother trying again, not even to tell him that O'Donnell wanted to talk to him. O'Donnell was a douche and Charles could do without him for a while.

However, Derek did text Hara back. *I think it best if you don't come to the game. I think things are too complicated.* He knew this would hurt Hara. It hurt him to type it. But what was he supposed to say? That he thought maybe the owner was crazy and might hurt her if she showed up? Who would believe that?

The basketball player hated it when he felt out of control, when the usual rules didn't seem to apply to his day-to-day life, the one he'd so carefully carved out for himself, away from his family. Yet, here he was, helpless against the wave of events washing over him.

What can I do?

He could stop worrying about himself. He needed to focus on something else, anyone else. Except Hara. Thinking about her made him ache for something he had never realized he was missing.

—*—

Hara woke up in the hotel the next morning feeling hungover and dead tired. She had dropped into sleep a number of times, only to wake clutching at her chest and gasping, terrified by graphic nightmares about blood and corpses. Always it was Naomi, dead in a river. Dead in a car. Dead on a hospital room floor.

However, Hara had spent the night more awake than asleep, thanks to her brain being unable to shut off. She'd thought about everything that had happened, everything that could happen, and everything that should happen. Like Derek knocking on her door and crawling into her bed at one in the morning. That should have happened. It didn't.

Instead, she'd received a text telling her not to come to the game. That Derek didn't want to see her. *I knew things were hard between us,* she thought, *but not that hard.* What, he couldn't be within a hundred feet of her?

She shut her eyes, pulled the perfectly weighted white quilt up to her chin, and ran her feet over sheets that must have been made from million-dollar silkworms. While she could appreciate the exquisite comfort of the hotel bed, her body still suffered. Her head hurt, her stomach was a mess. She'd had two martinis delivered to her room last night. Maybe three. The queasy feeling should have meant something fun happened the night before. It didn't.

She dialed room service and asked for tea, toast, and eggs. A setting for one.

Then she called the hospital.

"Can you please transfer me to room 419? Naomi Martin's room?"

After a few seconds, the voice on the other end of the line came back. "I'm sorry, we don't have anyone here by that name."

Panic rushed through Hara. "I know she's there. Will you please look again?"

"Room 419 has a patient by another name, and Naomi Martin is not listed in any other room. But let me check with a nurse on that floor. One minute, please."

One of the nurses from the night before answered the phone. "I remember you. Your friend is stable, don't worry. Sorry for the confusion. But she has been transferred to another hospital."

"What? Why? Where?" Ever the journalist.

"I can't say." But then the nurse's voice dropped to a whisper. "I will tell you she is in a swanky private hospital with one-on-one, twenty-four-hour care."

"Oh my God. Are you saying she's in a psych ward?"

"No! I can't give you any more information, hon, but she's in good hands."

Hara breathed a huge sigh of relief. Charles must have stepped up, even if he was just throwing money at a problem. It was a lot of money. She left a message on Naomi's cell for her to call when she felt up to it, or if she needed anything.

The young reporter took her time getting ready for the game. She might as well enjoy the room while it lasted. She was not in a hurry to leave the comfort and safety of the swanky digs. What was waiting for her today? A tornado?

Hara decided to ask the front desk if they had a flashlight she could borrow. Maybe a helmet. A floaty. And an EpiPen. A few days ago, Hara had thought small, nipple-size Band-Aids were the most important items to have in her bag. How her priorities had changed.

Her phone rang. It was her mother.

Oh goody. More high drama.

"Mom? What's up?"

"Hara."

The hackles on the back of her neck rose. Her mother's voice was low, clogged.

"What is it?"

"Your dad. He's in the prison infirmary. His roommate Jonas just called, said he'd found him unconscious in their cell. He says he was beaten pretty badly, Hara." Willa's throat clicked audibly. "Thomas is awake now. Jonas says he's been asking for you, that you can call directly into the infirmary. I have the number."

It took Hara a second to find her tongue. "How bad is it?"

"They had to intubate him while he was unconscious. Some broken ribs punctured a lung. That's all they've said."

"I . . . I can get on a plane. I can be at the prison tonight. It'll be late, but I can get there."

"Don't bother. No one is allowed in to see him. But you can call, talk to his doctors. Here's the number."

Hara's shaking hand dropped the pen a few times but she finally got the number down. "But they kept him at the prison? Didn't take him to the hospital? That's a good sign, right?"

"I don't know, Hara. You call. I'll have my phone with me if you want to talk again afterward."

Hara knew shit was real because her mother was calm. Hara, on the other hand, felt like she was about to spin out of control.

The man who answered the infirmary phone introduced himself as an intern, but Hara knew she was likely talking to a prison worker, someone who'd probably been a junkie and was highly skilled with needles so they gave him a job in medical. That's who was taking care of her father.

"They've taken the tube out of his throat and he's awake."

"How does he look? Is he going to be okay?"

"He's stable but started coughing up blood. He's got internal bleeding. We've got an ambulance on the way. Salem Hospital can deal with this better than we can." There was some shuffling in the background. "Hold on. He wants to talk to you. Make it quick."

Oh God. How was this even real?

"Baby girl?" His voice was a barely audible, crackling whisper.

She immediately burst into sobs. "Daddy!"

"Don't cry. Hara, stop. I have to tell you something." He coughed, a painful, hacking sound.

She gulped and bit her tongue, trying to put the stopper back in the bottle. She managed to push back the sobs, but the tears would not stop.

When he started up again, his voice was even quieter. "Listen. You have to leave Boston. O'Donnell did this to me."

"What?" She couldn't find her voice. Her question came out below a whisper.

"He said if you don't leave and stop investigating Butler, he's going to kill me."

It took her a second to understand what he said. "Daddy, they have got you on heavy meds. You're talking crazy talk."

"You know I'm not." He coughed and then groaned. "I don't care about me. But he's going to hurt you if you pursue this."

"Pursue what? This is nuts! We're talking about a mom taking money for her kid to go to college. Yeah, O'Donnell knew about it, but there is no way he's killing someone to keep that quiet. It's not that big a deal. Besides, why in the hell would he be going after *you?*"

"He's been rigging games. He was doing it years ago; I took his bets. But I didn't turn him into the Feds when I was arrested. That was how I talked him into giving the contest interview to you, figured he owed me."

Long, painful coughing.

My father. Protector of the predators. So proud.

Thomas took a second to catch his breath and then continued, "I didn't know he'd started rigging games again, but he thought I knew, once you started asking more questions."

"Daddy. I—"

"Stop. It's not your fault. But I didn't know about his gaming until I started getting roughed up in here, told I needed to keep my mouth shut. One of his hired goons let it slip." He was struggling to talk but kept going. "Honey. It's Charles. He's throwing games. O'Donnell is afraid that's the story you're chasing."

"I can't—" Hara breathed heavily for a minute. Pieces clicked into place. How could she have been so wrong about a person? Even after it had become obvious that Charles was a jerk, she'd given him leeway, thought there was more to the story. Well, there had been, but not in the way she thought. "I understand. Daddy, do you have someone to watch out for you there?"

"I'll be okay. If you get your ass on a plane. Leave now."

"Okay, Daddy. I will."

"The ambulance is here. I have to go."

"Why are they moving you? What's going on?"

"Come home."

The phone clicked off.

CHAPTER 19

Angry people are not always wise.

—*Pride and Prejudice*

She called her boss. Carter got her on the next flight out, leaving in a few hours.

But the one person she really, *really* needed to get ahold of was not picking up the phone. She had to talk to Derek.

Derek had no idea how dangerous O'Donnell was. If he decided to defy the owner and go for the shots, he could get hurt, too. O'Donnell had a lot riding on these games and wasn't afraid to use force to get his way. Picturing her father lying on a gurney in an ambulance, Hara had no doubt he'd have her father killed if he heard another peep from an Isari. But would he have the balls to go after someone high profile, like Derek? Hara had no way of knowing.

O'Donnell operated so far outside of her normal she had no idea what to expect.

Her calls and texts continued to go unanswered. Derek

was either ignoring her or he was at the stadium, warming up. He wouldn't get her messages until after the game.

She tried not to let fury at the situation overcome her common sense . . . but she could let it propel her into action, instead of just sitting around being a victim. There was no finding a positive spin this time. Hide out at the hotel, maybe lose herself in the comfort of one of her Jane Austen novels, maybe freak out, or she could try to find the ballplayer, warn him. Throwing the last of her stuff in a suitcase, she decided she had just enough time for a quick stop at the stadium. It should be easy enough to blend in with ten thousand fans. *I can be in and out.*

Hara shoved her phone into her pocket, made sure she had on a bra under her sweatshirt, and dug out her press pass. Then she headed for the door.

–*–

"Hara, are you all right? You look funny," asked Eddie.

She was standing next to the Fishers' tunnel into the arena, pressed to the wall by press row. TV reporters were setting up their cameras and players were warming up; there was a lot of activity to mask her presence.

"*You* look funny." She'd bought a Fishers baseball lid on the way in. With her long hair pooled under the hat and her sweatshirt hood drawn high around her neck, she prayed she could get in and out without anyone noticing her.

Eddie had spotted her in a flat second.

She would never make it in the CIA. But this wasn't good. She didn't want to put her father in more danger.

"Uh. Okay." The redheaded reporter frowned at her.

"Sorry. Yes. I'm fine. Just a lot of drama in the last few days." Maybe Eddie could slip Derek a note?

"I was worried about you in the flood. Did you guys do okay?" He leaned into her. "How crazy is it that you had Darcy driving you around!" He could not mask the pout in his voice. "Are you dating him?"

Clearly, Eddie had the emotional maturity of a fifth grader. No way could she trust him with a message for Derek. Eddie would for sure read it and then he'd be dragged into the mess. Hara continued to scan the floor for Derek, making sure she didn't miss him as he emerged from the tunnel, while also preparing to bolt if she saw O'Donnell.

Trying not to freak Eddie out, and ignoring the relationship question, she said, "The trip was a little sketchy."

A little sketchy. She almost laughed. Her friend had almost drowned in an inch of water and Hara was nearly sliced in half by a stop sign.

"The wind was nuts. We saw cars being dragged by the current." *We barely made it to the hospital.* "I was grateful to get back to a warm, dry bed." *With Derek Darcy curled up around me.* "Yesterday was a lot calmer." *If you're not bothered by the sight of your friend—the same friend who was knocked unconscious the day before—lying on a bathroom floor, bleeding out. Or if you're not bothered by the fact that the man you abhorred three days ago has started to take up a hell of a lot of real estate in your heart, yet that same man won't be involved with a reporter.*

"I spent some time at my hotel, writing." *And researching the background of Boston's favorite basketball player, trying to think of a way to talk about his mother's bribery scandal without bringing him down, despite the fact that Charles got his young mistress preggo, and, oh yeah, he's a cheating motherfuck . . . which I know because my daddy, coughing up blood, told me about it, and how O'Donnell is an even worse, shysty motherfucker, willing to hurt people. And he's had Charles throwing games. Charles fucking Butler!*

She shrugged, trying to shake the hamster in her head free from the spinning wheel of thoughts, and continued, "Eh, I just don't know, Eddie. Boston is a crazy fucking town. It's making *me* crazy. I'm ready to go home. How are you doing? Working on any exciting stories?"

The *City Gazette* reporter launched into a rant against Boston's Zamboni drivers and how their strike was going to lead to the downfall of hockey, even though, he claimed, anybody who could drive a lawn mower could do their job. Eddie, yakking away, did not notice when she deactivated her interaction mode and went totally inside her head, seeking to understand what motivates humans, while continuing to keep an eye out for Derek.

Neither of them was paying attention to the spectators behind them.

–*–

Derek was suiting up in front of his locker when Charles arrived. The room was filling with Fishers, voices bouncing off the walls.

"How you feelin'?" It was hard for Derek to keep the snipe out of his voice. He had left the apartment while Charles was in the shower. He hadn't been in the mood to talk to him. He still wasn't in the mood to talk to him. He was supposed to go out there and half-ass it, just to make Charles look good? Derek had finally made it off the bench, his playing was hot . . . this was fucked up.

Charles didn't answer, just shook his head and threw a duffel bag on his chair. Pulling out his gear, he said, "Just tried to call Naomi. Her pops won't let me talk to her. Like I'm nothing."

"No kidding."

"Whatever, dude."

O'Donnell and a few owners walked into the room with the coach and the manager. As the administration filed through, heading toward the coach's office, O'Donnell glared first at Charles and then Derek. The group left a stink of cologne in their wake.

Derek finished lacing up his sneakers and grabbed a ball. "You guys are really stealing the joy from this game."

"Derek, this is a big deal. It's my life. Please, be my wingman today."

"I'm always your wingman. I thought you were mine. Turns out, you aren't looking out for anybody but yourself." Derek left before he threw the ball at his best friend's head.

Emerging from the tunnel, his heart skittered. Hara was there, five feet from him, looking adorable in a sweatshirt and a hat. He'd hoped she wouldn't come to the game, knowing O'Donnell wanted her gone. Yet, here she was, and he just wanted to put down the ball, go to her, and carry her out the door.

She saw him. Her blue eyes widened and she started to smile, but then it faltered. She offered a small half wave instead, which he returned with a nod. Then she beckoned to him.

He hesitated, knowing it was best if he stayed away. But he could also be an adult and politely say hello.

An image of her popped into his head, sitting on his counter, her robe open, her head thrown back. He could smell her. *Oh, hell no. Not right now.* Getting hard in the middle of the court, right in front of press row—that would play well in the papers. Besides, the sex scenario was done for. Hara was a reporter and she was going home and there would be no more touchy-touchy. Derek had to let this go.

He stood up, straight, alert. Madeline Bingley. One look at her hatchet face and the iron melted out of his pole. The blonde assistant was making a beeline for the reporter, a grim look on her face.

–*–

Hara turned to see what Derek was staring at over her shoulder.

"Hello," said Madeline, more of a threat than a greeting. "Mr. O'Donnell would like to speak to you."

Oh shit.

Next to her, Eddie ignored the tense subtext and said, "Hi, Ms. Bingley, would you mind giving me a minute of your time? Maybe give me your take on the team roster—"

"Hara?" Madeline didn't even look at Eddie, only kept her gaze steady on Hara as she nodded toward the tunnel. "Let's go."

"Maybe Eddie should come with me. He'd love to meet an owner. Wouldn't you, Eddie? Wouldn't you love to meet Mr. O'Donnell?"

Before he could answer, the assistant said, "Some other time." She put a hand on Hara's shoulder and squeezed. Her nails dug in. "How's your father, by the way?"

"Um. Good. Thanks." The message was received. Hara could hear the blood thudding in her ears. "Eddie, could you save me a seat? I'll be back."

"Actually, Eddie, she won't be." Madeline, her nails still dug into Hara's arm, pulled her toward the tunnel entrance. "Come on, little miss reporter. Can't keep the big man waiting."

Hara felt a rush of gratitude when Derek was suddenly between them and the tunnel. "What's up, Madeline? You seem like you're in a rush."

"This is none of your concern, Mr. Darcy. Please, go practice like a good little boy. Mr. O'Donnell will be watching."

"You know, I think I'm just gonna go ahead and tag along." He towered over the assistant, the ball tucked casually under his arm.

His biceps were bulging, Hara noticed gratefully. She could physically take down the assistant herself, but she had no idea what O'Donnell would do to her father if she didn't comply. She was going to have to do some sweet talking, real fast.

Madeline appraised the player coolly. "Fine." To Hara, she said, "Come along," maintaining her grip.

"You can let go of me," Hara said calmly. "I'm coming." She wouldn't do anything to put her father at risk.

Derek followed without saying a word.

If I was a good human, I'd warn him off. She should tell him to run. Hara knew what O'Donnell was capable of and Derek had no idea. The sound of the growing crowd in the stadium above thrummed in the cement walls around them.

As they passed the locker room, the door opened. Charles stepped out. "What are you doing, Madeline?"

"You know what I'm doing, Charles."

Hara's eyebrows lifted. How could she have been so wrong about somebody? She would never again trust her instincts.

"Is this really necessary?" Charles asked.

"Is what necessary?" asked Derek, folding his arms.

Madeline ignored both of them. Hara allowed herself to be herded farther down the tunnel, toward the entrance to the private garage, and then through the doors. Her best hope was that O'Donnell would see she was being compliant.

—*—

Derek couldn't understand why Hara was letting herself get pushed around, especially by that snotty little bitch. *This is all too fucking weird. I don't like it.*

Charles stepped into the doorway, not letting Derek pass. "Let's go out and warm up. You don't want no part of this."

"You're right. From the beginning I've wanted no part of this, whatever *this* is. But you're my friend and I figured I'd stick by you, no matter what. I'm changing my mind, though." He stepped up to Charles, got in his face. Charles was taller, but Derek was more solid and ready to fight. "Why'd Madeline take Hara to the garage? I thought O'Donnell wanted to see her. What's going on?"

"Just stay out of—"

Over the sound of the music and stomping feet just above them, Derek distinctly heard a scream come from the parking garage. He shoved Charles to the side, hard. While his teammate regained his balance, Derek barged through the door.

There was Hara, her baseball hat and glasses knocked to the ground, straining to get away from O'Donnell. The old man was behind her, gripping her arms behind her back.

And, oddly, Madeline stood in front of the girl, holding up a picture. The photo looked to be of a bloody, beaten man, but Derek didn't take the time to look closely.

He strode over to O'Donnell and picked the old man up by his shirt, breaking his grip on Hara. "I'm going to fuck you up. Believe it, you wormy fucker."

Just then, something crashed into the side of his temple and his world went gray, then solid black.

CHAPTER 20

I have not been used to submit to any person's whims . . .
I am not to be intimidated.

—*Pride and Prejudice*

Hara watched in horror as Derek's long frame teetered and then crumpled to the ground. Charles towered over his friend, holding a short steel pipe. There was blood on the tip.

"What the hell, boy!" O'Donnell screamed. "He's supposed to play tonight!"

Madeline was wide-eyed. "This is not supposed to happen."

"How could you?" Hara said. No one was listening. Derek's eyes were closed. Just like Naomi's. "What is wrong with you people?"

Why in the hell am I just standing here? She took a step, ready to break into a sprint, when her arms were pinned behind her back once more. She twisted and jerked, struggling against his grip. When O'Donnell had grabbed her the first time, she'd been surprised and frightened, but her mind still hadn't believed what was happening, that she was being held against her will. She'd been too meek. Now, here was Derek, lying at her feet.

Her brain screeched into full alert, the fight-or-flight reflex pumping adrenaline into her veins. But, even so, she was unable to break free, the goddamn old man stronger than he looked, probably from hours of golfing and weird sex marathons.

For half a second, she wanted to burst into tears. Where were the garage attendants? Why didn't Derek wake up? Then, the rage she'd felt sporadically in the past two days returned, took root and bloomed, and gave her clarity.

Madeline still stood in front of Hara, the photo of a bloody Thomas Isari crumpled in her hands. Hara kicked, as hard and fast as possible. She swung her foot up between the assistant's legs, connecting with the tiny woman's crotch. There was a satisfying thud. Stunned and in pain, Madeline cried out and fell back a step.

Before anyone had time to react further, Hara bent forward at the waist then whipped her head back, smashing O'Donnell in the face with the back of her head. He shrieked, high-pitched, and suddenly her arms were free.

Hara jumped away.

Charles was there, between her and the door, holding the pipe in his hands, but he was swaying and staring down at Derek.

She tried to leap past him, but he caught her. "Let me go!" she yelled, twisting and trying to find a bare patch of flesh to bite.

"You do *not* let that bitch go, Charles," said O'Donnell, blotting the blood from his nose with a white lapel kerchief. "Hara, calm down. Madeline, stop whining." His assistant was bent over and groaning, tears of pain running down her cheeks. A snot bubble hung from one dainty nostril. The owner handed her his handkerchief. "Wipe your nose. Jesus. And go get the car."

Madeline limped away, glaring at Hara.

Hara was disgusted by the people and their blood and snot and evil actions. She was also disgusted by the heavy body odor coming off Charles. He had his arms wrapped around her like steel bands, holding her firmly against him.

Time seemed to pause, everyone silent, when Derek groggily got to his feet. "Let her go," he said to his teammate.

"I'll take you down again, man. Stay down." Charles's voice sounded like it was coming from far away.

"You fucking backstabber. Think you can take me if I don't have my back turned?" Derek didn't give anyone time to react, leaping onto Charles, knocking Hara out of the way. Unfortunately, right back into O'Donnell's path.

She swung around, fists up, and planted her feet. *I'm gonna beat down this asshole myself.*

But the old man faced her calmly, his arm outstretched, a small silver pistol held in a steady grip. Aimed at her.

Derek and Charles, unaware of the new development, fought furiously. They traded punches and kicks, tossing each other around. Two bears, brawling.

"Hara. You did this, you know," O'Donnell said, shaking a finger. He stepped close, his breath hot and moist on Hara's cheek, offering a stench of rotting leaves. "You and your father just couldn't leave well enough alone. You think a couple of blackmailers are going to outsmart me?"

"I didn't know anything! I didn't know the contest was rigged. And I didn't know your games were rigged until an hour ago. I was simply doing my job."

"Rigged?" A deep, loud voice vibrated the air around them.

It was then Hara realized Derek had Charles in a headlock and they had stopped fighting. He was staring at the gun in O'Donnell's hand. He flexed the arm around Charles's neck, his blood vessels and muscles bulging. "What do you mean the games were rigged? Charles?" Derek asked, confusion and anger darkening his eyes.

"You don't understand." His teammate slumped, limp in Derek's grip.

Derek shoved Charles down to the ground in disgust and scooped up the pipe. "What? What don't I understand?"

"Easy does it, son." O'Donnell cocked the trigger, the gun remaining on Hara. He took a few steps away from her. "This little girl would bleed out quickly, I'm guessing."

"I had to do it," said Charles, ignoring O'Donnell. The big man was on his hands and knees, his head swinging back and forth. "He had me over a barrel. He's been making me tank shots. Either that or he was turning me and Ma in for accepting the bribe. He'd bet against the team, knowing we were going to lose."

"Last year, the championships. We lost by two points."

It was hard for Hara to watch the hurt that ran across Derek's face.

"Yes. But it was because of him." Charles got up slowly, pointing to O'Donnell.

Derek swung back to Hara and O'Donnell, keeping Charles in his sight, while gripping the pipe, holding it at his side.

O'Donnell kept Hara between himself and Derek. "Well, let's not blame this all on me, Mr. Butler. You liked the money. You agreed to tank early *this* season so the house would bet against the Fishers. We'd just barely make the playoffs, and then win as the dark horse, taking another huge pot. With

Darcy here, a win was guaranteed. We just had to slow him up a bit in the beginning."

Hara felt cold sweat pour down her back. If O'Donnell was admitting to all this, then he wasn't worried they'd get away.

A car pulled up behind them. Hara turned to see Madeline, her white face a big O of surprise and fear, staring through the windshield at the now-awake Derek holding the pipe, while Charles was down on his hands and knees and O'Donnell held everyone at bay with a pistol.

The assistant threw it into first, stepped on the gas, and screeched past them.

"You cunt!" O'Donnell howled.

They watched as Madeline skidded around a corner and shot out of sight. *The bitch isn't stupid, anyway. What are the chances she'll send help?* But Hara knew it was absurd to hope the assistant had suddenly grown a moral compass.

O'Donnell waved the gun at them, refocusing quickly on Hara. "Now, I could shoot you all right here, but I'd rather not. Dragging bodies around is hard work. Charles, I'm assuming you'll play and keep quiet. You have the right attitude. But you two . . ." He took a step toward Hara.

Derek jumped in front of her.

Everything happening here was her fault. Hara didn't want this. She didn't want Derek to get hurt because she'd been stupid enough to leave the basketball court with Madeline, and stupid enough to believe she'd be safe even while knowing the owner had her father badly beaten. Hara started to edge around him, hoping to maybe draw O'Donnell's attention back to her.

Derek moved with her, used to shadowing other's movements. But then he broke contact and moved a step closer to the old man. "Give me the gun," she heard him growl.

O'Donnell seemed unfazed, pointing the gun at Derek now. "Dead bodies may be inevitable."

This is not happening. She started again to dart out from behind the brave basketball player when there was a blur of motion in her periphery.

Charles landed in front of O'Donnell, grabbing for the gun.

The gun went off. Charles took a few stutter steps and then fell.

Hara froze, confused, terrified. Before she knew how to react, Derek moved, quick as a lion, this time grabbing O'Donnell by the hair and yanking him off his feet. At the same time, he knocked the gun out of his hand.

"Charles! Charles, are you okay?" Derek yelled, though not turning his attention from O'Donnell. He threw the team's owner roughly to the ground and put a knee in the middle of his back. "Stop squirming or I'm going to smash your fucking head into the concrete." He tapped the pipe next to his head, making the owner flinch.

Hara ran to get the pistol and came to a stop a few feet from them, just out of reach, while training the gun on O'Donnell's head. Her hands were steady, though slightly sweaty. "It's okay, Derek, I got this." A grin stretched tightly across her face, which was weird because she felt only terror and despair. "I grew up on a farm, shooting rodents. Hear that, O'Donnell? I fucking love shooting rats."

Just behind them, Charles groaned. He lay on the ground, holding his chest, in the same fetal position Hara had found Naomi in yesterday. The blood pooling around him was just as dark and disturbing, as was the cloying smell of iron.

Derek removed his knee from O'Donnell and slowly stood. "I'd listen to her, jackass. Though I wouldn't mind seeing you get shot."

"Derek! You don't have to do this," gasped O'Donnell, one cheek pressed to the concrete, a smear of dirt across his forehead. "You've got a lot to lose if you let this go down. Instead, we clean up the mess and we all come out winners. Even this little cunt, if she can keep her mouth shut."

The air around Hara blurred as she moved, fast. In a split second, the bloated old man was writhing on the ground, spitting out blood and howling, a rabid animal. It took a second for her mind to catch up with her actions. She'd kicked O'Donnell in the teeth.

Breathing hard, she moved back to a safe distance, the gun still on him. "I'd like to say I feel bad about kicking a man while he's down, but I don't. My karma will probably survive."

–*–

Derek thought he might suffocate, his lungs refusing to take in a full breath of air. His body felt stuffed with mud and his mind was sluggish. The stadium security, police, and emergency medical personnel did a delicate dance around him and around Hara. She sat next to him; they were not far from the chalk outline and the large bloodstain that had seeped into the garage's concrete floor.

Charles Butler was dead.

My friend.

He'd bled out before the medics could reach him.

My friend.

Derek's thoughts refused to coalesce. He stared at his friend's blood on his hands. How much of this was his fault? The basketball player was surprised when droplets of water splashed onto the dark red pigmentation streaking his skin.

"I'm so sorry, Derek."

Hara. Her voice spread a soothing balm. He closed his eyes in gratitude when she reached up to his face and brushed her fingertips over his cheeks. It was then that Derek could feel the wetness. The drops of water diluting the blood on his hands had been tears. His tears.

He hadn't cried since he was a child. The ability to remain stoic and emotionally walled off had saved his sanity, as he'd grown up in the cold, toxic culture of his narcissistic and entitled parents. It had also helped him to strive to succeed on his own, no matter the battles he had to fight, no matter how sealed off from the world he became.

But right now, he felt busted open and wounded. He wasn't even embarrassed that Hara was here to witness it. Instead, alongside the endless waves of intense electric shocks of grief, he was deeply relieved to have a good-hearted, strong woman at his side, to willingly hold his hand as he stumbled through this dark moment.

This was such a profound shift in his approach to the world; he could do nothing but wonder at it. People he admired had the ability to alter themselves, to grow, so much so that there was something new to be observed in them every time they met. Derek had not known until now that he himself had the same capacity for change. If only Charles had discovered that quality in time.

The loss of Charles left a raw-edged hole, the sides crumbling away painfully. Charles had died, both literally and figuratively. Derek didn't have his friend now, and he had also lost the friend he'd thought he'd had, the man he'd thought he'd known. What was he going to do? Charles had been the only person he'd ever really let in.

Hara's hand was warm and real in his.

He knew then. Derek wasn't alone, not as he'd feared.

Basketball meant nothing. Money meant nothing. Fame and recognition meant nothing. His heart was still beating, and that was because of Hara. He wanted to see what it would be like to embrace love instead of pushing it away, and he felt like Hara might be the one. She was the only thing that felt right. That felt good.

–*–

Watching the gurney wheel away Charles's dead body, Hara felt a chill travel from the base of her spine to the top of her head. She'd believed his hype, that he was a decent guy. Charles was running in the wrong crowd and Hara had not sensed it at all. She was so stubborn she'd stuck with her first impression of him until it was too late.

And then O'Donnell killed him. That could have been her father. Hara sucked in a shuddering breath. Did Charles die because of her?

As she breathed in and out, comforted by the warmth emanating from Derek pressed against her side, her mind settled. No, she had not done this. Each of these men had made their own choices. Choices based in selfishness, even evil.

O'Donnell had been handcuffed and taken away in the back of a squad car. His weak cries of false arrest were quickly shut down, thanks to surveillance cameras in the garage. CCTV footage had also led to the quick apprehension of Madeline, who apparently sang like a canary when asked about her boss and his nefarious dealings. Karma. It had come around and bit these people in the ass.

It was hard to celebrate the justice of their demise, however, since her own father was part of this, and now he was in the hospital. The world wasn't black-and-white. Her father, a man she loved, also had made his choices and he'd chosen wrong, but he'd wanted what was best for her. He'd used morally challenged shortcuts to get there, to be sure. Thomas Isari was almost killed because he thought blackmailing O'Donnell would somehow have a positive outcome. He almost got Hara killed, too.

But at least her daddy had love in his heart. O'Donnell was a black-hearted monster. As a wealthy, white-collar criminal unused to adapting to others' rules, he'd suffer in prison and she had zero empathy.

The one person whom she'd initially judged as unworthy was the one who, in the end, turned out to be courageous, giving, and a worthwhile human. She squeezed Derek's hand, gently, and he gave her a grateful look that melted her heart. *Here is the one guy willing to literally throw himself in front of a bullet for me.* She had been going to walk away from him without trying to see if there was something there, just because she was afraid of rejection or looking stupid. From the beginning, she had told herself that Derek Darcy wasn't worth her time and then clung to that stupid impression despite all the evidence to the contrary. She'd desperately wanted love and companionship in her life but had used negative judgments of others to keep them at bay and protect her heart.

Hara realized then exactly how insecure and afraid of being hurt she was. Until that moment, she had not known herself.

Right now, though, it was Derek who was in pain.

"I'm so sorry." She enfolded his hand in both of hers, using her presence to comfort as best she could. He leaned against her and sighed, swiping at his eyes occasionally. After a few minutes, a detective approached and asked them to come to the station to give their statements.

Derek stood and helped her to her feet. His hands on her shoulders, he said, “Thank you. Thank you for saving my life. And thank you for still being here.”

“Where else would I be?” Hara pressed against him, and Derek pulled her tighter, bending down to give her a kiss. His beautiful copper eyes had her hooked even before his lips met hers, and the jolt was instantaneous. No matter the circumstances, no matter the history or the news stories, his energy was good and his heart was noble. She wanted more.

CHAPTER 21

My real purpose was to see you, and to judge, if I could, whether I might ever hope to make you love me.

—*Pride and Prejudice*

"Daddy? Can you hear me?"

Hara bent over Thomas Isari's inert body, hooked up to tubes and monitors on a bed at Salem Hospital. The guard at the door watched closely as she touched his face, wiping his brow. But he didn't stop her.

She kissed his forehead, trying to keep her tears in.

"Baby girl," came his whisper, his eyes still closed. "Am I dreaming?"

"No, Daddy. Open your eyes."

His eyes opened. Whatever else might be wrong with him, his gaze was sharp and clear.

"The doctors say you are doing better, that they stopped the bleeding. How do you feel?"

"You don't want to know." He sighed uncomfortably. "But, my God, I am so glad you are okay."

Hara had already called ahead and told her father that

he didn't have to worry about O'Donnell anymore. She'd also filled her mother in on all the details of the past week, so that both of her parents would get over the shock by the time she got home. Now, Willa sat in the corner of the room, a book at her side. She watched her daughter and her estranged husband with a smile. "Okay, Hara, don't wear him out. Come here." She held out her arms for a hug.

As Hara folded herself into her mother's embrace, the guard cleared his throat.

Seriously?

But he wasn't trying to stop them. Instead, the officer said, "Excuse me. You have another visitor."

Derek stood next to the guard at the door, a bouquet of flowers in his hand. The guard gave the flowers a cursory glance and then let the ballplayer through.

Hara's parents looked at him in surprise, as did Hara.

"Derek! Don't you have a game?"

"The franchise has me on suspension until they make sure I didn't have anything to do with throwing the games." He shifted back and forth uncomfortably. "I'm not worried, I'll be cleared."

Hara took the flowers and then paused awkwardly. Should she kiss him? They'd spent the night before together, after leaving the police station, and shared hours filled with tenderness and intimate conversation. And after Derek admitted that he was the one who put Naomi into private care and that he'd hired a lawyer for Charles's mother, there were also hours filled with amazing sex. She had flown out this morning, still not sure where they stood exactly, but very sure they would see each other again. Just not this soon. "I didn't think I'd see you for a few weeks."

Willa nudged up to Hara and put an arm around her

daughter's waist. "So! You're Derek Darcy. I am Willa Isari, Hara's mother." The tiny woman formally shook hands with the much taller man. "You'll be back on the team, then? For sure?"

"Mom . . ." Hara rolled her eyes. She thrust the bouquet into Willa's arms. "Here. Do you mind putting these in water?" Only her mother would take this moment to make sure Derek would be a suitable prospect, set up to take care of her daughter's financial needs . . . Little did she know, Derek didn't need to be playing ball to make money. More important, Derek didn't need to have any money at all in order for him to be a suitable prospect for Hara.

Her father coughed. She remembered herself and said, "Derek, this is my father, Thomas Isari."

Derek strode over to the side of the bed. "Nice to meet you, sir. I'm sorry it's under these conditions."

"We both know I helped create the conditions." Thomas paused and then held out his hand. "I'm the one who's sorry. My actions caused so much pain. I thought I was doing the right thing, trying to help Hara."

Hara had been afraid that Derek wouldn't shake with her father, the infamous criminal. But she needn't have worried. They shook, both eyeing each other carefully but respectfully.

"I can understand wanting to do what you can for your daughter, sir. And Hara is a special girl." Derek flushed when he said it and ducked his head, making Hara grin. It was so surreal, this six-foot-five man made of muscle acting like a shy little boy. Hara was relieved that Derek could be deferential, even to a felon who didn't really deserve it. Thomas had problems but he was her father and she loved him.

Willa gaped at Derek, no doubt stunned and delighted to hear a man "of means" give Hara a compliment. Coyly, Hara elbowed her in the stomach, and then stepped up to the ballplayer's side, holding her hand out. But he surprised her by stepping back.

"Oh, wait. I have something for you. The real reason why I came to Oregon."

Hara's heart pinged. She'd been under the impression that she was the real reason he'd come. Watching him pull a handful of newspaper articles out of a backpack, however, she was curious despite herself.

Derek handed the papers to her. "These reporters are botching the story." Then he paused a second and blew out a breath, as if still deciding something. But then he straightened his shoulders, determined. "I want you to interview me, Hara. To write the story of what happened. To write Charles's story. These news outlets are getting it all wrong. From the beginning, he trusted you to do a good job, and he was right. Only you can tell it the way it needs to be told."

She heard her mother gasp behind her.

The blood swooshed loudly through Hara's brain. Derek was here, with her family, he'd said she was special, and now he was trusting her with the story of the year. Maybe the decade. Her mother and father had heard him—they knew someone out in the real world thought she was worthy and capable. And that someone just happened to be Derek Darcy, star basketball player and the man she was very likely falling in love with.

Who am I kidding? I love him. I do.

"This could harm your career, Derek. It will serve to keep you in the eye of the scandal."

He tucked a strand of hair behind her ear. "I didn't do anything wrong. I should be able to weather this. If I don't, I'll survive. As long as you've got my back, I'm all right. I've got yours." Then he offered her a devilish grin, with just a hint of vulnerability in his copper eyes. If he was thinking like she was, he was probably remembering last night, when he'd wrapped himself around her back and held her tight. And caressed. And tantalized . . .

Hara Isari felt the *tick-tick-tick* of her heart, beating in time to the second hand of the old clock on the hospital wall. The universe had come through, given her a gift that was unconditional and welcomed. Not the interview. Her gift was Derek Darcy.

She didn't care about her parents or the guard or that she was back in a hospital, a mile from the prison. This was her story, the story of Hara, and she was going to make it a good one. She knew who she was, who she wanted to be, and who she wanted to share her story with. The reporter stood on her tiptoes and kissed the basketball player, long and hard.

ACKNOWLEDGMENTS

Thank you to the team at St. Martin's Press—Monique, Mara, Kelly, Ashley, Marissa, Sara, Naureen, and all the rest—for their work and support. It's nice having a strong group of women at our backs.

Thank you to romance-reader extraordinaire Breanna Stephens for her thorough and thoughtful critique. She is a gifted editor.

Also, thank you to our lovely and insightful beta readers Lynn Kyriss and Kathie Hightower.

Thank you to literary agent Chip MacGregor for continuing to make magic happen.

A huge thank-you to sports reporter Bill Oram, who covers the Los Angeles Lakers for the Southern California News Group. His advice and his humor were necessary and impactful. He'll be the first to tell you that any errors in regard to the culture, habits, or rules of a sports journalist or a basketball player belong to us.

ABOUT THE AUTHORS

Ziv Sade

EVELYN LOZADA is a high-profile American-Latina reality television personality, entrepreneur, author, and philanthropist. She is best known for her role on VH1's hit series *Basketball Wives* (2010–present), OWN's hit series *Livin' Lozada* (2015), as the author of *Inner Circle*, the first installment of the book series The Wives Association (2012), and as the creator of "Healthy Boricua," a Puerto Rican lifestyle guide to healthy living. She has become a national trendsetter, a "go-to" fitness expert, a jewelry designer, a fashion and beauty maven, social media royalty, and a stimulating voice and proactive supporter of causes that affect women and girls through the Evelyn Lozada Foundation. Evelyn is a Bronx native and a mother of two, Shaniece Hairston and Carl Leo Crawford, who currently resides in Los Angeles.

ABOUT THE AUTHORS

Grauwen Photography

HOLLY LÖRINCZ is a successful collaborative writer and owner of Lörincz Literary Services. She is an award-winning novelist of *Smart Mouth* and co-author of *The Everything Girl*, and of the bestselling novels *Crown Heights* and *A Day in Prison*. Holly currently lives in Oregon.